Murder at the Christmas Panto

The Canterbury Mysteries Book 2

Izzie Harper

ASIN for the ebook: B0FXB3GPXC

ISBN for the paperback: 978-1-9194366-0-9

This book is dedicated to:

Dr Oliver Lyell

Sonya Bigg

White Mill Vets

Chapter 1 MONDAY 15th December

It was ten days before Christmas and snow had fallen over Bramhurst, transforming the Kent village into something from a Christmas card.

Ellie Blix plonked an adoring kiss on Rebus' nose and left him in his bed. She pulled her woolly hat down over her ears, zipped up her fur-lined parka and locked the cottage door behind her. She trudged along the white pavement, her boots crunching softly with each step.

The shops in the high street were just opening. At the butcher's, strings of sausages looped like garlands across the window. Outside, the shopkeeper was putting the finishing touches to a handwritten board, publicising collection dates for Christmas meat.

'Hello, Ellie, love,' he said. He was in a blue-and-white apron.

'Morning, Jim.'

A sign in the window was advertising "Sylvia's pork and cranberry stuffing".

'I don't know what the secret ingredient is, but people are mad for your mother-in-law's stuffing.' He grinned. 'Can you ask her to drop in another batch?'

Ellie smiled. 'Will do.'

A cluster of coloured baubles leaned against a pyramid of pork pies, their golden crusts catching the warm glow from the fairy lights strung along the lintel.

At the florist, Christmas wreaths stood outside, half buried in snow, next to buckets of holly and mistletoe. Fairy lights blinked above the bakery door, and in the pet shop window, Duchess, the greyhound, was asleep in her bed in a woolly jumper.

Everywhere Ellie looked, the village was buzzing with festive excitement.

But for those who'd heard the news, a pall of disappointment hung heavy this morning because, after nearly three months of rehearsals, and with the show due to open at the weekend, Neville Snipe, the panto director, had cancelled Cinderella last night. Totally out of the blue.

The church hall was a pretty yellow brick building with a stone and flint dressing. This morning, when Ellie arrived, it looked forlorn, its windows dark except for the security light flickering over the main entrance. She would have been heading here tonight to meet her fellow production members for rehearsal. Instead, she was rushing to meet Neville so he could reclaim his property.

'Damn Neville Snipe,' she muttered, stomping a little harder as she strode along the pavement.

It was entirely his fault that Cinderella had been cancelled. The health and safety row with Reverend Jo had been completely unnecessary. Neville had wanted to cut corners on fire exits and first aid provision to save a few pounds, and Jo, as the guardian of the church hall, had quite rightly refused.

Belle Kersey was waiting by the hall porch, her window cleaner's van parked at the front of the building. Her ladder was already unloaded and leaning against the wall. She stood on the snowy path, cheeks pink from the cold, her breath forming little puffs in the frosty air. On her head, red and brown "reindeer antlers" drooped slightly to one side, the fur flopping in the snow. She had a takeaway coffee steaming in her hand.

'Morning,' she said, nudging a paper bag towards Ellie. 'Chocolate brioche. Emergency carbs. Coffee on the step.'

She gestured to the ground next to her feet. Her black, quilted jacket was flecked with snow. 'Ready for this cheerful task then?'

Ellie grimaced. 'About as ready as one can be for dismantling dreams. Three months of rehearsals, and it all ends with us packing away the fairy godmother's wand and Cinderella's glass slippers.'

Belle unlocked the door and grabbed her ladder. 'Could you bring my coffee in, Ells, please?'

Ellie nodded. 'Do we really think there's no chance of changing Neville's mind?'

Belle shook her head, antlers moving with her. 'And it's not just about him now, is it? Jo won't sign off on the production without adequate health and safety. And nor should she.'

The familiar smell hit Ellie as soon as they stepped inside: floor polish and the sausage rolls that they'd had last night.

Belle leaned the ladder against the wall in the corridor and followed Ellie into the main hall. On the stage, the set was where they'd left it last night, with the beautiful painted backdrops. Floor tape marked where set pieces were to be positioned.

'Are we going to take all this down and store it?' said Ellie, hearing and feeling the sadness that the question prompted.

Belle shrugged. 'Seems wrong, doesn't it? Let's get Neville sorted and then talk to the group. Decide what to do.' She turned to the corridor. 'I'll set the ladder up for him. Get this over with as quickly as possible.'

Ellie switched on the lights. The fluorescent strips flickered to life, harsh and unforgiving. 'All that work, all that excitement,' she called through to Belle.

'Not to mention the poor kids and parents who are going to be devastated,' Belle called back.

The ladder was quickly in position, and Belle joined Ellie in the main hall, their footsteps echoing in the large room. The pantomime set looked even more poignant under the stark lighting. The painted cottage where Cinderella was supposed to live with her stepsisters stood centre stage, its cheerful yellow door and pretty window boxes a mockery now.

'Where is he?' Belle checked her watch. 'He asked us to meet him.'

'Give him a few minutes,' Ellie told her.

'I can't hang around,' Belle added. 'I've got to get to Mrs Mitchell's multi-pane sashes before I do the GP surgery.

Her ginger cat thinks I'm the enemy and sits on the windowsill, swiping at me with her paws.'

Ellie pulled out her phone to check the last message from Neville.

'What did his lordship say then?' asked Belle sniffily.

Ellie read from his text. 'He'd be here by nine o'clock. Wants to collect his costumes and props from the loft.'

'That's alright,' said Belle. 'It's ten to.'

Outside, a car pulled up and a door slammed. The front door of the hall banged open. Heavy footsteps thudded along the corridor, accompanied by a voice raised in complaint.

'Typical,' he said. 'Absolutely typical. No one thinks to leave the heating on, do they?'

He appeared in the doorway of the main hall, stamping snow off his boots with unnecessary force. He was a large man with deep-set eyes, thinning black hair and a profoundly irritated expression.

'Neville,' Ellie said with forced politeness. 'Good to er... see you.'

'Well, I've got three boxes of costumes up in that loft, plus the props I paid for out of my own pocket. I'm not leaving them here to moulder away.'

Belle swallowed. She and Ellie came down from the stage and joined him. Belle gestured towards the corridor. 'I've set the ladder up for you. It's all ready to go. Do you want a hand?'

'About time someone showed some efficiency.' Neville brushed past them. 'I'll get my things myself, thank you. And then I'm done with this shambles. Three months of my life wasted because one person couldn't be reasonable about perfectly adequate safety measures.'

Ellie bit back a sharp response. Reverend Jo's safety concerns had been entirely justified. Neville's cost-cutting measures would have left them with blocked fire exits and no proper first aid provision. But there was no point rehashing the argument now.

'It's been *our* time too, Neville, with respect,' said Belle.

He ignored her.

'We'll leave you to it,' she called after him as he disappeared down the corridor. 'Give us a shout if you need any help.'

'I can manage *perfectly* well on my own, thank you,' came his curt reply.

Belle shook her head as his footsteps receded. 'Charming as ever.'

'Come on,' Ellie said, heading for the stage. 'Let's look at where we can store the set.'

They started examining the size of the backdrops and set pieces, discussing what would need to be dismantled and what would have to be discarded. There was plenty of space under the stage. However, the vertical supports restricted the usable width. Although the disappointment was fresh for Ellie and Belle, the work was oddly therapeutic, allowing them to focus on practical matters rather than the shock and sadness that hung over the whole enterprise.

'Just nipping to the loo,' Belle told Ellie, who carried on sorting and thinking about what to do.

Was this really it for their panto? Taking the set down and refunding tickets?

When Belle returned a few minutes later, she stood at the rear of the hall. 'It's such a shame,' she said. 'The backdrop really is gorgeous.' She took a couple of snaps on her phone and joined Ellie on the stage, running her fingers along the painted marble columns. 'Mike's got real talent. I couldn't design a set, let alone build it. Chloe was thrilled to help him decorate it.'

Chloe was Belle's daughter and Mike was the village carpenter.

'They did a great job,' said Ellie.

'How's the renovation going at the chapel?' asked Belle. 'Is the dancing detective pulling his weight?'

'Good.' Ellie always chuckled at Belle's nickname for Dave. She was relieved to discuss something other than the panto. 'Phase three starts tomorrow. The drying out is complete, and the roof and ceiling repairs.'

'Ooh. That *is* exciting.'

'Yes. We've got the steel frame going in first thing in the morning. It'll create the first floor. Once that's in, it'll start to feel like a home. Until now, it's felt like a shell.'

They carried on chatting.

From the empty corridor came the clunking sound of a hard sole on a rung. Neville's voice drifted through, muttering complaints about the ladder, the metal, the hatch, how tired he was. Then there was groaning, presumably as he heaved himself up into the loft.

Belle selected a playlist of carols and Christmas songs on her phone and put them on loudspeaker. 'Got to be better than listening to him grunting and groaning,' she said cheekily, and the two women smiled.

'At least he's getting on with it,' Ellie observed. 'With any luck, he'll be gone quickly and out of our lives forever.'

'Yes, hopefully,' said Belle.

They continued their work for around ten minutes, making notes about which pieces could be dismantled easily, and which would need cutting. Neville was in the loft, and they could hear him clomping across the floor over their heads, first at the front of the building, then at the rear.

'Sounds like a herd of elephants up there...' said Ellie, glancing up to the ceiling above them.

Belle increased the volume on her playlist, and sang along to Wham's *"Last Christmas"*.

Ellie assessed the cottage façade. This would need several people to move it safely. 'I think we should–' she began, then stopped as a sound came from the corridor.

A cry, brief but sharp, followed immediately by a tremendous crash.

The building seemed to shake with the impact.

'Good grief,' Belle said, standing still. 'What was that?'

They hurried off the stage and towards the corridor. The sound had definitely come from that direction. Perhaps Neville had dropped a box down the loft hatch?

As they entered the corridor, they saw him.

Neville Snipe lay crumpled on the floor at the base of the loft hatch, his body twisted at an unnatural angle. Blood was pooling in his hair. The ladder – Belle's ladder – lay beside him, one of its extending sections semi-retracted.

'Oh, my goodness,' Belle whispered.

Ellie knelt beside him, though she already knew it was too late. His eyes stared sightlessly at the ceiling, and there was a stillness about his expression that spoke of finality. She pressed her fingers against his neck anyway, searching for a pulse.

'Is he...?' Belle couldn't finish the question.

Ellie sat back on her heels, her hands shaking slightly. 'Dead. Yes.'

Above them, the loft hatch was open.

Belle was already reaching for her phone. 'I'll call 999.'

Ellie stood up slowly.

As Belle made the emergency call, Ellie found herself looking around the corridor with searching eyes. The ladder lay flat, its scuffed metal catching the light.

She looked up at the loft hatch again. It was a good ten or twelve feet from the floor, maybe more. Certainly high enough that a fall would be dangerous, even fatal.

'They're on their way,' Belle said, ending the call. Her face was pale, and she was gripping her phone like a lifeline. 'Police and ambulance.'

Ellie flinched as the back door slammed in the storeroom – a sharp crack that echoed through the empty hall, followed by the crunch of footsteps retreating into the snow.

'Who's that?' said Ellie. In the distance, she could already hear sirens approaching.

Belle dashed into the storeroom, Ellie following.

Outside, in the snow, Ellie made out a figure from behind: dark clothes, dark beanie. Clearly in a hurry.

The two women locked eyes.

'Have they been in here the whole time?' asked Ellie. She remembered Neville. 'C'mon. We need to wait with his body for the police.'

Back in the corridor, the stark reality was still there.

The loft hatch was open. Neville was sprawled beneath it. The ladder lay flat on the floor.

Ellie's stomach turned. Something wasn't right.

The ladder.

Belle had positioned it. She used ladders all day. She would've set the bolts in place securing the two halves, making sure it was safe. So, how had it retracted?

Chapter 2

The first patrol car arrived within minutes, followed by an ambulance. Two uniformed officers secured the scene whilst the paramedics confirmed what Ellie already knew – Neville was dead.

Belle stood by the notice board in the main hall, antlers askew, answering questions from a young PC who was eager to note everything down correctly.

Ellie sat on the stage, talking to another officer. Through the windows, flashing blue lights were painting the snowy car park in strobing colours.

A familiar Audi pulled up, and her stomach did an odd little flip. Dave.

Or Detective Chief Inspector Dave Blix, as his title was in this context.

He ducked through the doorway into the main hall, brushing snow from his shoulders and cheeks. His eyes found Ellie immediately, and something flickered across his face. Relief? Exasperation? Both, probably. They had, of course, been in this situation before...

He crossed to her in a few long strides. 'Ells. You two alright?'

'We're fine. Just shaken.'

He studied her for a moment, the detective's gaze that missed nothing, then seemed satisfied. 'Right. I need to see the body, then I'll want statements from both of you.'

More vehicles arrived. Crime scene investigators in white suits, carrying cases of equipment. A photographer. The church hall, usually so quiet outside amateur dramatics and Women's Institute meetings, buzzed with official activity.

Dave disappeared down the corridor, and Ellie caught glimpses of camera flashes, heard the murmur of professional voices.

Twenty minutes later, Dave returned with his phone out, ready to tap relevant points into his app. 'Let's start from the beginning,' he said, sitting next to her. 'Why were you here?'

Dave knew Neville had cancelled the panto – Ellie had told him the night before – so she explained about him requesting to collect his property, about Belle's offer of the ladder.

'The committee have been talking about getting one installed, but it takes ages for them to make decisions.'

'Uh-huh. What time did Snipe arrive?'

'Just before nine. We got here about ten minutes before him.'

'And you were where, exactly, when he went to the loft?'

'In here. On the stage, deciding what to do with the set.'

Dave made a note. 'Did you see anyone else arrive? Any other vehicles in the car park?'

'No. Just Belle's van, which was here when I arrived. Then we heard a car, Neville's presumably.'

'We'll get the CCTV. Were the two of you together in the main hall the whole time?'

Ellie nodded. 'Yes. Belle nipped to the loo for a couple of minutes, but apart from that, we were in here.'

'What about when you heard the fall? Describe exactly what you heard.'

Ellie closed her eyes, replaying it. 'A cry. Sharp, surprised. Then immediately a crash, like metal collapsing. The whole building shook.'

'How long between the cry and reaching him?'

'Seconds. Twenty, maybe thirty? We ran.'

'And the back door? You told the first officer you heard it slam.'

'After Belle called 999. Someone went out that way.'

Dave's finger hesitated over his phone screen. 'You're certain?'

'Well, we heard the door slam then saw someone leaving.'

'Did you get a good look at them?'

'No. Only from behind. No idea who it was.'

He made another note, his expression giving nothing away. Ellie recognised this version of her husband – the detective, not the man who'd kissed her goodbye that morning whilst asking her to add brandy butter and chocolate truffles to the shopping list.

When Dave finished with Ellie, he called Belle over, and took her through the same questions. Her answers matched Ellie's almost exactly. The timeline, the sounds, the person leaving.

'Tell me about the ladder?' Dave said.

Belle nodded. 'Professional grade. I use it every day. It's completely sound.'

'When did you last check it? Get it serviced, or whatever you do with ladders?'

'When I set it up for Neville. Force of habit. You don't get ladders serviced.'

'And you positioned it under the hatch yourself?'

'Yes. Made sure it was steady, extended it properly, slid the locks into place on both sides. I'm used to ladders from my job. And I felt slightly responsible for him, going up on my equipment.'

'Indeed.' Dave screwed up his mouth. 'But it was definitely secure?'

'Uh-huh. I'm up and down ladders all day long. It's second nature. It was ready to go up.'

'Was anyone with you when you checked the bolts?' asked Dave.

'No.'

He nodded. 'Did Snipe seem concerned about using it?'

Belle shook her head. 'He seemed more concerned about the heating not being on, but that's Neville for you. Complained all the time.'

Dave wrote for a moment, then looked up. 'Did either of you leave the main hall between Snipe arriving and hearing the fall?'

'Apart from me nipping to the loo,' said Belle, 'we were on the stage the whole time.'

'And the back door – it's usually locked?' asked Dave.

'Should be,' Belle said. 'There's a key kept in the storeroom, but most people use the main entrance.'

Dave put his phone away and stood. 'Right. We'll need formal statements, but that'll do for now. You can both head home. We'll be here most of the day.'

Ellie stood too, reading the signs. 'This isn't being treated as an accident, is it?'

'Early days yet.' His tone was professionally neutral, but she'd been married to him for over twenty years. She knew evasion when she heard it.

'Belle locked the two halves of the ladder, Dave. How could it have unlocked itself?'

He softened slightly. 'Go home, Ells, please. Let me do my job.'

She was halfway to the door when he called after her.

'Oh, and Ellie? Did the cast know Snipe had another production lined up? Pantomime in Whitstable, with rehearsals underway?'

'What?'

'The rat,' said Belle, joining Ellie. 'Did he engineer his row with Reverend Jo, then? Needed a way out of Bramhurst to take up the Whitstable gig?'

Dave's expression was carefully blank. 'Ah. OK. Sorry to be the bearer of more bad news. He was directing at Whitstable Playhouse.'

'A paid gig,' said Ellie. 'Even more reason for the cast and crew to be upset with him.'

Belle, who'd been removing her antlers, froze. 'I can't believe this.' She and Ellie locked gazes, both shaking their heads in disbelief.

'Right. I'll be in touch about those statements.' Dave headed back towards the corridor.

Five minutes later, Ellie and Belle stood at the front of the hall where they'd been an hour earlier, snow falling gently around them. The morning's festive atmosphere had been replaced by something altogether darker.

DS Carmichael joined them.

'He flipping well cancelled Cinderella on purpose,' Belle said slowly, trying to suppress her building anger. 'Made us all work for months for nothing. Got people buying tickets, just so he could clear off to Whitstable?'

'Apparently so,' agreed Ellie.

'Lots of people in this village had a very good reason to want him dead,' said Belle quietly but decisively.

Ellie eyed DS Carmichael.

Belle seemed to realise what she'd said. 'Not that I'm advocating murder, you understand,' she said, nervously eying Dave's sergeant.

Ellie looked back at the church hall, where white-suited CSIs were still working behind the crime scene cordon. Belle was right. Neville Snipe had made enemies of half of Bramhurst.

Had one of them decided to do something about it?

Chapter 3

Belle's van pulled away with a spray of slush, the other ladder on the roof rack. She'd muttered something about needing to keep moving, but Ellie had seen her hands shaking as she'd started the engine.

Ellie stood alone in the snow, trying to decide what to do. She watched a forensic services van perform an impressive manoeuvre to let a colleague park beside them.

Bramhurst looked pristine and innocent under a pale December sun. It was hard to believe a man had arrived an hour-and-a-half ago and was now dead. She felt... what? She didn't know Neville beyond his director role. She hadn't particularly liked him, certainly after he cancelled the production. But his death was a shock, and she felt sad for his family and friends. Plus – there was something eerie about Neville dying while she and Belle were in the room next-door. Ellie felt slightly... responsible?

As the snow fell on her face, she realised she wanted to know about Neville. Who was going to be hearing the news?

Except – hang on. The police were investigating. Did *she* want to investigate too?

She instinctively knew the answer to that – yes. She'd ring Sylvia and Zoe in a minute and run it by them.

It wouldn't hurt to visit Daphne, would it? Daphne Henderson ran the village shop and had been cast as the Fairy Godmother – a role she'd been thrilled about, having spent weeks perfecting her wand technique and learning lines. And if anyone would have strong feelings about Neville's betrayal, it would be Daphne.

Ellie felt better for making a decision, and she shuffled through the snow to the high street.

The shop bell jingled as she pushed through the door. The smell of newspapers and sweets greeted her, along with a wall of Christmas selections boxes and festive decorations.

Maya, Daphne's assistant, looked up from restocking the cigarette display. She was nineteen, studying at Canterbury Christ Church, and usually cheerful. Today, her face was pinched with worry.

'Morning, Mrs Blix. If you're after Daphne, she's not here.'

'Oh?' Ellie picked up a TV guide. 'When will she be back?' It was rare that Daphne was out of the shop during opening hours.

'Don't know. She got back from the church hall about an hour and a half ago and–'

'Wait. She went to the *hall*? What time was that?'

'About 8.45. She returned around fifteen minutes later.'

'Did she say why she was going?'

Maya shook her head.

Daphne was part of the cast. Maybe she'd decided to come and meet Neville, or to meet Ellie and Belle. Ellie would ask her. Then she remembered that Maya had said Daphne was still out. 'What did she do when she got back?'

'She went upstairs, got a phone call and dashed out again about twenty minutes after arriving back here. That would've been roughly 9.30am. Maybe a bit before.'

'Did she say where she was going?'

'No. Nor when she'd be back. Most unlike her.' Maya lowered her voice. 'Is it true the panto has been cancelled?'

Ellie nodded.

'That's terrible.' Maya seemed to gather her thoughts. 'It was sold out, wasn't it? We couldn't get tickets for the opening night or the next one.'

'Yes. Only a handful of seats left.'

'My little brother's going to be gutted,' Maya continued. 'Daphne was so excited about it. Practising her lines every spare minute. Kept asking me to test her.'

'She wasn't the only one.'

Belle had said her husband, Phil, had been walking round the house, learning his.

Maya's expression changed suddenly. 'Came charging in here this morning, he did. That Neville. Questioning Daphne.'

'Really. What for?'

Maya shrugged.

'When was that?'

'8.30ish. It was all very odd. He said, "Well, are you going to or not?" and Daphne replied saying, "No, I've already told you".'

Ellie frowned, repeating the question and answer to herself silently. 'So, they both knew what Neville was talking about? That suggests something had happened previously that he was following up on.'

'Yes, I thought the same thing.'

'Did she seem upset?' asked Ellie.

Maya pursed her lips, considering this. 'More like angry. But after he left, she grabbed her coat. Said she had to go out and asked if I could manage the shop.' Maya gestured to the empty aisles. 'Which was fine as we're not exactly rushed off our feet.'

Ellie thanked the young woman and left.

Outside, she stood on the pavement, watching her breath cloud in the cold air. Where would Daphne have gone? Maya would've known if she was in her flat upstairs, as she would've had to go through the shop to get to it.

She would ring Daphne and if she wasn't around, she'd visit Reverend Jo at the rectory. The vicar needed to know what had happened.

Chapter 4

Ellie's call clicked straight onto Daphne's answerphone, so she left a message and walked over to the rectory, which was next to the church, St Mildred's. St Millie's, they called it.

She crunched up the gravel drive and rang the bell. Bramhurst's rectory was a beautiful Victorian house with tall chimneys, its windows golden against the drifting snow.

Jo's Harley-Davidson gleamed proudly. Hopefully, she was in.

Reverend Jo Smythe answered, still in her running gear, cheeks flushed and hair scruffy. 'Ells. You just caught me. I was about to jump in the shower. Come in, come in.' She frowned. 'What's up? You look terrible.'

The hallway was warm and cluttered in a comfortable way – a pair of wellies by the door. A dog lead on the table, along with Jo's motorbike keys and helmet, and a stack of parish newsletters waiting to be delivered. On the floor, were various workman's tools: a drill; a bag of saws; a box with compartments containing what looked like every nail and screw size possible. Definitely not Jo's unless she'd taken up a new hobby.

'Mike's here, building me some storage in the lounge,' Jo told Ellie. 'I'll put the kettle on.' She led Ellie into the kitchen. 'You look like you need it.'

'You haven't heard then?'

Jo paused, hand on the kettle. 'Heard what?'

Ellie told her about Neville.

The kettle, which she was filling, clattered into the sink, splashing water over the worktop and up the wall.

'Dead?' Jo switched the tap off and left the kettle where it had landed. She traced a small cross in the air and said in a solemn voice, 'May the Lord receive Neville Snipe into the arms of His mercy, and grant him rest eternal in His peace. May light perpetual shine upon him, and may those who mourn be upheld in grace and comfort. Amen.' She took a deep breath, releasing it slowly, then cupped her hands over her mouth. 'What happened?'

Mike appeared in the doorway, tucking a pencil behind his ear. 'Everything OK? I heard a cra–' He must've seen

Ellie's expression. 'What's happened?' He was a tall man, similar age to Ellie, with a friendly face and mousey hair.

Ellie filled him in. 'Next we knew, Neville was on the ground, beneath the hatch, with the ladder beside him.' She told them about the bolts on the extension. 'Dave arrived so the police are treating it as suspicious.'

Jo thumped down on a chair at the kitchen table.

Mike followed suit.

'Good grief,' said Jo. 'Sounds like someone unlocked the ladder. I mean, Neville and I had our differences... But I never for one moment...' Her thoughts seemed to trail off, and she shook her head. 'Dead? I can't believe it. Can you?' She looked first at Mike then Ellie. 'I suppose, having seen him, you probably... Oh, how awful.'

Ellie told them about the back door slamming and the person fleeing.

'Could it have been a homeless person?' suggested Mike. 'Been kipping at the hall perhaps?'

'It's possible,' said Ellie. 'It's so cold.'

Jo seemed to gather herself and returned to making tea. 'I've not had word of anyone around the hall but I'll ask about.' Her hands moved slowly through the familiar ritual. Kettle on. Mugs. Milk from the fridge. 'This is such a shock. His poor family.'

Ellie nodded. 'Did he mention anything to you about another production? In Whitstable?'

Jo set sugar on the table and sat down. 'No.' She frowned. 'Why?'

Ellie relayed Dave's bombshell news.

'Have they started rehearsals then?' asked Jo.

'So Dave says,' replied Ellie.

'Perhaps he was planning to go onto that production after Cinderella?'

Ellie shrugged.

'If not, that would mean...' Jo's eyes widened 'he cancelled our production to take up the other one... and hasn't been honest with us all.'

'Good grief,' said Mike. 'That's not good practice, is it?'

Jo's face cycled through confusion, realisation, and finally anger. 'I'm not sure he was bothered about "good practice". I'm now wondering if the row he manufactured with me about health and safety, all that business about me being unreasonable, about costs – was just an excuse?'

'We don't know yet,' said Ellie. 'But – possibly.'

'He made me the villain over the whole thing.' Jo's voice was tight. 'Half the village thinks I'm some sort of politically correct, bureaucratic nightmare who killed Christmas.'

'They don't,' said Ellie. 'They know you.'

'And all along, he was just manoeuvring his way out?'

'We don't know for certain,' Ellie reiterated.

Jo stood abruptly and reached for her phone. 'Well, let's find out, shall we?' She tapped and scrolled, found a number, and pressed call. The phone was on speaker.

Ellie heard it ring three times before a bright voice answered.

'Whitstable Playhouse, Rachel speaking.'

'Hello, this is Reverend Jo Smythe from St Mildred's in Bramhurst. I'm calling about your pantomime.'

'Oh, yes? How can I help?'

'I wanted to confirm – who's directing it?'

A pause.

'That's Jack in the Beanstalk and it's Neville Snipe. We're very excited. Is this regarding tickets or–'

'Is Mr Snipe starting rehearsals soon? I was hoping I could volunteer at the theatre.' Jo pulled an embarrassed face and made the sign of the cross.

'He's already started in the afternoons.'

'Thank you, you've been very helpful.' Jo ended the call and set the phone down carefully. 'Well then.'

'So, it's true,' said Ellie.

'What a creep,' Mike added. 'The way he treated Chloe was bad enough.'

Jo sat back down, her tea forgotten. 'He engineered the whole thing. Picked a fight he knew I couldn't back down from, made himself the victim, and cleared the way to Whitstable.' She looked up at Ellie. 'The police know, you say?'

Mike glanced at Ellie.

'Dave told Belle and me about the production. I'm sure they'll be looking into the implications.'

'Technically, everyone who worked on Cinderella could become a suspect,' said Jo. 'Everyone who gave up their time, learned lines, built sets, made costumes.' She rubbed her face. 'Everyone who trusted him.'

'Yup,' said Mike.

'I see what you're saying,' said Ellie, 'but think whoever has done this *has* to have more of a motive than just Neville cancelling the panto and already having started the Whitstable one.'

Through the window, Ellie could see the church tower rising against a silver sky. Somewhere in the village, Dave and his team were piecing together Neville Snipe's final moments; delivering tragic news to his family.

And somewhere else, someone was trying to hide the fact that they'd been at the village hall that morning...

'Changing the subject slightly,' Ellie asked, 'have either of you seen Daphne today?'

Jo shook her head. 'Not since rehearsals, last night when Neville delivered his bad news about the panto.' She turned to Mike.

'Same,' he said. 'I walked out with her after that. Why?'

Ellie explained about Daphne having gone to the hall, back to the shop and now gone out somewhere.

'I wonder where she was dashing off to,' said Jo. 'Someone in the village will know. She's so rarely out of the shop when it's open.'

Ellie finished her tea and stood up. 'I should let you both get on.'

'Yes, I'll crack on with your cupboards.' Mike stood up.

'Could I have a quick look at them before I go?' asked Ellie. 'Sorry – hardly a priority under the circumstances but we need some storage at the cottage.'

They followed Mike into Jo's lounge. Lengths of timber and board were stacked against the wall. Some of his tools were in a bag. A hammer, saw, and a drill sat in a line.

'You're a neat worker,' said Ellie. 'Dave will like that.'

Mike smiled.

Ellie took a couple of photos to show Dave, and thanked him. 'Very stylish,' she said to Jo.

The two women walked to the front door.

'Ells? If you're going to investigate, be careful. It sounds like this wasn't an accident...'

'Oh, it wasn't.'

'Well, that means someone in Bramhurst is a killer.'

Outside, the winter sun was low and weak. Ellie walked back through the village, past the shops and the pub with its promise of warmth and Christmas music.

And as Ellie left her conversations with Jo and Mike behind, her thoughts drifted to Daphne. What had that cryptic conversation with Neville been about? And why *had* she gone to the hall?

Chapter 5

The bookshop café was blissfully warm after the chill of the street. Ellie claimed a table by the window and ordered a flat white, watching the village go about its business. A resident hurried past with her shopping, head down against the cold. A delivery van double-parked outside the butcher's.

Normal life, carrying on whilst crime scene investigators worked a few hundred metres away.

Ellie pulled out her phone and typed "Neville Snipe Kent" into Google. If he'd been directing locally, surely he'd have some kind of presence? Theatre people usually did.

The results came up quickly. A LinkedIn profile listing various recent productions across Kent and London, some amateur, others professional. A mention in a Whitstable Times article about their upcoming pantomime. And then, further down, a Facebook profile with public privacy settings.

Ellie clicked through. The profile picture showed Neville in a director's chair, looking pleased with himself. The cover photo was more interesting – a family snapshot of what looked like a summer barbecue. Neville with his arm around a woman in her fifties, two younger women flanking them. All smiling.

She clicked on the "About" section. Lives in Rough Common. Married to Patricia Snipe. The two daughters – Charlotte and Talia – both tagged in various posts, both appearing to be in their twenties.

Rough Common. That was just outside Canterbury, a ten-minute drive at most. Close enough that Neville could have easily been travelling to Bramhurst for rehearsals.

Ellie sipped her coffee, pondering what steps she could take. Dave would be visiting the family soon, if he hadn't already. Breaking the news, asking his careful questions. She couldn't exactly turn up on their doorstep a couple of hours after the man died.

But Whitstable was a different matter entirely.

She dialled Sylvia's number. Her mother-in-law answered on the second ring, slightly breathless. 'Ellie, darling...'

Ellie heard creaking.

'I've just heard...the most extraordinary thing... from Margaret at the library.'

'Everything alright? You sound out of breath.'

'Yes. I'm on my rebounder. Ten minutes boosts circulation and lymphatic drain–'

'What on earth's a rebounder?' It occurred to Ellie she could do with one.

Sylvia was famous for her health fads and spiritual initiatives.

'Mini trampoline... Anyway – is it true about... Neville Snipe?'

'I'm afraid so. Belle and I found him.'

'Good heavens... How perfectly dreadful.' A pause. 'Was it an... Hang on.'

Ellie heard shuffling and the thud of feet landing.

'I'm off now. Was it an accident?'

Ellie glanced around the café. Two other customers, neither paying attention. 'The police are investigating.'

'Ah.' Sylvia's tone shifted, taking on the particular quality it acquired when she scented a mystery. 'I see.'

Sylvia had been married to a detective, and like Ellie, knew all too well that CID officers were only called in if the first responders suspected the death wasn't an accident.

And you're calling because...?'

'I think we need to look into this. I didn't like him but the poor man died while we were in the room next-door, playing carols and being not very complimentary about him.'

'Oh, Ells. You can't feel guilty. You weren't to know there was a murderer in the building...'

Ellie gave a startled splutter, and set her cup down before it tipped.

'Where would you like to start?' came Sylvia's question.

This was one of many things that Ellie loved about her mother-in-law. No hand-wringing about propriety or leaving things to the police. Just immediate engagement with the problem at hand and a willingness to help.

'Neville has a wife and two daughters. They live locally.'

'Too soon,' Sylvia said immediately. 'We can't descend on a newly bereaved family. Dave would have our heads, quite rightly.'

'Agreed. But there's another angle.' She told Sylvia about Neville directing at Whitstable Playhouse.'

'While he was supposed to be directing in Bramhurst?'

'Exactly,' said Ellie. 'And he didn't tell them about our production.'

'Duplicitous man.' Sylvia's voice held a note of contempt. 'So, we visit Whitstable.'

'Can you get away?'

'For something like this – absolutely. Shall I pick you up from Stream Cottage? Say, twenty minutes?'

Ellie finished her coffee and headed out, walking briskly home through the village. The morning light had faded, and it had started snowing again. In Thimble Lane, Ellie's neighbour had her fairy lights on in the window.

She nipped into Stream Cottage, greeted as usual by an ecstatic Rebus.

'Hello, boy. Have you had a nice snooze?' She took him for a quick leg stretch and made a sandwich. She was stuffing the last mouthfuls when Sylvia pulled up.

'Right then,' Sylvia said. She was still wearing her sportswear. She pushed open the driver's door for Ellie to get in. 'Let's see what we can discover at Whitstable Playhouse.'

The drive took thirty minutes in the snow, winding round corners and through villages. There was a snarl-up at the entrance to the garden centre, where people were piling in – despite the weather – to buy their Christmas trees and were excitedly loading them onto car roofs.

As they drove down Borstal Hill, Whitstable appeared grey and windswept, the sea churning under heavy clouds.

The playhouse sat in the middle of the small town, a large art deco building that had been converted from a church into a theatre in the eighties. Its pristine white façade seemed even whiter in the snow.

Inside, the foyer was warm and smelled of coffee and old velvet. Posters advertised the upcoming pantomime – Jack and the Beanstalk, running through February. Neville Snipe's name was listed as director.

A young woman sat at the box office, scrolling through her phone and munching a bag of crisps. She looked up as they approached, plastering on a professional smile. 'Good afternoon. Are you here about tickets?'

'Actually,' Sylvia said smoothly, 'we're here about Neville Snipe. I'm Sylvia Blix, and this is my daughter-in-law, Ellie. We're from Bramhurst Players.'

The woman's smile faltered. 'Oh. Has something...?'

'I'm afraid Mr Snipe has pas–'

'He's been taken unwell,' Ellie interjected forcefully, aware they should leave it to the police to notify death. 'This morning,' Ellie said in a softer voice, noticing the young woman's expression. 'We're trying to piece together some information about his recent work.'

'Unwell?' The woman – her name badge read "Rachel" – sat back. 'But he was only here yesterday.'

'Were... are you aware that he is also directing a production in Bramhurst?' Sylvia asked.

Rachel shook her head slowly. 'No. He never mentioned it.'

'Does he have a contract with you?'

'I'd have to check with the manager, but I think so.' Rachel bit her lip. 'He didn't say anything about another production.' She picked up her phone. 'Let me call Martin. He's our manager. He'll know.'

She stepped away, voice low.

Ellie and Sylvia examined the posters while they waited. Jack and the Beanstalk looked professionally done, with proper publicity shots and a cast list that included several local names.

Rachel returned after a few minutes. 'Martin says he's going to check Neville's contract.'

'While we're here, can you tell us about the rehearsals?' Ellie asked. 'How are they going?'

Rachel glanced towards the auditorium doors, as if checking they were alone. 'Honestly? Not great.' She lowered her voice. 'Neville is... how can I put it? Demanding. Very exacting about how he wants things done. Some of the cast find him difficult.'

'Demanding how?' Ellie asked.

'Shouting, mostly. If someone forgets a line or misses a cue. He goes off on one.' Rachel lowered her voice. 'Last week, he had a massive row with one of our actresses. Proper screaming match in the middle of rehearsal.'

Sylvia crept forward. 'Do you remember what it was about?'

'Something about her costume, I think? Or maybe her performance as Jill. She wanted to interpret the role one way, he insisted on another. It got quite heated.' Rachel looked uncomfortable. 'She stormed out. Didn't come back for the rest of the session.'

'What's her name?' Ellie asked, lapping up the young woman's lack of discretion.

'Lauren. Lauren Blackwell. She's local, does a lot of amateur stuff around here.' Rachel pulled out her phone again and seemed to change her mind. 'I can't really give you her number but, if you want to contact her, she has a website showcasing her acting. The number is on there.'

'That's helpful, thank you.'

Ellie wondered what Sylvia made of the news. A screaming match at rehearsal, a week before Neville's death. That was certainly worth following up.

Rachel smiled faintly. 'Poor Neville. He can be a nightmare, but I hope he recovers quickly.'

Outside, the wind had picked up, carrying the salt smell of the sea. Sylvia and Ellie walked back to the car in silence.

'So,' Sylvia said once they were inside, 'Neville was working two productions, told neither about the other, and had recently had a blazing row with an actress here in Whitstable.'

'Plus, he cancelled the Bramhurst production in a way that questioned Jo's integrity, and made half the village furious with him.'

'Suspects are stacking up rather.' Sylvia started the engine. 'What do you want to do about this Lauren Blackwell?'

Ellie pursed her lips, turning over thoughts in her mind. A woman who'd argued publicly with Neville a week before his death. A woman who did amateur theatre in the area – which meant she might well have connections to Bramhurst.

'I think,' she said slowly, 'we need to find out exactly what that row was about.'

Sylvia smiled and pulled out of the car park. 'I was hoping you'd say that.'

The drive back to Bramhurst took them along the same roads, the Volvo's headlights cutting through the snow.

Ellie's phone buzzed – a text from Dave.

Will be home late. Lots to sort. Have you've been investigating already?

She smiled and typed back: *Would I do that?*

His response came immediately: *We both know the answer to that. Please DO NOT interfere.*

Ellie slid her phone in her pocket and looked out at the passing hedgerows. The killer would be hoping Neville Snipe's death would be written off as a tragic accident. But the more they dug, the clearer it became that Neville had made enemies wherever he went.

The question wasn't whether someone wanted him dead. It was: which one of them had finally done something about it?

Chapter 6

Sylvia dropped Ellie back at her house just as a neighbour was coming out on the other side of Stream Cottage.

'Terrible business at the hall,' said the man, who was sweeping snow off his path. 'Is Mr Blix investigating, dear?'

Ellie nodded, always amused by her neighbour's insistence on referring to Dave as "Mr Blix" and her as "dear".

'I walked past the hall with the dog on the way to Perch Meadow. Crime scene tape. Ambulance. Do you know what's happened?'

Ellie summarised briefly, Sylvia behind her.

'Awful. Let's hope they find whoever killed him quickly.'

'Yes,' said Ellie.

She let Sylvia and herself in. The cottage was warm and welcoming, light spilling from the kitchen window, but Ellie's mind was already racing ahead to the next steps.

'We need more background on Neville,' she said, removing her coat. 'On Bramhurst Players, on who might have had reason to want him gone.'

'Agreed.' Sylvia hung her coat next to Ellie's. 'Though it's rather a long list at present.' She tapped her mouth thoughtfully. 'What about Zoe? She's marvellous at digging up information.'

Ellie's daughter worked at a local wildlife rescue centre, but one of her lesser-used talents lay in online research. Give Zoe a name and an hour, and she'd come back with a complete dossier.

'Good idea. I'll ring her now.'

Zoe answered on the third ring, her voice echoing slightly. 'Mum? Everything alright?'

'Where are you?'

'Recovery room. Waiting for a seal to wake up properly after his surgery. He's had an abscess drained, poor love.'

In the background, Ellie could hear voices. 'I won't keep you long. We wondered if you could help with some research.'

'Is this about the murder? Rory texted saying something had happened at the village hall.'

Rory was Daphne's son.

'How does *he* know it's murder?' Ellie made a mental note to have a chat with him.

'Not sure. His mum probably. She knows everything.'

'I was half-expecting him to turn up at the hall with his tripod and phone actually. Do one of his TikTok lives...'

'He's covering another case, I think,' Zoe replied. 'But he mentioned being worried about his mum. I didn't catch it fully.'

'Actually, we're looking for Daphne. Don't suppose he mentioned where she is.'

'Nope. Sorry. So, presumably it *is* a suspicious death?'

'Well, *I* think it's murder.' Ellie told Zoe about Belle positioning the ladder. How it was half-retracted when Neville "fell".

'OK. What do you need?'

Ellie smiled. Her daughter's enthusiasm for crime-solving had definitely come from Sylvia's side of the family. 'Everything you can find on Neville Snipe. Background, previous productions, any controversies or arguments. And anything about Bramhurst Players – their history, past directors, that sort of thing.'

'Consider it done. The seal's going to be woozy for a while yet, but a colleague is coming to take over shortly and

I've got my laptop. I've got some social media to do for the centre but that can wait. I'll text you what I find.'

'Thanks, lovey.'

'No problem. Oh, and Mum? Be careful. We don't know what we're dealing with yet.'

Ellie ended the call and turned to Sylvia. 'She's on it. But we need local knowledge too. History that won't be online.'

'Belle,' Sylvia said immediately. 'She's lived here all her life, knows everyone through the window-cleaning business. If there's gossip or background worth knowing, Belle will have it.'

Chapter 7

Home for Belle was a terraced house near the primary school. She answered the door to Ellie and Sylvia in joggers and an oversized jumper.

'Come in. You'll have to excuse the state of the place.'

The lounge was cosy and cluttered in a lived-in way. A Christmas tree stood in the corner, decorated with an eclectic mix of ornaments that looked like they'd been collected over decades. Artwork covered one wall – landscapes and portraits in watercolour and pencil.

'Chloe's at the yard,' Belle said, moving a stack of window-cleaning invoices from the sofa. 'She's got a job as a stable hand, mucking out the horses and riding. Loves it, she does. Apart from having to get there for 8am.'

Zoe had loved horses too.

'I did Mrs Mitchell's windows and came home. I had a couple of jobs booked for this afternoon, but they cancelled because of the weather. Can't say I was sorry, to be honest. This thing with Neville... It's got me feeling strange. Has it you?' She glanced at Ellie.

'Yeah. It's partly why we've decided to investigate.'

'Ah. I wondered if you would.' She nodded. 'Have a seat. Can I get you anything? Tea? Something stronger?'

'I'm fine, thank you,' Sylvia said. 'We wanted to pick your brains about Bramhurst Players.'

Belle settled into an armchair, tucking her feet under her. 'Sure. I thought you might. Naturally, everyone's talking about Neville. The whole village knows by now.' She paused. 'Is it true that he'd lined up another job?'

'Worse than that,' Ellie replied. 'He'd already started it. At Whitstable Playhouse.'

Belle's mouth fell open.

'We've just come from there and he's been rehearsing their panto in the afternoons whilst working on ours in the evening.'

'Sneaky so-and-so. Sorry, but really.' Belle shook her head. 'So, what do you want to know?'

'The history of the group,' Sylvia said. 'Who ran it before Neville?'

'That was Janine Blackwell. She was director for, oh, must be fifteen years? Maybe longer. Started when her kids were small, carried on even after they'd grown and left home.'

Ellie felt a prickle of recognition. 'Janine Blackwell?'

'That's right. Nice woman. Popular too. Really brought the group together, made it something special. We did proper productions under Janine – musicals, Shakespeare, comedies. Everyone loved her.'

'Why did she leave?' Sylvia asked.

Belle's expression clouded. 'Her mother is elderly and moved in with Janine and the family. Needs a bit more help now. Janine wanted more free time to spend with her.'

'That's kind of her.'

'Absolutely.'

'How did Neville end up taking over?'

'Daphne recommended him to the committee.'

'*Daphne?*' Ellie couldn't help screeching. 'There's something going on with her. Did she know him then? Were they friends?'

'Dunno.' Belle's voice held a note of bitterness. 'But I wish she'd told us we were getting a tyrant who'd upset my daughter and cancel everything the moment something better came along.'

'Hmm,' said Sylvia. 'Where does Janine live?'

'Here in Bramhurst. She's got a grown-up daughter. Lauren.'

Ellie's pulse quickened. 'Lauren Blackwell? Of course.'

'Yes. She does theatre, like her mum. Amateur dramatics all over Kent. Very talented, apparently, though I've never seen her perform.'

'Does Lauren live with her family still or...?'

Belle thought for a moment. 'Whitstable, I think. Or maybe Tankerton. Somewhere on that stretch of the coast, anyway. Why?'

Ellie glanced at Sylvia, seeing her own thoughts reflected back. 'We've just learnt that Neville had a row with an actress at Whitstable Playhouse last week. This was Lauren.'

Belle's eyes widened. 'Are you sure?'

'The woman at the box office gave us her name.'

'Blimmin' heck.' Belle sat back, processing this. 'So, Lauren's been working with the man who took over from her mother, and they were arguing?'

'It seems that way. Although not quite arguing. Apparently he suddenly started having a go at her.'

'What about?'

'Something to do with her performance. Or her costume. The details were vague.'

Belle was quiet for a moment, staring at the Christmas tree lights. 'You know, after Janine left Bramhurst Players, there was a bit of disappointment about the succession. Some people thought Lauren might take over the directing. She'd grown up in the theatre, knew the group inside out. But she didn't put herself forward.'

'So, Neville got the job instead,' Ellie said.

'And proceeded to run things completely differently from how Janine had. Stricter, less collaborative. Got a few people's backs up, but nothing too serious. Until he replaced Chloe as Cinderella, and then this health and safety business with Jo.'

Ellie's phone buzzed. A text from Zoe: *Lots to tell you. Call when you can or can meet?*

'We should probably let you get on with your day,' Sylvia said, standing. 'Thank you. You've been tremendously helpful.'

At the door, Ellie gave Belle a hug.

Belle caught Ellie's arm as they were separating. 'You do know I secured the two bolts on the ladder, don't you? Made sure it was in place properly.'

'Of course.'

'How could it have collapsed then? Bolts don't move themselves.'

'Quite.'

'I use that ladder several times a day. I *definitely* locked it properly.'

'Don't worry. Presumably that's part of what the police are investigating. Someone must've undone them.'

'Like the person we saw leaving from the back door?' said Belle.

'Very possibly. Incidentally, what do you remember about them?'

'Oh, blimey. Dark clothes? Beanie?' She screwed up her face while she tried to recall. 'That's about it.'

'Same here. They've got to be a person of interest. Leaving like that.'

Belle nodded slowly.

Ellie and Sylvia left.

Outside, the temperature had dropped sharply. Frost was already forming on top of the snow, glittering under the streetlights.

Sylvia pulled her scarf tighter. 'So, Lauren Blackwell, daughter of the previous director, was working with the man who replaced her mother. Who then cancelled Bramhurst's production – the group her mother built up and ran for fifteen years.'

'That's quite a collection of grievances.' Ellie kicked at some snow on the kerb. 'Any other ideas?'

'We need to find out who the person was that you and Belle saw leaving the hall in a hurry. Rule them out or in.'

'Yes. The police have the luxury of being able to call in and view CCTV. We'll have to knock on doors.'

Ellie's phone buzzed again. Another text from Zoe: *Call me ASAP. Found something about Neville.*

'Shall we go to the pub?' Ellie said. 'Zoe's got intel. We can warm up a bit and see what Zoe's discovered.'

'Sounds good.'

Ellie texted Zoe: *Meet us at the Hop Picker's Rest as soon as you can get there. We need to agree on what we're doing.*

From Belle's, they walked through the quiet village, past windows lit by twinkling fairy lights and glowing Christmas decorations. The two women walked in companionable silence, speaking every now and then to discuss questions they had.

As they trudged through the snow, Ellie couldn't help wondering whether the killer was someone from Bramhurst, or someone from Whitstable – or someone connected to both.

It was going to be a complicated case. She could feel it.

Chapter 8

The Hop Picker's Rest sat at the far end of the high street, a thatched building with tiny leaded windows. Ellie pushed through the door, Rebus, who they'd collected en route, trotting beside her. The cockerpoo's tail wagged, knowing there was the possibility of crisps coming his way.

Christmas music was playing. Lights and baubles twinkled on a tree.

Sylvia claimed a corner table away from the bar where they could talk without being overheard.

Zoe arrived moments later, bringing an enthusiastic puppy on a lead. 'Marple, sit.' The chocolate cockerpoo dropped obediently, though her eyes remained fixed on Zoe, waiting for her reward.

'She's filling out, isn't she?' Ellie said, eager to stroke the puppy's ears.

'Yes.' Zoe dispensed the treat. 'She's five months now and still thinks she's tiny.' Zoe removed her coat and sat down. 'Right. I've got loads to tell you.'

A waitress appeared, and they ordered hot chocolate with marshmallows on top. It was one of the new management's specials.

'Before we start,' Sylvia said, 'we should agree on what we're doing with regards to Neville's death. Are we going to investigate properly, or just gather information to pass to Dave?'

Ellie took a breath, glancing at her two fellow sleuths. 'I think we need to investigate. The police will do their job, but they won't have our insider knowledge and... how shall I put it?'

'Cheek?' suggested Zoe.

She smiled at her daughter. 'Something like that. But also, they won't know the history of the Players, or the personalities involved. We've been part of the backstage crew for the last few months. And Belle will be able to fill us in on everything.'

'Agreed,' Zoe said. 'Plus, Dad's going to follow procedure. That takes time. Warrants. Official interviews under caution at the station. We can move faster, ask questions casually. It might seem a bit nosy to some people but that's OK.'

'Exactly,' said Sylvia. 'We can do things he can't.' She beamed. 'Then we're decided. We're going to investigate.'

'So,' Ellie pulled out a small notebook from her coat pocket, 'what are our priorities?'

'Background on Janine Blackwell,' Sylvia said. 'Whether her daughter harbours resentment towards Neville. What the row was about. Find out if it was just artistic differences or something deeper.'

Zoe nodded. 'I found quite a bit online. Janine is a big deal in local theatre. Productions all across the UK. Glowing reviews, photos with stars. People really love her. She's very much in demand.'

'We need to talk to them both,' Ellie said.

'Then there's whoever was at the village hall this morning,' Sylvia added, 'and left by the back door. We need to know who that was.'

'Mike suggested it could've been a homeless person who'd been sleeping at the hall and got disturbed.'

'Very possible,' said Sylvia.

Ellie wrote quickly, the list growing. 'And Daphne. Why did she rush to the hall? What phone call did she receive? Sounds like she and Rory had a chat about the hall. Maybe he rang her?'

Their hot chocolates arrived.

'Don't forget any recent arguments Neville had with other cast members,' Zoe said.

'And with anyone else,' Sylvia added, picking up and chewing bits off a giant marshmallow. 'It sounds like he made enemies easily.'

'Do you have to make that noise?' asked Zoe, pulling a pseudo-disgusted face at her grandmother.

Sylvia ignored her and took another bite of her marshmallow.

They sat in silence for a moment, the enormity of their task settling over them. Under the table, Marple had given up sitting and was sprawled across the floor, licking the table leg.

'We've got a lot of ground to cover,' Sylvia observed.

'That's OK,' Ellie said. 'Zoe, can you keep digging into Neville's background? Theatre connections, past productions, any patterns of behaviour?'

'Already on it. I've found his Facebook, some reviews, a couple of newspaper mentions.' Zoe paused, pulling out her phone. 'Actually, there's something else. Something I only just realised.'

She scrolled through her contacts and held up the screen. A photo showed a young woman in waterproofs, cradling a seal pup.

'That's Talia. She volunteers at the centre. Comes in twice a week, helps with feeds and cleaning.'

Ellie leaned closer. It was one of the two women she'd seen on Neville's Facebook.

'Talia Snipe is Neville's youngest daughter,' Zoe told them. 'I didn't make the connection until I saw his Facebook properly. She's tagged in loads of his posts.'

'Poor girls,' Sylvia said. 'How dreadful for them, losing their father.' She paused. 'From an investigation point of view, it could be handy though to know Talia.'

'She wasn't in today – it's her uni day. She does marine biology at Kent.' Zoe bit her lip.

Ellie considered this. 'What's your relationship like?'

'Friendly. We chat while we're working. She's nice, quiet. Loves the seals.'

'When you see her, listen carefully,' Sylvia told Zoe. 'Be sympathetic. If she mentions her father's work or any family tensions, make a note. But this needs to be gentle – she's just lost her father.'

'Yeah, Gran.'

'So that's one possible source,' Ellie said. 'If Talia opens up. But we can't rely on it, and we need to give her space.'

'What about Lauren?' Sylvia asked. 'Do we contact her directly?'

'I think we have to.'

Under the table, Marple had rolled onto her back, paws in the air.

'Right then,' Sylvia said. 'Lauren first, or Janine?'

'Janine,' replied Ellie. 'If we understand why she stepped down as director and how Neville got appointed, we'll have better questions for her daughter.'

'Where does Janine live?'

Ellie checked her notes. 'According to Belle, in Bramhurst. Near the woods and Pear Tree Meadow.' She was still getting to know the village and all its different parts.

'Then we start with Janine,' Sylvia said. 'Tomorrow morning?'

'What about now?' Ellie said. 'If she's home. The trail gets colder the longer we wait.'

'Alright with me,' Sylvia replied.

Zoe finished her drink and stood up. 'I need to get back. One of the rescue seals is being moved to the main pool tomorrow, and I want to check on him.' She bent to clip on Marple's lead. 'Keep me posted?'

They watched Zoe leave, the puppy bouncing at her heels. Through the window, they could see her loading Marple into her van.

The door opened and Mike arrived, a bag over his shoulder. He approached the bar, waved at Ellie, exchanged a few words with the landlord and returned to the main entrance, where he proceeded to take the door off its hinges. He carried it outside and began shaving off wood from one side with a plane.

'You know, Zo didn't mention Finn once,' Sylvia observed. 'Does it sound unkind to say I hope he doesn't come back to Kent for Christmas?'

Ellie smiled. 'No. Dave and I said the same thing last week. I think it's helped, getting Marple. And she *did* mention Rory to me earlier.'

It wasn't that they wanted Zoe to get together with Rory. They just didn't want her to keep pining for Finn if he'd moved on.

Sylvia finished her drink. 'Come on then. Let's go and find out what Janine can tell us.'

Chapter 9

Janine Blackwell's house sat in a row of ancient cottages on the outskirts of Bramhurst. The lane curled between hedgerows heavy with rosehips and frost, its surface dappled with pale winter light. At the far end, beyond the last cottage gate, it opened into Holly Wood and a meadow covered with fresh snow. The house was rendered and painted white, and had a front garden with a picket fence round it. In the snow, it looked a picture of festivity.

Ellie and Sylvia parked behind a mud-spattered Land Rover and stood for a moment, watching the scene before them.

Two women in matching bobble hats were building a snowman in the front garden. The younger – Janine, presumably – was rolling a substantial middle section whilst the older woman patted snow onto what would become the head. A chocolate labrador bounded between them, barking joyfully and occasionally destroying their work with enthusiastic paws.

'Biscuit, no. We've just done that bit.' Janine laughed as the dog launched itself at the snowman's base. She looked up and spotted Ellie and Sylvia. 'Hello. Can I help you?'

'Janine?' Ellie called up the slope. 'I'm Ellie Blix. This is Sylvia. We're from Bramhurst Players. Could we chat to you for a few minutes?'

Janine's smile faltered slightly, but she gestured them up. 'Of course. Come in. You'll have to excuse us – we're being terribly childish.'

The older woman turned, revealing a face weathered by age but brightened by lively eyes. She must have been in her eighties but moved with agility. 'Lovely to meet you. I'm Hattie. Do come inside before you freeze.'

The hallway was warm and cluttered in a comfortable way. Wellingtons and walking boots lined up by the door, coats hung on hooks, a walking stick propped in the corner. Biscuit shook snow everywhere and was banished to the kitchen with good-natured firmness.

'Let me put the kettle on,' Hattie said, already heading towards the back of the house. 'Janine, take them through to the sitting room.'

The room was cosy, with orange flames flickering in a wood burning stove and family photographs covering every available surface.

Janine gestured them to sit and pulled off her bobble hat, revealing wavy blonde hair in a long bob.

Ellie recognised her now. They'd met briefly once, walking their dogs.

'So,' Janine said, settling into an armchair, 'what brings Bramhurst Players to my door? I haven't been involved for nearly a year now.'

'We know,' Ellie said. 'We're actually here about your replacement. Neville Snipe.'

'Ah.' Janine's expression suggested she'd heard plenty about Neville's tenure. 'How is he? Still making enemies left and right?'

Sylvia glanced at Ellie, who took a breath. 'I'm afraid Neville died this morning. At the village hall.'

Janine sat very still. 'Died? How?'

Ellie explained briefly. 'The police are investigating.'

'Good Lord.' Janine looked genuinely shocked. 'That's awful. I mean, he wasn't my choice for the new director role, but I wouldn't wish something like this on the man.' She was shaking her head gently in disbelief.

'The thing is,' Sylvia said gently, 'we're trying to understand Neville's relationships in the theatre community. Who might have had issues with him.'

Janine's laugh was short and humourless. 'That's rather a long list, I'm afraid. Neville had the unfortunate habit of making enemies.'

Hattie appeared with a tea tray, setting it down with a clatter. 'Are you talking about that dreadful man who took over from you? I told you he'd be trouble, darling.'

'Yes, Mum. He's dead, apparently.' She mouthed 'sorry' to her guests, gesturing to her mother with her gaze.

'Oh dear.' Hattie poured tea into mugs. 'Well, that's very sad.' She handed drinks round. 'Sugar? Milk?'

Once Hattie had settled into her own chair with Biscuit at her feet, Janine continued. 'I'd heard rumours about Neville for years. He has – had – a reputation in the local theatre circuit. Difficult to work with, prone to taking credit for other people's ideas, and work. Not always reliable about payments.'

'Yet he became director at Bramhurst,' Ellie said.

'Yes. That was... complicated.' Janine stirred her tea thoughtfully. 'He got in via Daphne Henderson. She put in a good word for him.'

'Belle mentioned this,' said Ellie. 'It seems extraordinary.'

'She persuaded the committee to offer him the post. I was consulted, of course, and I expressed my reservations. But Daphne was very keen. Said he had extensive experience, excellent references, would bring a professional touch to our productions.' Janine's tone suggested she'd had doubts about all of this.

'Did she say why she was so keen for him to have the role?' Sylvia asked.

'Not really. Just that she'd known him years ago and thought he deserved a chance.' Janine sipped her tea. 'I should have pushed back harder. But I was in the process of stepping down anyway, and honestly, I thought maybe the rumours were exaggerated. People can be very catty in amateur dramatics.'

'Were they exaggerated?' Ellie asked.

'No. If anything, they underplayed the issues. Within a month, I was hearing complaints. He was autocratic, dismissive of people's ideas, unpleasant when anyone questioned his decisions.'

'But nobody challenged him?'

Janine shrugged. 'That's the trouble with volunteer organisations. Once someone's in post, it's hard to remove them without causing a massive row. Easier to just put up with them and hope they improve.'

Hattie snorted. 'Or hope they fall off a ladder, apparently.'

'Mum, please.'

'I'm sorry, darling. I know you'll tell me off again, and blame my dementia, but the man sounds perfectly horrid. These nice ladies wouldn't be here asking questions if he'd been a decent human being.'

Janine looked slightly embarrassed but didn't argue. 'My daughter had first-hand experience of his rudeness.'

'We heard,' Ellie confirmed. 'Jack and the Beanstalk.'

'She was thrilled to get the role of Jill. Good part, she's perfect for it. Then, last week, Neville suddenly started being rude about her acting.'

'Just like that?' Sylvia asked.

'Uh-huh. In front of the entire cast, during rehearsal. Told her she had all the charisma of a lump of mud.' Janine's voice was tight with controlled anger. 'She was mortified. Twenty-six years old, and reduced to tears in front of strangers.'

'That's appalling,' Ellie said.

'It's typical Neville, from what I've heard. He enjoyed humiliating people. Made him feel powerful, I suppose.' Janine set down her mug. 'Lauren was furious. She's got her mother's tongue, I'm afraid. They had a dreadful row, apparently. Half the cast heard it.'

'What did she say to him?'

'I don't know exactly. She was too upset to tell me everything. But she used some choice language, I gather. Told him he was a talentless hack trading on other people's work, that sort of thing. Then she stormed out.'

Biscuit chose this moment to get up and pad over to Ellie, resting his head on her knee with a soulful expression. She scratched behind his ears automatically.

'The strange thing,' Janine continued, 'is that Lauren's genuinely talented. She's been performing since she was a child, learned everything from me. For Neville to cast her and then insult her like that makes no sense. Unless...'

'Unless what?' Sylvia prompted.

'Unless he never intended to keep her. Maybe he cast her knowing he'd drop her, just to be cruel. Or maybe someone else wanted the role and put pressure on him. I honestly don't know.'

Hattie leaned closer, her expression shrewd. 'Or maybe your Lauren reminded him too much of you, dear. You said he didn't like being questioned, and heaven knows your daughter's not one to keep quiet when she sees something wrong.'

Janine considered this. 'Perhaps. He certainly knew who she was – knew she was my daughter. Maybe that was part of it.'

'Where does Lauren live?' Ellie asked.

'In Whitstable. On Harbour Street. Above the fish and chip shop. She carried on with her role because she's professional but she was embarrassed, I think, and angry. I've tried to tell her it's not her fault, but you know how it is when you're young. Everything feels like the end of the world.'

'Do you think she'd talk to us?' Sylvia asked.

Janine looked from Sylvia to Ellie. 'About Neville? Probably. She'll be upset that he's dead – Lauren's got a good heart, even if she's got a temper – but I can't imagine she'll pretend to be devastated.' She paused. 'Why are you asking all this? The police must be doing their own investigation.'

'They are,' Ellie said carefully. 'But we were there when it happened. We found him. And now everyone's asking questions, making assumptions. We thought it might help to understand the full picture.'

Janine stood and walked to the window, looking out at the half-finished snowman. 'I feel guilty, you know. I should have fought harder to keep him out. Or at least warned people more explicitly. But I thought…' She turned back to them. 'I thought maybe he'd change. Or maybe I was wrong about him. You want to give people the benefit of the doubt, don't you?'

'You can't blame yourself,' Sylvia said firmly. 'Neville's choices were his own.'

'I know. But still.' Janine returned to her chair. 'Is there anything else you need to know?'

'Just a couple of further questions,' Ellie said. 'Neville was directing two plays simultaneously. Well, he was before he cancelled our panto here. Did Lauren know about that?'

Janine frowned. 'She must've done. Obviously, she knew he was directing the one in Whitstable. And when Neville humiliated her in front of everyone, she mentioned that he'd sacked Chloe and given someone else her part. So – yes. She did.'

Ellie was wondering what that meant. How many other people knew he was rehearsing two plays?

'Finally – do you know if Neville had any particular enemies? Anyone who seemed especially angry with him?'

'Apart from my daughter and Chloe, you mean?' Janine smiled wryly. 'I honestly don't know. I've kept my distance since stepping down. Heard bits and pieces through the grapevine, but nothing specific.' She paused. 'Though, as I'm sure you know, from what I understand, the whole of Bramhurst Players are furious about the cancelled panto. Children disappointed, money wasted, all that work for nothing. If you're looking for people with reasons to be angry with Neville, I'd start there.'

They finished their tea with small talk about the snow and Christmas plans. Hattie insisted on sending them away with some of the mince pies she'd made that morning.

'Lovely to meet you,' Hattie called from the doorway. 'Do let us know if we can help with anything. This sleuthing business sounds rather fun.'

'Sorry,' said Janine. 'Mum's condition has...' She didn't finish her sentence and gave an embarrassed smile.

In the car, Sylvia unwrapped a mince pie and took a bite. 'Well. That was definitely worth the trip.' She bit into the pie. 'Mmm. Buttery.'

'Daphne recommending Neville for the job,' Ellie said, starting the engine. 'Despite Janine's concerns. Why would she do that?'

'Because of a romantic history perhaps? Some misguided loyalty?'

'Or because he asked her to, and she couldn't say no.' Ellie pulled out onto the lane, windscreen wipers clearing fresh snow.

'Perhaps she regretted it,' suggested Sylvia. 'Decided to do something about it?' She finished her mince pie. 'And then there's Lauren. A screaming match with Neville a week before he dies. That's quite a coincidence.'

'We need to talk to her. And to Daphne.' Ellie glanced at her mother-in-law. 'Dave's going to be furious with us, you know.'

'Darling, he's always furious with us. It's practically tradition.' Sylvia smiled. 'Besides, we're just asking questions. It's not as if we're tampering with evidence.'

'Not yet, anyway.'

They drove back towards Bramhurst through the snow-covered countryside, the winter sun already setting though it was barely four o'clock. Somewhere ahead, a killer was hoping Neville's death would be written off as a tragic accident.

But the more questions they asked, the clearer it became that Neville Snipe had made enemies wherever he went. And someone had finally decided that enough was enough.

Chapter 10

It was a short drive back to the high street from Janine's house, through lanes narrowed by snow. Ellie pulled up outside the village shop just as the streetlights flickered on, casting cream pools across the white pavement. 'Let's speak to Daphne before Lauren,' she said, unbuckling her seatbelt. 'Given Daphne recommended Neville to the Bramhurst Players' committee despite Janine's warnings, we need to know why.'

'And whether she regretted it,' Sylvia added.

The bell jingled its merry tune as they entered. The shop was full of people grabbing up Christmas wrapping paper and cards.

Rory was behind the till, entering numbers into the lottery terminal for a customer. He gave Ellie a polite smile.

'Helping your mum out?' Ellie asked him.

'Something like that.' He turned to the next customer. 'EuroMillions or National Lottery?' He scanned the slip and printed the ticket.

Daphne appeared from the back room. Seeing them approach, something flickered across her face. Not quite alarm, but close.

'Ellie. Sylvia.' She set down her pen carefully. 'We're just about to close.'

'We were hoping to have a quick word,' Ellie said. 'About Neville Snipe.'

'I can handle things here, Mum...' Rory's tone was helpful.

Daphne's expression closed like a door slamming. 'I don't want to discuss him.'

'We understand it's difficult–' Sylvia began.

'No, I don't think you do.' Daphne's voice was tight. 'I've already told the police I don't wish to talk about him.' She turned towards the back room, seemingly not realising Ellie and Sylvia were following her.

Ellie surveyed the area. Boxes stacked against the walls. A formica table and chairs. 'Daphne, we're not trying to upset you. But Belle and I were there when it happened. We found Neville.'

'Then you should leave it to the police.' Daphne gathered up a couple of mugs from the table and started to walk towards the doorway, a clear dismissal. 'I'm sure they'll do their job.'

'We know you went to the hall yesterday morning after Neville came into the shop,' Sylvia said quietly. 'Why?'

'That's my business?'

'Have you told the police?'

'No.' Daphne leant up against a stack of crisp and biscuit boxes.

'Was his death a shock?'

'Of course.' Daphne looked up, and her eyes were bright with what might have been tears or anger. 'Whatever you might think, Neville's death is a tragedy. I won't pretend otherwise.'

Ellie studied her carefully. Daphne's usual warmth had vanished, replaced by a brittle defensiveness. They'd always been on good terms. Daphne had been welcoming to Ellie when she'd moved to Bramhurst three months ago; always had a kind word and the latest village gossip. This coldness felt wrong – and like a different person.

'We spoke to Janine this afternoon,' Ellie said gently. 'She mentioned that you recommended Neville for the director's position.'

Daphne's jaw tightened. 'Did she?'

'She said you were quite insistent about it. Even though she had concerns.'

'Janine *always* has concerns. She's cautious to a fault.'

'But you knew Neville,' Sylvia pressed. 'From before. Is that right?'

'I knew him years ago. A lifetime ago.' Daphne's fingers were drumming on the side of one of the mugs. 'And yes, I put in a good word for him. I thought he deserved a chance. I was wrong. Is that what you want to hear?'

'We're not trying to–'

'Then what *are* you trying to do?' Daphne's voice rose slightly. 'Stand in my shop asking questions like you're the police? I've already had them here this morning, asking where I was, what I knew, whether Neville and I had any disagreements. As if I'd...' She stopped, pressing her lips together.

'As if you'd what?' Ellie asked quietly.

'Nothing. Forget I said anything.' Daphne reached into her jacket pocket and pulled out a tissue, dabbing at her eyes. 'Look, I appreciate that you found him, and I'm sure that was awful. But I really don't want to discuss this. Not with you, not with anyone. I just want to be left alone to get on with my life.'

Sylvia tried once more. 'Daphne, if there's something you're worried about–'

'I'm not worried about anything except running my shop and getting through Christmas.' Her voice had taken on a trembling quality. 'Now, unless you're buying something, I'd appreciate it if you'd leave. I have stock to put out before closing.'

Ellie had seen the shelves when they arrived, all recently restocked, the shop immaculate as always. Daphne was lying, and not very well.

'Of course,' Ellie said.

Sylvia picked up a packet of custard cream biscuits from an open box. 'I'll pay for them on the way out.'

'We didn't mean to upset you,' Ellie said.

'I'm not upset.' Daphne's smile was pained, tight with no warmth. 'I'm just busy. Now – would you please leave?'

The bell jangled behind them as they left, somehow sounding less cheery. Through the window, Ellie could see Daphne standing in the doorway into the back room, motionless, tissue clutched in her hand, staring at nothing.

'Well, what do you think is going on there?' Sylvia asked, once they were safely in the car. She placed the biscuits on the dashboard.

'She's hiding something.'

'Oh, undoubtedly. But what?' Sylvia pulled out her phone and made a note. 'She was defensive, emotional, lying about being busy. Classic guilty behaviour.'

'Perhaps she feels bad about recommending Neville,' said Ellie. 'And doesn't want people knowing why she did.

It's as if he had a hold over her.' Ellie started the engine and pulled away from the kerb. 'She admits knowing him from years ago. I wonder if they have some sort of romantic history. It's the only thing I can think of that might explain her loyalty. What if Neville has been exploiting it somehow?'

'Blackmail?'

'I'm thinking: manipulation. Emotional pressure. Coercion. "Remember what we meant to each other, help me out for old times' sake." That sort of thing.' Ellie navigated the corner by the pub. 'And then once he had the director job, he kept pressuring her for something else. Support against Jo, maybe. Or money.'

'She refused him the morning he died,' Sylvia said slowly. 'Maya said Neville came to the shop before going to the hall. What if that was one demand too many?'

'I wonder why she went to the village hall...' Ellie paused. 'It sounded like that "no" was pretty final.'

They drove in silence for a moment, past the church where lights blazed from the windows. Choir practice, probably, preparing for Christmas services.

'I'm sure Dave will interview her again,' Ellie said. 'He'll get more out of her than we did.'

'Perhaps. Though sometimes people are more willing to talk to amateurs than police.' Sylvia smiled. 'We're less threatening. More like concerned friends than official investigators.'

'She didn't seem to find us very friendly just now.' Ellie was trying to think how she could have a quiet word with Rory.

'No. Which suggests we touched a nerve.' Sylvia made another note. 'We need to find out more about her history with Neville. When they knew each other, what happened between them, why she'd feel obligated to help him decades later.'

Ellie pulled up outside her cottage and killed the engine. Through the window, she could see lights on in the kitchen. Dave must be home already.

'I should go in,' she said. 'I want to know if there have been any developments.'

'He won't tell you. Are you going to fill him in on what we've learnt?'

'Of course. Although it'll probably make him furious.'

Sylvia laughed. 'Good luck with that, darling. I'll see you tomorrow. We should try to talk to Lauren, if we can locate her.'

'Agreed. And I want another go at Daphne when she's had time to calm down.' Ellie was considering speaking to Rory. See what he knew. He was a true crime podcaster, after all, and a very thorough one.

'There was a sadness to Daphne. Did you notice?'

'Yes,' Ellie said. 'I agree. It's worrying.'

She watched Sylvia drive away, then gathered her things and headed inside.

Chapter 11

The house was warm and smelled of toast. Dave appeared from the kitchen, ramming a piece of white bread slathered with strawberry jam into his mouth. He looked both pleased to see her and resigned to whatever she was about to tell him.

He kissed her cheek and uttered something unintelligible.

'Ugh. You're all sticky.'

He chewed and swallowed. 'Sorry. Starving. I asked how your day was.'

'Interesting. You?'

'Long. I've been interviewing half of Bramhurst.' He studied her face. 'Why do I get the feeling you've been doing the same thing?'

'Because you're a brilliant detective?'

'Because I know you, more like.' He gestured towards the kitchen. 'Come on, you can tell me about it while I eat. We're going to the quiz this evening, aren't we?'

'Yup. If you still want to.'

'So, what've you been up to? Hopefully you haven't been sneaking around behind my back.'

'I *never* sneak.'

'No, you investigate openly and thoroughly, which is somehow worse.' But he was smiling as he said it, and Ellie felt a rush of affection for this man who understood her compulsions even when they drove him mad.

In the kitchen, she told him about Janine and Hattie, the snowman and the labrador, the story of Lauren's humiliation. She told him about Daphne's defensive reaction, her refusal to discuss Neville, the tears that might have been real or performance.

Dave listened, making a mug of tea for Ellie and asking occasional questions.

'So, Daphne recommended Neville to the panto group,' he said finally. 'Despite warnings. That's interesting.'

'She said you spoke to her.'

'This morning. She claimed she barely knew him, just thought he seemed qualified.' Dave put his mug and plate in the dishwasher. 'Sounds like that wasn't entirely truthful.'

'She knew him years ago. Romantic history, we suspect.'

'Then she lied to me.' Dave's tone was mild, but Ellie knew that look. Someone had just moved up his suspect list. 'I'll need to speak to her again.'

'She's very defensive. And upset.'

'Guilty people often are.' He turned to face her. 'Ells, I know you want to help. And some of this is useful background. But please be careful. Neville was murdered–'

'At least you've admitted it now.'

'The ladder didn't show signs of sabotage, but the locks had been pushed back,' he confirmed, 'the way they are when you want to fold up the ladder.'

'Yep. We noticed that.'

'It collapsed under Neville's weight.' He paused.

Ellie shivered.

'Someone knew what they were doing.'

'Lots of people in the village use ladders,' Ellie said quietly.

'We certainly have a few on our list. In addition, we've got most of the panto cast and crew, along with everyone else who was in or near the village hall yesterday morning.' Dave took her hands. 'Which is why I need you to be careful. No confronting potential murderers in car parks, no heroic solo investigations. Promise me.'

'I promise.' She squeezed his hands. 'We're just asking questions.'

'Questions that might lead to answers someone doesn't want revealed.' He kissed her forehead. 'Don't forget that. This person is dangerous. The pathologist says Neville had already sustained a head wound before the fall.'

In the bath fifteen minutes later, Ellie went over everything they'd learned. The list of suspects was growing: Daphne had recommended Neville, and had history with him. She was defensive and upset about his death. Lauren had been publicly humiliated by him and had a screaming match. Belle's daughter had been dumped from the lead role. The ladder was Belle's and she'd been present at scene...

Had one of them watched him fall to his death or pushed him?

Chapter 12

The Hop Picker's Rest was packed by the time Ellie and Dave arrived. The Monday night quiz was a village institution, and the new landlords had thrown themselves into it with enthusiasm. Darren stood behind the bar pulling pints whilst his wife Alex moved between tables, collecting glasses, chatting with customers and taking team names for the quiz.

The pub had been transformed for Christmas. Fairy lights draped every beam, tinsel wound around the brass beer pumps, and a towering tree stood in the corner, decorated with what looked like decades' worth of ornaments. Carols played softly under the buzz of conversation. The fire roared, casting dancing shadows across the flagstone floor.

Rebus scurried over to the fireplace and stretched out on the hearth like a furry draught excluder. He didn't even bother to check in with the couple sitting at the table there.

'Over here,' Belle shouted, waving from a table near the dartboard. She'd saved them seats, drinks already waiting – a pint for Dave and a glass of prosecco for Ellie. Her husband Phil sat beside her, still in his work clothes.

'Evening,' Phil said, standing to clap Dave on the shoulder. 'Ready for another spectacular win?'

'A hundred per cent,' Dave said, grinning. He and Phil were both intensely competitive, something which Ellie and Belle ribbed them about endlessly.

Ellie slid into her seat and took a grateful sip of her fizz. The pub was warm after their brief but chilly walk from the cottage.

The atmosphere was determinedly festive but there were mutterings all around them about Neville's death – a shadow hanging over the village. Was it wrong for them all to be here, drinking, socialising, laughing when his body was at the funeral director's?

Her sense was – no. They weren't celebrating his death. And tragedy tended to make people cling to their loved ones and their regular routines.

'How's Chloe?' Ellie asked Belle quietly.

'Upset. She's at a friend's, which is probably for the best. Gives her some distance from all the gossip.' Belle's expression was carefully neutral.

At the next table, a group of teachers from the local primary school were deep in conversation, voices low but urgent.

Several of the cast and crew were there. Mike, who'd built the set, sat at a table with Rory Henderson and Reverend Jo. A vivacious young woman was with them, wearing a baseball cap on back-to-front. Five other members of Bramhurst Players were on the next table: Marie-Hélène and Paul from the bakery; Rebecca, the bookshop owner; Margaret Fleming who ran the wool shop was with her husband and Gideon, a local historian.

Alex appeared at their table with menus. 'Evening, folks. We've got a curry special tonight – chicken korma, lamb rogan josh, or vegetable jalfrezi. All served with rice, naan, and poppadoms.'

Ellie and Dave ordered food and settled in as Darren called the pub to order. He was a large man, tall too, with an even larger voice, perfectly suited to pub quizzes.

'Right then, everyone. Welcome to our Monday quiz night. We've got five rounds: general knowledge, music, sport, history, and a special round on local knowledge.' He paused for effect. 'Which given you lot are all local, you'll no doubt find easy. However, given recent events, I thought we'd keep it light.'

Murmurs rippled around the bar.

'Alex has given me all the team names,' said Darren, glancing at his list. 'Who on earth is "the Raging Numpties"?'

Phil waved his arm in the air.

The first round was straightforward general knowledge. Capital cities, famous paintings, which planet was closest to the sun. Ellie and Dave worked well together, and Phil surprised everyone by claiming to know the collective noun for flamingos.

'Flamboyance,' he said smugly. 'I read it in Chloe's nature magazine.'

The music round required identifying songs from their opening bars. Belle proved good at this, much to Phil's amazement.

'Since when do you know nineties indie rock?' he asked.

'I was young once, Philip. Hard as that might be to believe.'

The curry arrived during the sport round, steaming plates of fragrant food. Ellie had the lamb rogan josh, perfectly spiced and served with fluffy pilau rice. Dave tucked into a jalfrezi.

Around them, conversation was split between the quiz and Neville. It was impossible not to overhear fragments, mainly the result of speculation and overactive imaginations.

'... heard it was the ladder that failed...'

'... we all know who has ladders...'

'My mum saw police at Daphne's shop this morning...'

'Shame about the panto. The kids are so disappointed...'

The history round tested knowledge of British monarchs and Tudor architecture. Phil knew all the details of chimneys and fireplaces through the ages and carried them to a respectable score.

Then came the final round: local knowledge.

'Right,' Darren said, consulting his notes. 'This one's about Bramhurst and the surrounding area. Question one: What year was St Mildred's built?'

Easy. Everyone knew that. 1186, with Victorian additions.

Belle already had it down on their answer sheet.

'Question two: How many pubs are there in Bramhurst?'

Two. The second was the Crooked Lantern at the other end of the village.

'Question three: What was the theme of last year's village fête?'

'Ah, *le cancan*,' said Marie-Hélène. '*Mon dieu*, the laughter...'

Ellie remembered the chaos of the French can-can dancers.

"*Around the World in Eighty Days,*" muttered Belle.

'Question four: Who directed Bramhurst Players for fifteen years before stepping down last year?'

Ellie and Belle met each other's gaze, eyebrows raised.

Dave jotted "Janine Blackwell" on their score sheet.

'Question five...' Darren paused, and something in his expression suggested he knew this question was going to cause a reaction. 'Name five items that are part of the set for Cinderella.'

The pub went very quiet.

'That's easy,' said Mike 'given I made them all.' He scribbled on their score sheet.

Belle wrote: kitchen table. Cottage door. Ballroom backdrop. Pumpkin coach. The throne.

'Can we include the glass slipper?' shouted a student on one of the tables.

Conversation levels shot up. Some talking about the cancelled production. Others, the previous Cinderella performance they'd seen. People expressed disappointment about the tickets they'd bought.

Ellie glanced around and caught sight of Jo, standing very still near the bar. Her face drawn with sadness.

Darren collected answer sheets and began marking them with Alex.

Phil was arguing quietly with Belle about whether the cottage façade counted as one item or multiple, given it had a door and windows.

Ellie scanned the room, taking in the familiar faces. So many people, like Belle and herself, who'd been part of this year's production, which had ended in tragedy.

And then she saw Daphne.

She was tucked into a corner booth, almost hidden by the fruit machine. Alone, which was unusual. Daphne was normally sociable at pub events, and always had someone to chat with.

Tonight, though, she sat hunched over a large bowl-shaped glass, with three empty tonic bottles on the table, a barely touched sandwich in front of her.

Even from across the room, Ellie could see she looked terrible. Her face was pale, eyes red-rimmed, her usually neat hair a mess.

'Ells?' Dave's voice was quiet, concerned. He'd followed her gaze. 'You alright?'

'Look at Daphne. Why isn't she with Rory?'

He glanced over, and his expression shifted into detective mode. 'Oh dear.'

'Something's not right, is it?' Belle said, having noticed their attention. She kept her voice low, barely audible over the quiz. 'Been sitting there since before you arrived. Hasn't spoken to anyone.'

'Has she been drinking much?' Dave asked.

'That's her third,' Phil said. 'Large ones by the look of the glass. I've been keeping an eye.'

'Should someone check she's OK?' said Dave. 'Not me though. She'll think I want to question her again.'

'She won't want to speak to me either,' Ellie said quickly. 'I might nip over and have a word with Rory.'

'He must know she's here,' Belle added.

'All the same…' Ellie wriggled out of her seat and went over. 'Hi, everyone.' She smiled at the whole table, then Rory. She lowered her voice. 'Is your mum OK? We're worried about her.'

'We've asked her to join us twice, but she doesn't want to,' replied Rory.

'Shall I go and ask again?' said the young woman.

'Ellie,' said Mike, smiling proudly. 'I don't think you've met my daughter, Sadie. She's staying with me for a few days and again at Christmas.'

Sadie had a friendly face like her father. 'Last few times in my childhood bedroom before Dad gets a lodger.' She screwed up her mouth in a sad expression.

Ellie gave her an understanding smile. She remembered when Zoe had left home and she'd started doing Airbnb.

'I'll go,' said Rory. He got up and made his way over to Daphne. He had his back to them but they all saw Daphne shake her head vigorously.

Rory returned. 'She wants to be on her own.'

Darren was calling out scores now, so Ellie returned to her table. Teams groaned or cheered, depending on their results. 'In third place,' he said, "the Sweeping Changes".'

A cheer went up from the student table.

'Second place, "the Bramhurst Bees".'

Another cheer from across the bar.

'And in first place – someone beat this motley crew next time please or I'll have to ban them from entering – "the Raging Numpties"...'

Phil thumped the table.

'... who clearly think that if they keep changing their team name, I won't know who they are.'

'It was DCI Blix's suggestion,' said Phil affectionately. He collected their prize – a crossword puzzle with a picture of Canterbury Cathedral.

As the pub began to thin out, people heading home or to the bar for one last drink, Ellie watched Daphne push away her plate and stand unsteadily. She made her way to the door, not looking at anyone, moving slowly, like someone who just wanted to be anywhere else.

Belle caught Ellie's eye. 'Should we follow her? Check she gets home OK?'

At that moment, Rory got up and shot over to his mum.

'She'll be OK now,' said Dave.

Rory took her arm and steered her towards the door.

They finished their drinks, collected Rebus from the hearth, and said goodnight to Darren and Alex.

Outside, the temperature had dropped sharply. Frost was forming on top of snow, glittering in the evening light, and their breath steamed in the cold air. The Christmas lights hung in swags across the high street, strung from lamppost to lamppost – stars, snowflakes, flickering in the night air.

'What do you think Daphne knows?' Belle asked, pulling on her gloves.

'Something that's eating her up,' Ellie said. 'Did you see her face? That's not just grief. That's guilt.'

Phil put his arm around Belle. 'Come on, love. Let's get you home. Leave the detective work to the professionals.'

'*And* the amateurs...' Belle said, grinning.

Dave raised an eyebrow and muttered something as he turned up the collar of his jacket.

They walked along the lane towards home, footsteps crunching on frozen puddles, Rebus pulling on the leash to follow smells.

When they reached Belle and Phil's road, they said goodnight and parted ways.

Ellie and Dave continued walking.

'You're unusually quiet. What are you thinking?' Ellie asked.

'That we've got too many suspects and not enough evidence. That people are lying, hiding things, protecting themselves or others.' He kicked at a snow drift at the edge of the road. 'That this case is going to get messier before it gets clearer. I can feel it.'

'Do you think Daphne did it?'

'I don't know. I think she knows something. Whether that's who did it, or just information that's connected somehow, I can't tell yet.' He flicked snow off the railings by the old phone box. 'But tomorrow, I'm going to find out. Before anyone else gets hurt.'

Ellie nodded. She was thinking that it would be a good idea to get the whole cast and crew together. To discuss how they felt and support each other. And find out who knew what.

Her thoughts shifted to the chapel. 'We've got the frame being installed first thing tomorrow. That's going to be interesting.'

'Yes,' said Dave. 'Roll on the next phase of the renovations.'

Chapter 13
TUESDAY

Ellie had walked Rebus and was halfway through her second cup of coffee, about to head to the chapel to meet the builders to see the steel frame installed.

Today was the first day of the Christmas market. The seats outside the bookshop café had the best view of the high street, and Ellie had got settled near one of the heaters with a blanket, and a cappuccino and mince pie for breakfast.

The market was in full swing despite the early hour. Her gaze drifted from one stall to the next, watching their friends and neighbours enjoy themselves.

Wooden huts lined both sides of the street, their peaked roofs dusted with fresh snow. The coffee hut squatted on the pavement, its timber walls strung with fairy lights. Ellie kept getting wafts of roasted beans and hot milk, and the sweetness drifting from the pastry stalls nearby.

Steam rose from a glühwein stand where a man in a thick jumper stirred the spiced wine, the scent of cinnamon and cloves drifting through the cold air. Ellie kept checking to see if anyone was going to indulge at 8.30am.

Gideon was chatting to a woman in a red apron who was tending a brazier where chestnuts roasted, their shells splitting with little cracks as they cooked. The nutty, sweet smell mixed with everything else, created an aroma that was purely Christmas. Gideon handed over change and took a paper cone of edibles.

Next to them, another vendor served hot cider from a copper pot, whilst bratwurst sizzled on a griddle, fat spitting and popping.

Two huts along sold baked goods. Ellie could see mince pies stacked in pyramids. She could practically taste their buttery pastry. Gingerbread men hung from ribbons, some decorated with icing, others plain. Stollen sat on wooden boards, studded with fruits and dusted with snow-white sugar.

The craft huts were doing good business already. Mel from the pottery studio was browsing handmade wreaths. Dried orange slices hung on strings, their spicy scent just detectable when the wind shifted. Another stall displayed wooden decorations – stars, angels, reindeer – all hand-painted in traditional red and green.

Near the war memorial, a couple were opening a stall selling alcohol-infused cupcakes. Next to them a man in a Christmas jumper was showing Rory their various-sized drinking horns.

At the far end, a stall was making crêpes. Sweet and savoury. And, on another stall, a young woman handed two excited children marshmallows on a skewer to heat over a fire pit.

Christmas songs played from speakers hidden somewhere in the market – "*The Holly and the Ivy*" drifting over the chatter and laughter. Children darted between the stalls, parents calling after them. A man juggled three oranges near the fruit seller, making people laugh.

Ellie sipped her drink, watching it all. Despite everything, the village was still preparing for Christmas. Life carried on. It had to. The market opened. People bought their wreaths and their gifts and their gingerbread.

A few moments later, Zoe crossed the road, joining Ellie at her table, stamping snow off her boots. 'Talia Snipe just came to see me at the centre. Can we go inside and I'll tell you what she said? It's freezing out here.'

They relocated and Zoe removed her jacket and sat down. 'She wants to talk about her dad. *In confidence.*'

Ellie set down her mug. 'Oh?'

Zoe settled at the table, Rebus padding over to rest his chin on Zoe's knee in greeting.

'She turned up this morning, saying she wants to keep busy,' Zoe said, scratching the dog's ears absently. 'Asked if we could talk somewhere private. I took her to the staff room.'

'What did she say?'

'That she needs to speak to someone about her father.' Zoe met her mother's eyes. 'I told her I couldn't agree to that. Not about someone who's just died, not without knowing what she wants to share.'

'Good.'

'I asked if she could talk to her mum or the police but she says no. Says she trusts me.' Zoe pulled a face. 'Which is lovely but also terrifying. What if she tells me something incriminating?'

'Did you ask her what this is about?'

'Sort of. She just said it's about her dad's death and her mum, and she's worried. Really worried, Mum. She looked like she hasn't slept.'

Ellie puzzled for a moment, weighing options. 'How did you leave it with her?'

'That I'd talk to you. That if she wants to speak to me, you'd need to be there too. And that depending on what she tells us, we might have to pass the information on. To Dad, probably.'

'How did she react?'

'She agreed. Said she'd meet us at lunchtime.' Zoe checked her phone. 'Hambrook Marsh. She's helping on the Stour today. Determined to keep herself occupied. River clearance project.'

'Bit cold for it.'

'I know. That's why I don't want to get freezing now. Some idiot has dumped a refrigerator in one section and, in another, a load of household waste. We've got to remove it before it pollutes the water and poisons the wildlife.'

Ellie glanced at the clock. Just after nine. 'That gives us three hours.' She smiled with pride. Zoe had become a proper conservationist.

'Do we tell Dad about Talia?'

'Not yet. Not until we know what she wants to get off her chest.' Ellie stood and stretched her back. 'If Talia's worried about her mother, there might be a good reason. Or she might just be frightened and confused. Either way, ambushing her with the police isn't going to help.'

'That's what I thought.' Zoe eyed the drinks board. 'But if she tells us her mum killed her dad, we have to tell him. Right?'

'Of course. But let's hope it doesn't come to that.'

Zoe ordered a drink and got Ellie a refill. They spent the next fifteen minutes in careful speculation, running through possibilities. What could Talia know? What had she seen or heard? And why wouldn't she go to the police?

'OK,' said Zoe. 'I need to get back to work. I'll meet you at Hambrook Marshes at midday. Park at Wincheap and walk through onto the marsh. The team is working on the section to the right.'

'See you there.'

Once Zoe had left, Ellie sent an email round to all the panto cast and crew, suggesting they meet at the hall. The police had released the crime scene. She floated a couple of times, including early the following morning. Hopefully, workers would be able to make that.

She put on her coat and hat, left the bookshop and began the walk to the chapel. And much as she was looking forward to seeing her future home, she also couldn't stop wondering what Talia wanted to confide.

Chapter 14

Dave was already at the chapel when Ellie arrived.

The thirteenth-century building looked magical in the winter sunshine, Gothic spires reaching up onto the sky, its ancient stone walls glowing golden against the snow.

The largest window – the beautiful arched one that had once held stained glass – gaped open, the glass carefully removed and stored. Through it, she could see the empty space inside, waiting to be transformed.

A grabber lorry stood in what would eventually be their garden, its mechanical arm extended upwards, a steel frame section suspended from chains. The driver sat in the cab, working the controls.

Dave stood near the chapel entrance, hard hat on, talking to the site foreman. He spotted Ellie and waved her over, his face lighting up with pleasure.

'Perfect timing,' he said, handing her a spare hard hat. 'They're just about to hoist the first section.'

Ellie put it on and stood beside him, watching as the grabber's arm swung smoothly round, manoeuvring the steel section towards the window opening. The frame was modular – prefabricated sections that would bolt together to create the first floor structure.

'It's really happening,' she said quietly.

'It is.' Dave squeezed her hand. 'Our home.'

The steel section slid through the window opening with inches to spare, guided by two builders inside who called instructions to the driver. Slowly, carefully, the frame was lowered into position.

'How long will this take?' Ellie asked.

'All the sections should be in place by end of day,' the foreman said. 'Weather permitting. Then we bolt them together, weld some and check everything's level. Anchor them into the stone walls and you've got your first floor.'

Another section was already being lifted, chains rattling as the grabber's arm extended. The machinery hummed and clanked, breaking the winter silence.

Ellie thought about those first weeks in the chapel, when they'd "camped" inside with sleeping bags on an inflatable mattress and a camping stove. The reality of converting a derelict building into a home had been overwhelming.

The cold, the dust, the damp, the sheer scale of work needed.

Then they'd moved into Stream Cottage while the major structural work happened. Temporary accommodation that had felt more permanent with each passing month.

But this – watching the steel frame sections being installed – made it real again. Made it feel like they were actually building something, not just talking about it.

'Once the frame is done,' Dave said, following her gaze as another piece swung through the window, 'the guys will be laying the floor and installing the staircase. And in no time, we'll be onto phase four, putting up the stud walls and starting the plumbing and electrics.' He turned to look at her, eyes bright with excitement. 'Our new home, Ells. *Actually* taking shape.'

Chapter 15

Over at the rectory, where Leonard and Sylvia lived, Sylvia checked the clock. She'd made a bumper batch of pork and cranberry stuffing for the butcher in Bramhurst. That was in the fridge to drop off later. There was a good forty-five minutes before Leonard's visitor was due. She had plenty of time.

Leonard had already left for St Mary's, fretting about flower arrangements and whether the brass needed another polish. 'He notices everything, that man,' he'd said, checking his collar twice before leaving.

Sylvia had nodded sympathetically, all the while thinking about her grey roots, currently quite visible after a recent economy drive and six weeks without a hairdresser appointment. If he was that observant...

She mixed the dye quickly in the bathroom and slapped it on. Twenty minutes to process. Perfect timing to do her face mask as well.

The green clay mask went on thick, covering her face from hairline to chin. She looked like a swamp creature. Leonard would have laughed. Good job he wasn't here.

She settled into the armchair by the window, feet up on the pouffe, and set her phone timer for twenty minutes. On her phone, she selected the diaphragmatic breathing track her yoga instructor had recommended and pressed "play".

'*Start by finding a comfortable position,*' said the instructor, '*placing one hand on your chest and the other on your stomach.*'

Sylvia centred herself in the chair.

'*Inhale slowly through your nose, focusing on breathing into your belly.*'

Sylvia liked this bit.

'*Your lower hand will rise while your chest hand stays still.*'

It was true. Her belly was really moving.

'*Now exhale slowly through your mouth or nose, and feel your stomach gently fall.*'

Yes. That was good.

'In... and out, letting your stomach expand and deflate as you breathe.'

A tiny snore erupted. Oops. Sylvia shifted her position.

'See if, each time you breathe, you can take in more air and exhale more.'

Wait. What did he say?

'Good. In through the nose, expanding the belly. Hold. Out through the mouth.'

She was on breath number forty-three when the doorbell rang, playing Leonard's *"Knock, Knock, Knockin' on Heaven's Door"*.

It was probably one of Leonard's diocesan deliveries.

The bell went again, firmer this time. The caller must know she was in. Perhaps it was Leonard and he'd forgotten his key. She was tempted to ignore it. Let him go round the back and get the spare.

Except. Hang on. What if it was something important? Or Ellie dropping something off?

She heaved herself out of the chair, switched off her breathing tutorial, completely forgetting about her appearance.

When she opened the door, the Archdeacon of Canterbury stood facing her on the doorstep in full clerical dress, looking both distinguished and slightly apologetic.

'Mrs... er... Chapman, is it?' His frowned suggested confusion.

'Yes.' Sylvia recognised him from a church magazine.

'I'm so terribly sorry to arrive early. My previous appointment cancelled, and I was rather cold, sitting in the car.' His expression shifted from apologetic to concerned. 'My dear, are you quite alright?'

Sylvia stared at him. Then remembered.

The hair dye. The face mask. Her roots covered in brown goo, her face an alarming shade of green.

'Oh, my goodness,' she managed. 'I'm so sorry. You weren't due until nine. I thought I had time to–' She gestured helplessly at her head, wondering what the archdeacon had thought.

'I should have telephoned ahead,' the man said quickly. 'How thoughtless of me. I'll come back–'

'No, no, please.' Sylvia's embarrassment was mixed with ingrained politeness. 'Do come in. Leonard's just popped to the church to check everything's ready for you. He'll be back any moment.'

She stood aside, acutely aware that she looked like something from a horror film.

The archdeacon stepped inside with the careful neutrality of someone pretending not to notice anything unusual.

'If you'd like to wait in the lounge?' Sylvia gestured to the right. 'Can I get you tea? Coffee? I'll just…' She pointed upstairs. '… wash this off. Won't be a moment.'

'Please, don't rush on my account.' The archdeacon started to move. 'Take all the time you need.'

Sylvia fled across the hall just as the front door opened and Leonard appeared, slightly flustered.

'Is that the archdeacon's car in the la–?' He stopped dead, noticing his wife's appearance. 'Good grief. You didn't–'

The archdeacon turned round.

'Your Grace.' Leonard's face shuffled from recognition to horror and then embarrassment. 'I wasn't expecting you until nine.'

'My fault entirely.' His hand went to his forehead.

Leonard absorbed the scene – the archdeacon standing in their hall, Sylvia in her dressing gown with dye dripping down her forehead and her face an apocalyptic green.

'Ah,' Leonard said faintly. 'I see.'

Sylvia met his eyes. The horror in them was almost funny.

'I'll just have a quick shower,' she said with as much dignity as she could muster.

'Yes,' Leonard agreed. 'That would be marvellous.'

'I could do with a seat actually,' said the archdeacon. 'Was nearly knocked over by a collie in the lane. Beautiful black-and-white bundle of fur.'

'Oh dear,' said Leonard. 'Tea. Let's get you a sweet tea and one of Sylvia's mince pies.

'Very nice owner. The dog had a stick as wide as a pew.'

Chapter 16

As agreed, Ellie reached Hambrook Marshes at midday. The area lay east of Bramhurst, a sprawling wetland where the River Stour wound through reed beds and willow carr.

Zoe was already there with Marple bounding about excitedly.

A team of people in high-visibility jackets moved along the riverbank. Another group stood waist-deep in the river, wearing full-body wader suits. They were pulling debris from the water – shopping trolleys, branches, plastic bottles, the detritus of human carelessness. Each piece was hauled to the bank and loaded into a container.

Ellie joined Zoe.

Further along the river, movement caught Ellie's eye. Two sleek shapes gliding through the water, barely disturbing the surface.

'Beavers,' Zoe said, following her gaze. 'They were reintroduced a while ago. Brilliant engineers. See that dam?'

She pointed to a structure of branches and mud spanning a narrow section of the river. It looked both chaotic and purposeful, nature's architecture at work.

'Amazing,' Ellie said.

One of the figures in the river waved. She was smaller than the others, her waders slightly too large, but she had an air of dedication. She said something to one of the team, who nodded, and made her way to the bank. Talia, presumably.

On the grass verge, she began peeling off the waders. Underneath, she wore thermal leggings and a fleece. Her dark hair was loose, and her face showed the flush of exertion.

'Thanks for coming,' she said, not quite meeting their eyes. 'I wasn't sure you would.'

'We're really sorry about your father,' said Ellie. 'Are you sure you should be at work?'

She nodded her head vigorously. 'I want to keep busy and be around other people. I talked to my sister last night. We're going to get together later in the week.'

'Let's walk,' Zoe suggested. 'Give you a chance to warm up.'

They followed a footpath that wound away from the working group, along the riverbank where the Stour ran clear and fast. Marple strained at her lead, desperate to investigate every smell.

Talia walked with small steps.

'I know this is awkward,' Ellie said gently. 'But Zoe explained the situation. We'll listen to what you have to say, and then we'll work out what needs to happen next. Together.'

'I can't go to the police,' Talia said immediately. 'Not yet. Maybe not at all.'

'Why not?'

'Because I'm worried I'll get my mum into trouble. And I don't know if...' She stopped walking, staring at the water. 'I don't know if she did anything wrong. But it looks bad. Really bad.'

Zoe touched her arm. 'Start from the beginning. Tell us what you know.'

Talia took a shaky breath. 'My parents were arguing. A few days before Dad died. I heard them.'

'Arguments happen,' Ellie said carefully.

'Not like this. Mum was saying she wanted a divorce. That she couldn't do it anymore, couldn't live with the stress and the lies and the debts.' Talia's voice cracked slightly. 'Dad was... horrible. Indignant, like how dare she.

Told her she was being ridiculous, that she owed him loyalty, that sort of thing.'

'That must have been difficult to hear,' Ellie said.

'I knew they weren't happy. But I didn't realise Mum wanted out.' Talia resumed walking, faster now, as if movement helped. 'Then, the morning Dad died...'

She trailed off. Ellie waited, knowing that pushing wouldn't help.

'Someone came to the house,' Talia said finally. 'A man. I was upstairs getting ready for uni. I heard the doorbell, heard Dad answer it. Then voices getting louder.'

'What were they saying?'

'The man was demanding money. Said Dad owed him, that he'd been patient but enough was enough. Dad was trying to calm him down, making excuses.' Talia pulled her fleece tighter. 'I went to the top of the stairs to see who it was as the same thing had happened a while ago.'

'Hang on a sec. What do you mean "the same thing happened"?'

'A week before that, a different man had come to the house asking for unpaid money. That was why I went to have a look. To see if it was the same person.'

'And it wasn't?'

'No. Definitely not. I could see them in the hallway. This man looked really angry. Mum was there too, listening from the kitchen doorway.'

'Did your dad give him money?'

'No. He said he didn't have it right then, that he'd sort it out next week. The man said that's what Dad had said last time, and the time before. Then the man left.'

'Going back to the man who came round a week before this, do you know when it was or remember anything about him?'

'It was at the beginning of December,' said Talia.

Ellie and Zoe exchanged glances. Two men had called at the Snipe's house, recently saying Neville owed them money. Yesterday, the second man was witnessed by both Patricia and Talia.

'Returning to Monday now, what happened after the man left?' Zoe asked.

'Dad went to get his coat and keys. He was muttering about having to deal with incompetent people, something about the village hall. I think he was going to meet you, wasn't he?' Talia looked at Ellie. 'You and Belle?'

'Yes. He was collecting his costumes from the loft.'

'Right. Well, he left and I thought that was it.' Talia stopped walking again. They'd reached a bench overlooking the river, and she sat down heavily. 'But then

Mum got her coat. She said, “I’m not having this. It needs sorting out once and for all. I’m going to the hall.” She got in her car and followed him.’ Talia twiddled her hair anxiously.

‘And those were her precise words?’

‘Yep.’

‘Was that all she said?’

Talia shook her head. ‘She said “How many more people are going to come to the house saying your father owes them money?” I left soon after that as I had a lecture and had to leave for uni. But all morning I kept thinking about it. The argument about divorce. The people owed money. Mum following Dad.’ Talia looked up at them, eyes bright with tears. ‘Then I got home and found out Dad was dead. And Mum wouldn’t talk about where she’d been that morning. Just said she’d been running errands.’

‘Have you asked her directly?’ Ellie said gently.

‘I can’t. What do I say? “Mum, did you follow Dad to the village hall and kill him?”‘ Talia wiped at her eyes. ‘I’m so scared. What if she did something? What if she went there to confront him about the debts and something went wrong?’ Her pitch was getting higher. ‘What if she killed him?’

Zoe sat down beside her. 'Talia, your mum wanting a divorce and following your dad does *not* mean she killed him.'

'I know. But the police will think it does, won't they? Motive and opportunity, that's what they look for. And she had both.'

'The police will investigate properly,' Ellie said. 'They won't just assume.'

'But they'll question her. They'll make it public. Everyone will know.' Talia's voice rose slightly. 'And what if she didn't do anything? What if she just went there to talk to him, to tell him she was serious about the divorce, and then left before anything happened? I'll have destroyed her life for nothing.'

Marple, sensing distress, pushed her nose against Talia's leg. The girl reached down automatically to stroke the puppy's soft ears.

'What do you want us to do?' Zoe asked quietly.

'I don't know. That's why I came to you.' Talia looked between them desperately. 'Can you... can you find out what really happened? Without involving the police yet? Just enough to know whether Mum's in trouble or not?'

Ellie sat down on Talia's other side. She took a breath, knowing Talia wouldn't want to hear this. 'I can't do that. I'm married to the detective in charge of this investigation.

What you've told us – your mother following your father to the village hall – that's information Dave needs to know. *Now.*'

'No.' Talia's voice was sharp with panic. 'Please. You can't tell him. Not yet.'

'I have to. I'm sorry, but I have no choice.' Ellie kept her voice gentle but firm. 'Your mother was at or near a crime scene. The police need to speak to her.'

'But she didn't do anything. I'm sure she didn't.'

'Then she has nothing to worry about,' Zoe said, though her expression suggested she knew how hollow that sounded. 'If your mum's innocent, talking to the police is the right thing to do.'

'They'll arrest her. Everyone will know. It'll destroy her.' Tears spilled down Talia's face. 'I shouldn't have told you. I should have kept quiet. Mum's going to kill me.' She cupped her hand over her mouth. 'I can't believe I just said that.'

Ellie put a reassuring hand on her shoulder and said firmly, 'You did the right thing. Keeping this secret would only make things worse. For you and for your mother.'

Tears dripped from Talia's eyes onto Marple's head.

'We did say we couldn't guarantee that we would keep your information confidential. Didn't we?'

She nodded.

'And you understand I can't keep information from a murder investigation. Yes? That would be irresponsible. Potentially dangerous.' Ellie met the young woman's eyes.

'Yes.'

'Your mum may not have gone to the hall. There might be evidence that clears her. She might have seen something that morning that could help identify the real killer. Every hour that passes without the police knowing she was there is an hour lost.'

Talia wrapped her arms around herself, rocking slightly. Marple pushed closer, whining softly.

'Will you at least... can you be there when he talks to her?' Talia's voice was small, defeated.

'That's not how it works. Dave will interview her properly, with another officer present. But I promise you, he's fair. He won't assume anything.'

'When will you tell him?'

'Straightaway. And – if possible – it's important you don't tell your mum that the police know about what she said. The police will want to get honest answers from her and if she's been tipped off...' Ellie paused, feeling guilty about what she was asking. 'How do you feel about that?'

'Like I'm betraying her.'

'You're in a very difficult situation,' said Zoe. 'I would feel the same if Mum had told me what yours told you.

But I'd hope that Mum would understand that I'd had to do the "right thing".'

Talia was quiet for a long moment, staring at the river. The beavers had disappeared, their dam standing solid across the water.

'I kind of wish I'd never said anything,' she whispered. 'But am also pleased I did.' She pawed at the ground with her boot. 'I won't tell Mum about our conversation. I just hope I haven't ruined our relationship forever.'

'You've been very brave.' Zoe squeezed her shoulder. 'And have one hundred per cent done the right thing.'

Eventually, Talia stood, wiping her face roughly with her sleeve. 'I should get back. They'll wonder where I've gone.'

'You can call me,' Zoe said. 'Anytime. Even if it's just to talk.'

'Thank you.' Her voice was flat.

They watched her walk back along the riverbank, her shoulders hunched, her movements mechanical. Back at the clearance site, she pulled on her waders and rejoined her team in the water, but even from a distance, Ellie could see the difference in her. The energy had gone.

'She hates us now,' Zoe said quietly.

'She doesn't really. We did the right thing.'

'I know. Doesn't make it feel any better.'

Ellie and Zoe collected their vehicles and went their separate ways.

As Ellie drove, her mind raced through what Talia had told them. Patricia following Neville. The man at the door, asking for his money. The argument about divorce. All of it pointed to motive and opportunity. But did Patricia have the means? Did she know about loft hatches and ladders?

Ellie passed the snow-covered sign for Bramhurst. Nearly home.

The phone rang. Zoe.

'What are you going to do?' Zoe asked through Ellie's speaker.

'I'm going to call Dave. Tell him everything. Then...' Ellie thought for a moment. 'Then we wait to see what the police find out. And we focus on the other suspects.'

'Lauren Blackwell?'

'Yes. If Dave's interviewing Patricia, we should talk to Lauren. Get her side of the story about the row with Neville.'

Ellie pulled up outside Stream Cottage.

'Do you want me to come?' asked Zoe.

'No, thanks, lovey. You've done enough today. Go back to work, check on your seals. Sylvia and I will handle Lauren.'

They rang off.

Ellie let herself in and made a mug of tea. She sat at the kitchen table and rang Dave.

He answered on the second ring, traffic noise in the background. 'Ells? Everything alright?'

'I need to tell you something. About Patricia Snipe.' She relayed everything Talia had shared: the divorce argument, the two men coming to the house, Patricia following Neville to the village hall.

Dave listened without interrupting, his breathing the only sound on the line now. 'Right,' he said when she finished. 'Where did you get this information?'

'Talia came to Zoe at the rescue centre. She's frightened her mother's involved.'

'And you've just told me, not given Talia time to talk to her mother first?'

'She's said she won't warn her mother, but she's upset and feeling guilty. Thinks she's betrayed Patricia, so you might want to speak to the mother quickly.'

'Thank you.' She heard him speak to someone, DS Carmichael perhaps. 'What are you planning now?' The question was casual, but Ellie heard the wariness beneath it.

'Sylvia and I thought we'd talk to Lauren Blackwell. Janine's daughter. The one who had the row with Neville at Whitstable.'

Dave sighed. 'Of course you did. Just... be careful. And if you find out anything relevant, tell me immediately. No sitting on information.'

'I won't.'

After they hung up, Ellie sat for a moment, tea cooling in her hands. She felt exhausted, and it was only early afternoon.

Rebus padded over and rested his chin on her knee, brown eyes sympathetic.

'Come on then,' she said, scratching his ears. 'Let's call Sylvia. We've got an interview to arrange.'

She selected Sylvia's number from her recent call list and pressed call. Her mother-in-law answered immediately.

'Ells. I was just about to ring you. I've been thinking about Daphne and what she's hiding.'

'Hold that thought. We've got a new development.' Ellie explained about Talia and Patricia.

'Good grief,' Sylvia said. 'Poor girl. But you were right not to sit on it.'

'I know. But now we need to focus on our other suspects. Specifically – Lauren Blackwell.'

'Yes, I've been thinking about her too.'

'Are you free this afternoon? We should drive to Whitstable, see if she'll talk to us.'

'Absolutely. I'll pick you up in twenty minutes. As it happens, I'll be rather pleased to escape. I'm in the doghouse with Leonard.' She shared what had happened with the archdeacon.

Ellie chuckled, picturing Sylvia answering the door in her dressing gown, with a face mask and hair dye on.

'And worse than my embarrassment,' Sylvia explained, 'the poor archdeacon had nearly had a fall and was already shaken…' She told Ellie about the collie with the giant stick.

Ellie gasped. 'Rebus went through a tree trunk phase. Nearly had me over a few times. Thank goodness the archdeacon was OK. He's not young, is he?'

They rang off, and Ellie stood at the front window, looking out at the grey December afternoon. They had suspects. They had motives. What they needed now was evidence. With any luck, Lauren Blackwell might provide exactly that.

Chapter 17

The main road into Whitstable was at a crawl from halfway down Borstal Hill. Holiday traffic. Christmas shoppers. Double decker buses and sludgy pavements. The high street was the same. While at a standstill, Ellie saw a giant, inflatable Santa billowing in the wind on the roof of the Peter Cushing pub.

'We need one of those at the rectory,' Sylvia joked.

'Best not put one up if you want to get out of the doghouse,' Ellie replied.

Once they'd parked, the two women walked back to the high street. They climbed the steps to the main entrance of the Playhouse, where posters advertised Jack and the Beanstalk in bold letters. Neville Snipe's name had been covered with a printed slip announcing "Harry Thornton, Director".

Inside, the foyer was warm and smelled of fresh paint. Through the open auditorium doors, they could see the beautiful red seats. Voices carried from the stage.

Sylvia peeked through the doorway while Ellie explained to the lady in the box office that they'd come to see Lauren.

They slipped inside quietly, taking seats at the back of the stalls. The auditorium was beautiful – all red velvet and gold leaf, restored to its former glory. The stage was lit, illuminating a painted backdrop of a cottage garden.

On stage, five actors were running through a scene. A young woman in jeans and a hoodie stood centre stage, hands on hips, facing a man in a cow costume that had seen better days.

'I won't sell Buttercup,' the woman declared. 'She's all we have left.'

'But Jack,' the cow-man replied in a mournful voice, 'I'm getting old. My milk's not what it used to be. Perhaps it's time.'

'Never.' The woman – Jack, clearly – threw her arms around the cow's neck dramatically. 'We'll find another way.'

A man in his forties stood in the front row, script in hand. He had ginger hair and wore a battered leather jacket over a Christmas jumper featuring a sequined reindeer.

'Good, Lauren,' he called. 'But remember, Jack's torn. She knows selling the cow makes sense, but her heart won't let her. Let's see that conflict in your face before the line.'

Lauren nodded and reset her position. They ran the exchange again, and this time her expression showed genuine anguish before the defiant words.

'Much better. Right, let's move on to the market scene. Dame Trott, you're up.'

A large man in a floral dress and ridiculous wig bounced onto the stage, and the rehearsal continued. The transformation from ordinary people in rehearsal clothes to larger-than-life pantomime characters was fascinating to watch. Dame Trott's comic timing was perfect, and the bean seller – played by a woman in her seventies who brought a wonderful slyness to the role – had the audience of cast and crew chuckling.

After twenty minutes, the director called a break. Actors dispersed, some heading backstage, others collapsing into seats to check their phones.

The director turned and spotted Ellie and Sylvia. His expression shifted from surprise to wariness. 'Can I help you?' he called, walking up the aisle towards them.

'We're looking for Lauren,' Ellie said, standing. 'Are you Mr Thornton?'

'I am. And you are?'

Ellie introduced them. 'We're from Bramhurst, where Neville Snipe was directing before he came here.'

Harry's expression softened into sympathy. 'Ah. Terrible business. I knew Neville slightly, years ago. Difficult man, but nobody deserves...' He didn't finish. 'You want to speak to Lauren about him?'

'If she's willing. We won't take much of her time.'

Harry glanced back at the stage where Lauren was scrolling through her phone, a bottle of water in her other hand. 'Is it about his death?'

'Yes.'

'Then I suppose you'd better. But keep it brief, please. We're already behind.' He raised his voice. 'Lauren? These ladies would like a word.'

Lauren looked up, taking them in with dark, intelligent eyes and an air of controlled wariness. She set down her phone and walked over.

'What's this about?'

'Neville Snipe,' Sylvia said gently. 'We understand you had a bit of a row with him here.'

Lauren's jaw tightened. 'I've already spoken to the police about this. It was humiliating.' She crossed her arms. 'In front of the entire cast, he told me I had all the charisma of a lump of mud.'

'What did you do?'

'I told him exactly what I thought of him. His directing, his attitude...' Lauren's voice was steady, but her hands were clenched. 'Then I left.'

Harry shifted uncomfortably. 'It was quite the scene, I gather. Very unprofessional of Neville.'

'He called me a spoiled amateur who couldn't handle criticism.' Lauren's eyes glittered. 'Said my mother had been overrated too, and nepotism wouldn't get me far.'

Sylvia made a small noise of sympathy. 'That's appalling.'

The three of them sat down.

'It's what Neville was like.' Lauren took a breath, visibly calming herself. 'Look, I'm sorry he's dead but I didn't kill him, if that's what you're wondering.'

'We're not accusing anyone,' Ellie said quickly. 'We're just trying to understand who Neville was, who he'd had conflicts with.'

'Then you'll be making a very long list.' Lauren uncrossed her arms slightly. 'Why are you asking? Are you with the police?'

'My husband's in charge of the investigation,' Ellie admitted. 'But we're here because we're involved with the Bramhurst production. We want to understand what happened.'

Lauren studied them for a moment, then seemed to make a decision. 'Neville made enemies everywhere he went. Here, Bramhurst, probably every theatre in Kent. He was talented enough to get hired, but too difficult to keep around long.'

'I gather he did something similar to another actress in Bramhurst,' Sylvia said. 'Chloe Kersey?'

Lauren's expression shifted. 'Yes, I heard about that. He promised her the lead in Cinderella, made her learn all the lines, then dropped her for someone else. Then cancelled the whole thing.' She took a gulp of air. 'Neville was a bully and a sadist. I'm glad someone finally stood up to him.'

'Did Neville have rows with anyone else you know of?' Sylvia asked. 'Either here or in Bramhurst?'

Lauren considered this. 'Here, just me as far as I know. But he mentioned having trouble with someone in Bramhurst. A woman who kept bothering him.'

'Do you know who?'

'He didn't say a name. Just complained that she wouldn't leave him alone, that she thought they had some special connection from years ago.' Lauren frowned, remembering.

Ellie and Sylvia caught each other's eye. Daphne. It had to be.

'He said she was delusional, living in the past. That he'd used her to get what he wanted and now she was becoming a liability.'

'When was this?' Ellie asked.

'A few days before his row with me. He didn't tell *me* specifically. A few of us were having coffee before rehearsal in the café, and he was in a foul mood. Going on about people who didn't know their place.' Lauren's mouth twisted. 'I should have seen it as a warning. Nobody was safe from his venom.'

'Did he say what she wanted?'

'No. Just that she kept asking him to do things, make decisions that weren't his to make. He found it amusing at first, then irritating.' Lauren picked up her water bottle. 'Is that helpful?'

'Very,' Ellie said. 'Thank you for talking to us.'

'No problem. Look, I know I might seem guilty. A row with the victim a week before he dies? Very suspicious. But I was nowhere near Bramhurst the morning he died. I was at home here in Whitstable, sleeping off a hangover after a friend's birthday party.' She smiled without humour.

'Can anyone vouch for you?' asked Ellie.

'Er... well, no-one was with me, but I did a video call with a mate, Debs, from the couch around nine. I'm sure she'll be able to confirm I was at home from my lounge furniture and decorations. I've given her contact details to the police.'

That was good. Dave's team would be checking Lauren's alibi.

Harry checked his watch. 'Ladies, I really need to get back to rehearsal.'

'Of course. Thank you for your time.' Sylvia got up, and Ellie followed suit.

Lauren walked them to the auditorium doors. 'I hope you find out who did it. Not because I care about justice for Neville, but because whoever it was probably had a very good reason. I'd like to know what it was.'

Outside, the wind off the sea was brutal, cutting through their coats as they hurried back to Sylvia's car.

'Wow,' Sylvia said once they were safely inside.

'The woman who wouldn't leave him alone,' Ellie said, 'who thought they had a special connection. That's got to be Daphne.'

'Yes. We know Neville used her to get the director position...' Sylvia started the engine and turned up the heating. 'I wonder what she was asking him to do? What decisions?'

'Go along with Reverend Jo's requests regarding health and safety, maybe? Or something else entirely.'

'Lauren seemed remarkably sanguine about Neville's death.'

'She's angry and hurt.' Ellie buckled her seatbelt. 'And she's young. But I tend to believe her about being at home the morning Neville was killed.'

'Which leaves us with Daphne and Patricia as our main suspects.' Sylvia pulled out of the car park. 'Also: Chloe. All with motives. And whoever was at the hall.'

Ellie watched Whitstable disappear in the wing mirror of Sylvia's car.

'We need to talk to Daphne properly,' Ellie said. 'Find out exactly what hold Neville had over her, and what she was asking him to do.'

'She won't want to talk to us,' replied Sylvia. 'She made that clear yesterday.'

'Then we'll have to find a way to make her.' Ellie paused. 'Let's leave her while we think of an approach. Shall we visit Chloe? See what she's got to say about Neville?'

'Good idea.'

Ellie pulled out her phone and sent Dave a text updating him on what Lauren had shared.

The response came quickly: *Thanks.*

They drove back towards Bramhurst through the winter afternoon, past fields white with snow and villages huddled against the cold. The case was getting more complex, not clearer. More suspects, more motives, more lies and half-truths. Would they ever find out who had killed Neville?

Just as they turned into Thimble Lane, Ellie's phone rang.

Talia.

'Mrs Blix, you know you do this private investigating thing?'

'Uh-huh.'

'Well, would it help if I formally asked you to investigate Dad's death on my behalf?'

'Er...' said Ellie, weighing up what Talia was suggesting.

'I mean, then you can legitimately ask to interview witnesses. People like – my mum.'

Chapter 18

Ellie dialled Belle's number as Sylvia navigated Bramhurst's narrow streets.

Her friend answered on the third ring. 'Ells? What's up?'

'Is Chloe at home? Sylvia and I wondered if we could speak to her.'

A pause. 'About Neville?'

'Yes. We've just been talking to Lauren Blackwell, and some things came up. We need to hear Chloe's side of the story.'

'Right. Yes, she's here. Just got back from tobogganing with some friends at the Magical Glade.'

'OK. We'll be there in twenty minutes.'

When they arrived, Belle's house looked cheerful in the gathering dusk, lights blazing from the windows and a holly and fir wreath on the front door. Belle opened it before they could knock, ushering them inside where warmth and the smell of spiced fruit and pastry greeted them.

'She's in the kitchen,' Belle said quietly. 'I've just made some mince pies. Go easy on her, yeah? She's still a bit raw about the whole thing.'

Chloe sat at the kitchen table, hands wrapped around a mug, her cheeks still flushed from the cold. Ellie had met her several times before at the rehearsals and at Belle's house, but had never considered her age. She was early twenties, she guessed; the same spirited eyes as Belle.

'Chloe, love,' Belle said, taking a seat beside her daughter. 'Ellie and Sylvia want to ask you about Neville.'

Chloe's expression hardened. 'What about him?'

'We're trying to understand what happened,' Ellie said gently, sitting across from her. 'Specifically, why he gave you the part of Cinderella and then took it away.'

'I wish I knew.' Chloe stared into her hot chocolate. 'One minute I was the lead, learning my lines, so excited I could barely sleep. The next, he was telling me I wasn't suited to the part.'

'Can you tell us exactly what happened?' Sylvia asked. 'At the rehearsal where he fired you?'

'I had to miss that evening,' Ellie explained. 'The dog rolled in fox poo and had to go in the bath.'

Chloe smiled and took a deep breath. 'It was only the second proper rehearsal. We were running through the kitchen scene – you know, where Cinderella's being treated like a servant by her stepsisters. I thought it was going well. I knew all my lines. Everyone else was reading theirs from their scripts. My timing was good. The other actors seemed happy.'

'What was Neville doing?'

'Watching from the front row, like he always did. Taking notes. He seemed fine at first, nodding along.' Chloe's hands tightened on her mug. 'Then suddenly, maybe ten minutes in, he stood up and shouted "Stop. Stop." Everyone froze.'

Belle reached over and squeezed her daughter's hand.

'He came up onto the stage,' Chloe continued, her voice shaking slightly. 'Walked right up to me and said, "No, no. It's not working. You're not right for this part. I'll have to find another leading lady." Just like that. In front of everyone.'

'Did he give a reason?' Ellie asked.

'No. I asked him what I was doing wrong, what I could improve. He just said I didn't have the quality he was looking for, that he'd made a mistake casting me.' Chloe looked up, eyes bright with remembered humiliation. 'I ran out of the hall in tears. Couldn't face anyone. Couldn't understand what I'd done wrong.'

'You hadn't done anything wrong,' Belle said fiercely. 'He was a cruel, manipulative...' She caught herself. 'Sorry. Go on, love.'

'I didn't go to the next rehearsal. Couldn't face seeing whoever he'd given my part to. Mum went though, didn't you?'

'Yeah. He turned up with Frances. Said he'd given her the role. She's from Rough Common too.'

'Did Neville explain why he'd made the change?' Sylvia asked Belle.

'Just said Frances "better embodied his vision for the character".' Belle's tone made it clear what she thought of that. 'But there were *rumours*...'

'What kind of rumours?' Ellie waited impatiently.

'That Frances was his new romantic interest.' Belle lowered her voice, though it was just the four of them. 'Everyone knew things weren't good between Neville and Patricia. Rumours of infidelity on his part, money troubles. And suddenly this young woman appears, gets the lead role, and Neville's all over her. Arriving and leaving with her. Extra rehearsals, private coaching sessions, that sort of thing.'

'Did anyone confront him about it?' Sylvia asked. 'Or her?'

'Not directly. People were uncomfortable, but amateur dramatics groups don't exactly have HR departments.' Belle's expression was grim. 'And Neville had a way of making anyone who questioned him feel like *they* were the problem.'

Chloe had been quiet, but now she spoke up. 'Was that why he did it? Dropped me for her because they were... involved?'

'We don't know, love,' Belle said. 'But it seems likely.'

'That's even worse,' Chloe whispered. 'At least if I wasn't good enough, that would make sense. But to be dropped because he wanted to give the role to someone he fancied? That's just...'

'Appalling,' Ellie finished. 'And completely unprofessional. I'm so sorry you went through that.'

Chloe wiped at her eyes with the back of her hands. 'After he cancelled the whole production, part of me was relieved. At least I didn't have to watch Frances perform the role that should have been mine. Is that awful?'

'It's human,' Sylvia said gently.

Belle stood up and moved to the kitchen counter. 'I tried to find Frances earlier, actually. Drove through Rough Common after work, thought maybe I could track down her house, see if she knew anything useful about Neville. None of us know much about her. She's never come along to drinks. Kept herself to herself.'

'Any luck?' Ellie asked.

'No. Rough Common's not that big, but I don't know her surname and there's no central village to ask around in. Just houses scattered along the roads.' Belle busied herself making fresh hot chocolate. 'Though I did see something odd when I got back to Bramhurst.'

'Oh? What?'

'Daphne Henderson getting her labrador out of the car at the Magical Glade.'

The Magical Glade was a wood in the village that had been set up for the festive season to be a "winter wonderland". It had pretty walkways, lit by lamps and fairy lights, an ice rink and, with the recent heavy snow, a toboggan run had been created.

Belle glanced at the clock – just gone 3.30pm. 'This was about half an hour ago. She was putting the dog on a lead, heading into the woods.'

Ellie and Sylvia exchanged glances.

'The Magical Glade isn't far,' Ellie said, turning to Sylvia. 'Shall we go and see if she's still there? As it's all lit up, it won't matter if it's dark.'

‘I’ve got to get back. Leonard needs me for some meeting.’

Ellie stood up. ‘That’s OK. Thank you, Chloe, for talking to us. It can’t have been easy.’

‘It’s fine.’ Chloe managed a small smile. ‘I hope you find out who did it.’

Outside, Sylvia had started the car.

Ellie found herself saying, ‘I wonder if Daphne will talk to us properly this time.’

Chapter 19

Ellie rang Zoe as soon as they left Belle's house.

'Hey, lovey. Are you still at work?'

'Nope. On my way home from Harbledown. Had an early start so I'm finishing early.'

'Can you meet me at the Magical Glade ASAP?'

'Why? What's happening?'

She explained that Daphne was there. 'I'm hoping that bumping into her with the dogs might encourage her to tell us the truth. Be less confrontational for her.'

'Sneaky. I like it. Give me ten minutes. I'll see you there.'

Ellie stopped at Stream Cottage to collect Rebus, who bounded into the jeep with enthusiastic tail wagging. The cockerpoo loved any excuse for an adventure, and the mention of "woods" got his tail rotating like a propeller.

By the time they reached the car park at the Magical Glade, Zoe's van was already there, pulled up beside

Daphne's Volvo. Zoe stood by the open back doors, practising "sit", "stay" and "lie down" with Marple. The chocolate cockerpoo puppy wriggled with barely contained energy.

'Any sign of Daphne?' Ellie asked, letting Rebus out.

'Not yet. But her car's still here, so she must be.'

The car park was full, with families, couples and dog walkers arriving and leaving continually. Snow-frosted evergreens and twinkling strings of lights had turned the purpose-built glade into a Christmas card scene.

Straight ahead, a cluster of wooden cabins were selling drinks and snacks. To their left, the ice rink stretched beneath a canopy lit by lanterns, its surface gleaming like glass. Skaters of all ages glided round, some clinging to the railings and each other; others sailing round confidently.

Beyond the cafe was the toboggan run, where Chloe had been with friends. The snowy track was edged with safety barriers. Children's laughter carried on the frosty air as sleds skimmed down the slope, the whole scene glowing with Christmas cheer.

'If she's not back in ten minutes, we'll just walk the dogs anyway,' Ellie said. 'The paths are clear so it's fine for paws.'

Ellie and Zoe stood stamping their feet against the cold, watching the path. Both dogs were tugging at their leads, desperate to investigate all the fascinating woodland smells.

'There,' Zoe said quietly, gesturing across the car park.

A figure emerged from the trees, backlit by the remaining twilight. It was Daphne walking slowly, her labrador plodding beside her. The dog had a greying muzzle but was snuffling about in the snow and pushing a stick.

Daphne saw them and stopped. Even from a distance, Ellie could see the flash of recognition, followed by eye-rolling resignation.

Ellie and Zoe walked forward to meet her.

'This isn't a coincidence, is it?' Daphne's voice was tired.

Ellie smiled warmly. 'That we're both walking our dogs in this beautiful spot? How are the woods? The toboggan run looks great fun.'

Daphne sighed.

Marple bounded over to Daphne's labrador, sat by his head and started licking his ears and muzzle.

Zoe crouched on the ground, making sure the older dog was OK with the puppy's exuberance. 'He's a gorgeous boy. How's his paw now? It's always a relief when the grass seed season is over.'

Daphne chatted about her dog and inquired about Marple. Oscar and the puppy were now rolling around in the snow together.

'Can we buy you a hot chocolate?' Zoe asked her. 'Rory and I had one here the other day and it was delicious. They've got heaters too.'

Ellie smiled again, happy for Zoe to take the lead.

They filed over to the cabin. Ellie bought hot chocolates while Zoe and Daphne sat with the dogs. She heard them talking first about Rory's podcast then the beavers along the Stour.

'There are certain spots they like,' Zoe explained to Daphne. 'The sheltered stretches where the water moves slowly, with soft banks and plenty of trees like willow.' She got out her phone and showed Daphne some of her photos. 'Neville's daughter volunteers with us. Talia. She's been helping us clear the river.' She chatted away about Talia's university degree and told Daphne about the refrigerator that someone had dumped in the water.

As Zoe talked, Daphne glanced at Oscar, who had one end of a rope toy and was playing tug-of-war with Rebus while Marple dive-bombed them both. Daphne had her hands wrapped around her cup. In the dim light of the cafe, she looked older than her sixty-odd years, lines of worry etched deep around her eyes and mouth.

'I knew Neville before I was married,' she said eventually. 'Forty years ago. We were both involved in amateur dramatics in Canterbury. He was charming back then, attentive when he wanted to be, and attractive. Very different from the man he became.'

'You were together?' Ellie asked. This was what they'd suspected.

'Briefly. I was in love with him. Properly, stupidly, madly in love.' Daphne's face flickered with bitterness and pain. 'It wasn't mutual, sadly. I realised that eventually. But for a while, I thought we had something special and would get married, have children, live in a rose-covered cottage.'

'What happened?' Ellie asked.

'He met Patricia and dumped me. Told me I'd been "fun". I was devastated. Took me months to get over him. I say "get over". In truth, I don't know I ever did. I think I've probably been in love with him my whole life.' Daphne sipped her hot chocolate.

It was one of the saddest things Ellie had ever heard.

'I married someone else eventually. A good man. Had my son. Built a life and have been very happy. Thought I'd left all that nonsense with Neville behind until Rory's father died a couple of years ago.'

So, grief had made poor Daphne vulnerable.

'And then Neville came back?'

'Yes. About a year ago. Not that he'd ever gone anywhere. He just hadn't been in touch.' Sadness streaked across her face. 'He contacted me through Messenger on Facebook, all friendly and nostalgic. Said he'd love to see me and catch up. Lots of flattery. He'd heard I was involved with Bramhurst Players and he was looking for a directing position. Would I put in a good word?'

'And you did.' They knew this already, but it was useful to hear Daphne confirm it.

'Yes.' Daphne's voice was heavy with regret. 'I told myself I was just helping out an old friend. That the past was past. But really, some part of me was still that stupid girl who'd been in love with him all that time ago. I thought maybe...' She stopped. 'Oh, it's so ridiculous. And embarrassing. I'm a sixty-year-old woman.'

'Perhaps you thought he'd changed?' Ellie asked gently. 'Or that *you* had?'

As Daphne had been talking, it had sounded like Neville had undertaken a form of grooming.

'I should have known better. Janine warned everyone that he had a reputation for being difficult. But I persuaded the committee anyway. Told them he had experience, references, that we'd be lucky to have him.' Daphne closed her eyes. 'Biggest mistake of my life.'

'What happened after he got the position?'

'At first, nothing. He was grateful, friendly. Kept up the act. Then the production started, and I saw what he'd become. Cruel, manipulative. The way he treated Chloe Kersey – dropping her from the lead role for no good reason. Fawning over Frances. The way he spoke to people. I realised I'd inflicted a monster on the village.'

'Did you confront him?' Zoe asked.

'A few times. Told him he needed to be more respectful, that people were complaining. He laughed at me. Said I'd done my part getting him the job, and now I should stay out of his way.' Daphne's hands tightened on her cup. 'Then came the row with Reverend Jo about health and safety.'

'He wanted you to support him,' Ellie said, remembering what Maya had told them in the shop.

'He *demanded* I support him. Told me I owed him loyalty. That after what we'd shared all those years ago, I should stand by him.' Daphne's laugh was hollow. 'What we'd shared? A three-month fling that meant everything to me and nothing to him.'

Ellie let Daphne's words settle between them for a few moments, hoping they might ease some of their friend's pain.

'But you refused.'

'I told him Jo was right. That the safety concerns were legitimate and he was being unreasonable. He didn't like that.' Daphne looked at Ellie directly now. 'The morning he died, he came to the shop again. One last attempt to make me change my mind, to agree to pressure the committee into sacking Jo. I refused. Told him I was done being manipulated by him.'

'What did he say?'

'That I'd regret it. That he'd make sure everyone knew I'd been the one to recommend him, that any fallout from the cancelled production would be my fault.' Daphne's voice shook slightly. 'He was furious. Then he left for the village hall.'

'And you followed him,' Ellie said carefully.

Daphne nodded. 'Not immediately. But after he left, I kept thinking about it. About how this was all my fault, how I'd brought this man into our community here in Bramhurst. I thought if I could just talk to him one more time, make him see reason, maybe he would continue with the panto. I couldn't bear the thought of all the disappointed children and families, all our wasted work.'

Sympathy rose in Ellie. Neville had manipulated Daphne in a cruel way.

'So, you went to the hall.'

'I drove there, yes. Parked outside briefly. Sat in my car trying to work up the courage to go in.' Daphne stared at her hands. 'But then I thought, what's the point? He'd made his decision. Nothing I said would change his mind and he couldn't be trusted. So, I left.'

'You didn't go inside the hall?' Zoe asked.

'No. I sat in the car for a few minutes, then drove away. Went back to the shop.'

'When you were at the hall, did you see anyone else?'

Daphne frowned. 'Just Patricia briefly in her car on the other side of the road. Belle's van was outside and Neville's car.'

Ellie studied her carefully. 'When did you find out he was dead?'

'Rory rang me. He'd seen the ambulance and police cars arrive at the hall. I knew it had to be Neville.' Daphne met her eyes. 'I felt guilty. Still do. Not because I killed him, but because I was glad I wouldn't have to deal with his manipulation anymore.' She took a tissue from her coat pocket and dabbed at her eyes.

'That's understandable,' Ellie said quietly.

Marple climbed onto Daphne's lap, peering at the upset woman with innocent amber eyes framed by long, brown lashes.

Daphne gave the puppy a kiss on her nose.

'You *definitely* didn't go into the hall?' asked Zoe.

'No. I went there but didn't go in.' Daphne finished her hot chocolate and crushed the paper cup in her hands.

'Thank you for telling us all this,' Ellie said finally. She paused, giving Daphne a few moments to decide whether she wanted to say any more. 'Have you given this information to the police?'

'Not yet. I'll drop the dog home and go to the police station now. Will it help? With finding who really did it?'

'It helps us understand the full picture,' Ellie replied. 'That matters.'

Daphne gathered up the dog's lead. 'I should get Oscar home. Usually, I'm telling people that he's old and doesn't like the cold anymore, but he's loved playing with your two dogs.'

'You have told us the truth, haven't you?' asked Ellie.

The older woman turned back, her expression unreadable in the dimming light. 'If you're asking whether I'm capable of killing someone, I honestly don't know. I never thought I was. But I hated him, Ellie. Really hated him. So maybe I'm capable of more than I thought.' She paused. 'But no. I didn't kill him. I just half-wished someone would. And then someone did.'

They watched her walk back to her Volvo and drive away. Her taillights disappeared around the bend, leaving them alone in the café area.

'Wow,' said Zoe. 'That was quite a story. And poignant. Do you believe her?'

Ellie thought about it. 'I believe she hated him. I believe she went to the hall that morning. We didn't see her inside but whether she went round the back...' She shook her head. 'I don't know.'

'Hmm.'

'Dave will check CCTV, timelines, all of that. If she's lying, he'll find out.'

'Poor woman,' said Zoe. 'Carrying all that around for forty years.'

'First love can be like that. Especially when it ends badly.' Ellie got up. 'Come on. We promised these dogs a walk. Let's give them a good run in the woods before we go home.'

They followed the path into the Magical Glade, lanterns illuminating the way. The air smelled of earth and pine and cold.

Rebus and Marple bounded ahead, sniffing everything, tails wagging furiously. Their joy was infectious, and despite everything, Ellie felt some of the day's tension ease.

'Do you think we're getting anywhere with this?' Zoe asked after a while. 'Or are we just making things more complicated?'

'Honestly? I don't know. But we're uncovering truths people have been hiding. That has to count for something.'

They followed the main path through the ancient woodland. The trees were stark against the snow, bare branches reaching up to the darkening sky. Beautiful and slightly eerie.

As Ellie drove back to Bramhurst, her mind turned over everything they'd learned. Daphne's story rang true – the manipulation, the guilt, the relief at Neville's death. But the sense Ellie had got was of when someone is partly telling the truth, partly telling a story. And she wasn't sure which parts fell into which category.

Had Daphne really stayed in her car and driven away? Or had she gone into the hall, gone up into the loft and confronted Neville one final time? Sabotaged the loft ladder and let him fall from the loft hatch?

Chapter 20

Ellie was halfway through chopping vegetables for dinner when a thought struck her. She set down the knife and reached for her phone, ignoring Rebus' hopeful look. The cockerpoo had stationed himself strategically near the chopping board, ready to pounce on any dropped morsels.

'Not for you, greedy guts.'

She scrolled to Talia's number and pressed call. The young woman answered promptly, sounding wary.

'Ellie?'

'Talia, hi.' She asked her how the rest of her day had gone. 'Quick question – yesterday morning, when that man came to your house demanding money from your dad. Did you take a photo of him by any chance?'

A pause. 'Yes. Why?'

'Can you send it to me? And do you remember if your dad referred to him by name?'

'Geoff, I think. Dad said something like "Geoff, please, be reasonable." Hang on. The photo's somewhere here amongst lots of animals.' Ellie imagined Talia scrolling. 'Ah. Here we are. Shall I WhatsApp it to you?'

'Please.'

Ellie's phone quickly pinged with a message.

The photo showed a man in his sixties, stocky build, dark hair, beard and moustache, wearing a dark fleece with a logo on it saying "FLEMING ELECTRICAL". Trousers with multiple pockets and reinforced knees. His face was flushed with anger, jaw set, hands gesturing emphatically. The image was slightly blurred, taken quickly from an upstairs window, but clear enough.

'Great. Thanks, Talia. The time stamp is 8.01am. Is that what you remember?'

'Yeah. I'd just had a shower.'

Ellie studied the photo whilst stirring the pasta sauce. She didn't recognise the man and hadn't dealt with any electricians in the village yet. But Belle might – she knew everyone in the area through her window-cleaning business.

She forwarded the photo to Belle with a message: *Do you know this man? Geoff? Went round to Neville's the morning he died asking for money owed.*

The reply came within minutes: *Yes, we know Geoff. Sending to Phil for intel on debts. He knows all the tradespeople.*

Ellie continued cooking, browning mince, adding garlic and herbs. The kitchen filled with warm, savoury smells. Rebus gave up hope of dropped food and relocated to his bed by the radiator.

Her phone pinged again. Belle: *Phil says Geoff lives near the golf course. He's ringing him now.*

Ellie's pulse quickened. An electrician. Someone who would understand electronic systems, wiring, equipment. Someone who would know how ladders worked – and how to make them fail.

She was setting the table when Belle called back.

'Right,' Belle said without preamble. 'Phil's just spoken to Geoff. Apparently, he rewired part of Neville's house. The ground floor. Plus did all the electrical work for the pantomime – lighting, sound system, the works. Neville hasn't paid him for either job.'

'How much does he owe?'

'Six grand.'

'Blimey. That's a lot of money.'

'Yep. And Geoff's retiring soon. He told Phil he's been patient about it, kept asking politely, sending invoices, reminders, being professional. But that morning – the morning Neville died – he'd had enough. Drove over to Neville's house and confronted him.'

'We know. Talia saw it, and so did Patricia.'

'Phil says Geoff's mortified about losing his temper. Says he's not normally like that, but he's got bills to pay.' Belle paused. 'He swears he didn't kill Neville though. Says he left the house and went to another job in Bramhurst.'

'Did Phil believe him?'

'Yes. Phil says Geoff's a lovely bloke. Salt of the earth. Been patient for months when most people would've kicked off ages ago.'

Ellie thanked Belle and ended the call. She stood looking at the photo on her phone. Geoff Fleming, electrician. Owed £6,000. Angry enough to confront Neville at his home. And then what?

The front door opened and Dave appeared, bringing a blast of cold air, and snow on his boots. Rebus bounded over to greet him, tail wagging furiously.

'Hi, love,' Dave said, bending to ruffle the dog's ears. 'Something smells good.'

'Spaghetti bolognese. Five minutes.'

'I'm not stopping. I just popped in to get my phone charger. I've got to go back to work.'

Ellie showed him her phone. 'Do you know this man?'

Dave studied the photo, his expression shifting into detective mode. 'Where did you get this?'

'Talia Snipe sent it to me. It's the man who went to their house the morning Neville–'

'I know who it is, Ells.'

'Neville owed him six grand.'

Dave nodded. 'I know.'

'Oh, good.' Ellie recalibrated.

Dave went on. 'A couple of residents have reported seeing trucks in the vicinity of the village hall on the morning Neville died. Nothing specific yet though.' He looked up from his phone.

She told Dave about the 8am time stamp on Talia's photo. 'If Geoff was going to the hall, that would've given him forty-five minutes to get from the Snipes' house back to Bramhurst.'

'I'm just about to interview him.'

Ellie touched his arm. 'Phil says Geoff's a good guy. Patient, decent, not the type to lose his temper normally.'

'Neville owed him money. A lot of money.' Dave's tone was gentle but firm. 'He kissed her forehead. 'You did well finding out about him. But I need to go.'

Dave disappeared into the lounge, grabbed his charger and left.

Ellie switched the bolognese on low and sat in the living room, staring at her notebook. She sifted through all the suspects, all the motives, all the lies and secrets and half-truths.

Outside, snow had started falling again, soft flakes drifting past the window. Christmas was just over a week away. The village should be preparing for celebrations, attending carol services, knocking back mulled wine and hanging up their stockings.

Instead, they were caught up in a murder investigation, secrets being dragged into the light, relationships destroyed by old betrayals and new suspicions.

She grabbed her phone. Dialled Belle. 'Hey. Have you eaten yet?'

'No. I've just got in. Phil and Chloe have gone ice skating. Are you offering food?'

'Home cooked bolognese. And... a spot of detective work?'

'Ooh. I don't know which appeals most. I'll be round in ten.'

'And Belle? Could you bring a ladder?'

Chapter 21

Belle arrived at Stream Cottage in no time, her van pulling up with the spare ladder strapped to the roof rack.

'Right then,' she said, manhandling the ladder through the front door. 'Where d'you want this?'

'The landing,' Ellie replied, pointing up the stairs. 'There's a loft hatch up there. Not as high as the one at the hall, but close enough.'

They hauled the ladder upstairs, Rebus following with intense interest. The cockerpoo sat on the top step of the stairs, head cocked to one side, watching these strange human activities with quizzical brown eyes.

'He thinks we've lost our minds,' Belle observed, positioning the ladder directly under the hatch.

'He might be right. Food first? Then detective work?'

'Fine by me. I haven't eaten since lunch.'

Belle checked the ladder carefully, testing each foot was secure on the carpet, making sure the extending sections were properly locked. She gave it a shake. Solid.

'This is what I did that morning. Positioned it, checked it, made absolutely certain it was safe.' Belle looked up at the hatch. 'Then I left it there for Neville.'

'And he climbed up without a problem,' Ellie said. 'Right. Let's eat.'

Twenty minutes later they'd both eaten a plate of steaming pasta and had returned to the landing.

'So, let's do the climbing bit.' Belle moved confidently. After all, she'd spent her entire working life on ladders. At the top, she pushed open the hatch, which swung back on its hinges with a creak.

'We definitely did hear him, didn't we?' Belle called down. 'Moving about above our heads, muttering about dust and storage? I'm rather regretting playing Christmas songs so loud now.'

Ellie froze.

'Ells?'

A memory surfaced, something Ellie had heard but hadn't been able to place at the time. They'd been on the stage in the main hall, discussing the set pieces. Carols had been playing on Belle's phone. And through that music, through the walls and ceiling, she'd heard footsteps.

Not one set of feet.

Two.

'Come down,' she said slowly. 'Come down a minute.'

Belle descended and stood beside her. 'What's up? I was burbling away up there and you went all silent on me.'

'That morning. We heard Neville up in the loft.'

'Yes. Stomping about, banging things.'

'There were two sets of footsteps.' Ellie closed her eyes, trying to recapture the exact sound. 'I couldn't place it at the time. But now I remember. Two sets of feet clomping about above our heads.'

Belle's eyes widened. 'You're sure?'

'Yes. Not just Neville. Someone else was definitely in that loft with him.'

They stared at each other as the implications sank in. Someone had been up there with him. Someone who'd lain in wait, or who'd climbed up after Neville.

'We need wine to help us think about this,' Belle said decisively.

'Good idea,' agreed Ellie, fully aware that it wasn't a good idea at all. 'It's nearly Christmas, after all.'

Ellie fetched a bottle from the kitchen and two glasses. They sat on the landing, ladder looming beside them, and Belle poured generous measures.

'Right,' Belle said, taking a sip. 'Someone was up there with Neville. So, what happened?'

'Let's think it through,' said Ellie. 'Scenario one: he tripped and fell down the hatch, somehow bringing the ladder with him.'

'Yup,' said Belle. 'I can get on board with him dislodging the ladder. He was a hefty chap. Just not the ladder bolts unlocking themselves.'

'Scenario two: he was pushed.'

'Same issue with the ladder.'

'Scenario three. Someone confronts him up there. The argument gets heated... We've still got the ladder problem. If someone was in the loft with him, they cannot simultaneously have been on the ground releasing the bolts on the ladder extension.'

They sipped wine in thoughtful silence, Rebus settling down between them with a contented sigh.

After a few minutes, Belle got up and climbed the ladder again, more slowly this time, wine glass still in hand. At the top, she leaned through the hatch opening, looking around the loft space above and pulling herself up into it.

'If I'm up here,' she called down, 'and someone else comes up – either through this hatch or another one – we're in quite close quarters. Not much room to move around.'

'So, a confrontation could be scary,' said Ellie.

Belle dropped down through the hatch back onto the ladder. 'There's proper flooring in the loft at the hall. You can walk about OK and store a good amount of stuff.'

The front door opened downstairs. Dave's voice called up: 'Belle? Your van's sticking out a bit. A delivery driver's just struggled to get past. Do you want to tuck it in a bit more?'

'Oh crikey,' Belle whispered to Ellie. 'The boss is back.'

Dave appeared at the bottom of the stairs and stopped dead, taking in the scene. Ladder under the loft hatch. Belle halfway up it with a wine glass. Ellie sitting on the top step of the stairs with another glass, Rebus sprawled next to her.

'*What*,' Dave said slowly, 'are you doing?'

'A re-enactment,' Ellie said. 'We're trying to figure out what happened in the loft.'

'*With wine.*'

'Small celebration. We had a breakthrough.'

Dave closed his eyes briefly, dramatically, as though trying to summon patience. 'Belle, can you please come down from that ladder?'

'I'm fine. I know my way around ladders.'

'You've been drinking.'

'Half a glass. I'm well within safe limits for ladder climbing, honestly, Officer.' Belle took another sip to prove her point.

Ellie held her breath. Dave must've come straight from the station and forgotten to remove his chief inspector hat when he came in.

Dave looked at Ellie. 'Can you please tell your friend to get down from the ladder?'

'Don't involve me,' she replied. 'She's a grown woman and a professional window cleaner. If anyone knows ladder safety, it's Belle.'

'Window cleaners don't typically drink while working.'

'I'm not working,' said Belle defiantly.

Ellie patted the step beside her. 'Come and have some wine,' she said to Dave. 'We've made an important discovery.'

Dave stood in the hall at the bottom of the stairs, clearly torn between police officer instincts and the knowledge that arguing with both of them was pointless. Finally, he shook his head.

'I'm shattered. I'm going to put the kettle on. I don't want to know about ladder experiments while drinking. When you're done, come and tell me about this discovery. Safely. At ground level.' He retreated to the kitchen. They heard the kettle being filled and switched on.

Belle finished her wine and set the glass carefully on the landing floor. 'I don't think the dancing detective is very happy with us.'

'No,' said Ellie. 'Anyway – back to the problem. How would the person have got down to a) release the bolts and b) leave?'

Belle climbed back up to the top of the ladder and looked through the open hatch. 'From up here, if the killer wanted to get out of the loft, the best way would've been to climb down the other hatch...'

'What *other* hatch?' Ellie squeaked.

'The one in the storage room on the other side of the hall,' Belle explained.

'I had no idea there was one there.'

'That's because you're a Bramhurst newbie, my dear, Ells.'

Ellie felt the tickle of excitement. This was important.

'So, we're looking for someone who knew about the second hatch,' Belle summarised. 'Someone who could get up into the loft and into position before Neville arrived, and down again to release the ladder locks.'

'Didn't you say Geoff did the electrics for the panto?'

Belle nodded.

'He'd probably have known about the extra hatch then.'

'Oh, no. He's one of us, Ells.'

'He had means, motive and opportunity.' Ellie's thoughts shifted to Dave. 'I'm sure the police will have searched the hall for access routes, but I'd better check Dave knows about the one in the storeroom.'

'If he's accepting tips from drunken ladder climbers...'

Ellie smiled. 'I wonder who else would've known about the second loft hatch,' said Ellie.

'Pretty much anyone who'd worked on the building recently. But especially tradespeople. Electricians, decorators, roofers, general builders.'

'All of whom will use ladders regularly.'

They looked at each other, the implications hanging heavy between them.

Downstairs, Dave was heating up soup and making toast. The smell of it drifted up.

Belle carried her ladder back down to her van.

Rebus followed them hopefully, clearly disappointed that the interesting human activities were ending.

In the kitchen, Dave was buttering toast. He looked up as they entered.

'Done?'

'Yes. And we found something important.' Ellie sat at the kitchen table. 'That morning, when we were in the main hall and Neville was up in the loft. I heard *two* sets of footsteps. Not just him. Someone else was definitely up there with him.'

Dave set down his knife. 'You're certain?'

'Yes. It didn't dawn on me at the time that that's what I was hearing, but having done our re-enactment...'

Belle let out a giggle.

'Well, now I'm sure. Two people were moving around above us.'

Dave was quiet for a moment, processing this. 'So whoever came to kill him, lay in wait in the loft, then came down via the hatch in the storeroom, released the bolts on the ladder, and left via the back door once Neville had fallen.'

He knew about the second hatch then.

'That's what we think,' said Ellie.

'Which means the killer knew the layout of the building well enough to plan an escape route.' Dave pulled out his phone and made notes. 'That narrows it down. Not to one person, but to people with specific knowledge.'

'We were thinking – tradespeople,' Belle said.

Dave finished his notes and looked at both of them. 'Thank you. This is useful. But please, no more amateur reconstruction experiments. Especially not with alcohol involved.'

'It was just a glass,' Belle protested.

'Still. We've already had a death from a ladder. I don't want any more.' His tone was gentler, acknowledging that they'd found something valuable.

After Belle left, Ellie sat on the stairs thinking. They'd found another piece of the puzzle. And slowly, surely, the truth was beginning to emerge. But there were a couple of things she still couldn't get her head round.

She pulled her parka on and shouted to Dave, 'Just popping out. Won't be long.'

And she slid out of the front door.

Chapter 22

The church hall looked abandoned in the night-time gloom, snow piled against its yellow brick walls. Ellie crunched through the fresh fall up the path to the main door and stood for a moment, watching snowflakes. The police had released the building after cordoning it, but a fragment of remaining blue-and-white crime scene tape fluttered on the gate.

Ellie had a key from rehearsals. And there was no alarm system. The key turned smoothly and she slipped inside, stamping snow off her boots in the dim corridor.

The heating was off, and the building felt hollow, expectant. She found the light switches and the fluorescent strips flickered to life, making her blink. The main hall stretched before her, empty stage at the far end, the painted Cinderella set still standing like a ghost of what might have been.

She turned away from it and headed for the storage room.

The door stood ajar. Inside, the room was cluttered. Folding chairs were stacked against one wall, trestle tables leaned in a precarious tower. In the corner, a plastic bin had a fluffy, pink pencil case in it, a fluorescent yellow tennis ball, a ruler, a half-drunk bottle of Ribena, a hammer and a packet of Blu Tack. Next to that, inexplicably, was a large garden parasol with faded stripes.

Ellie took a couple of photos, and crossed to the back door. It was solid wood with a modern mortice lock. She tried the handle. Locked. She examined the frame and lock mechanism, looking for signs of damage or tampering. Nothing.

So, the killer had either found it unlocked – unlikely in a community building – had a key, or knew where one was kept. She glanced around the storage room. A key cabinet hung on the wall near the door, but it was locked too. No helpful spare keys dangling from nails.

She stood with her back to the door and looked across the storage room to its entrance, mentally tracing the route to where Neville had fallen in the main corridor. Twenty feet? Twenty-five? Not far, but far enough that someone in here wouldn't be immediately visible to people in the main hall.

The killer must have kept themself contained within this space. Arrived through the back door, climbed the electric ladder into the loft, waited for Neville, then descended and left the same way. No need to venture into the hall proper. No risk of being seen by her and Belle on the stage.

Smart. Calculated.

Ellie turned her attention to the ceiling. The loft hatch was obvious once you knew to look for it – a square panel with a small control box mounted on the wall beside it. Three buttons: up, down, stop.

She pressed the 'down' button.

Nothing happened.

She pressed it again, harder, as if that would help. Still nothing. She tried 'up' in case the system worked backwards. The control box emitted a faint beep, but the hatch remained stubbornly closed.

'Come on,' she muttered impatiently, examining the control box more carefully. There was a small switch at the bottom, currently in the 'off' position. She flipped it to 'on' and the box lit up with a green LED.

She pressed 'down' again.

With a mechanical whir, the hatch swung open and the ladder began to descend, unfolding in smooth sections until it touched the floor with a gentle click.

'Yes.' Ellie grabbed the sides of the ladder and started climbing.

In the distance, a siren wailed. Perhaps there'd been an accident in the snow...

She reached the top of the ladder and hauled herself into the loft, fumbling for a light switch. Her fingers found it and the space flooded with light.

The loft was larger than she'd expected, stretching the full length of the building. Proper boarding here – solid plywood sheets creating a safe floor surface. Boxes were stacked along one side, labelled in faded marker pen: Christmas decorations, summer fête bunting, Jubilee flags. Racks of costumes on hangers. To one side, three boxes bore the name: Neville Snipe.

She oriented herself, trying to calculate distance and direction. The main corridor hatch should be... that way. She walked carefully across the boards, counting steps.

The siren was closer now. Maybe there'd been a burglary.

If the killer had come up from the storeroom, as they expected, it would only have taken them a few seconds to get to the hatch in the main corridor.

The sirens cut off abruptly, replaced by the slam of car doors and the crackle of police radios.

Heavy footsteps pounded into the building. Voices shouted, echoing through the empty hall.

'All clear in here.'

What was going on? Who were they looking for?

They were heading for the storage room at speed.

'Yes, sir. We're here now. Intruder in the loft space. The electric ladder's been activated.' A pause. 'OK. See you in a sec.'

'In here,' came another voice.

Ellie froze, aware now that the police had to be looking for *her*. They must have thought she'd broken in.

'Police,' an officer shouted. 'Whoever's up there, come down now with your hands visible.'

She made her way back over to the hatch she'd come through.

'This is your final warning. Come down immediately.'

Ellie poked her head through the opening, peering down.

Dave stood directly below, looking up at her, his expression one of profound irritation.

Two uniformed officers stood next to him at the base of the ladder, one with his hand on his baton, the other speaking urgently into his radio.

'Ellie,' said Dave, in the tone of a man whose patience had been tested beyond endurance. 'What on earth are you doing here?'

Chapter 23

Dave's Audi was warm and quiet after the chaos of the village hall. Ellie buckled herself in and tried to think of something to say that wouldn't make things worse.

Dave started the engine and pulled out of the car park without a word.

They drove through the village in silence, streetlights casting orange pools across the snowy road. The heating hummed. The wipers scraped intermittently across the windscreen.

'No wonder,' Dave said finally, 'you didn't say where you were going.'

'I didn't think anyone would suspect me of breaking and entering.'

'No. You didn't think.' His hands were tight on the steering wheel, his jaw set. 'What were you looking for? What was so important that you had to break into a–?'

'I have a key. Jo gave me one. It wasn't breaking in.'

He navigated the corner by the church. 'Did you stop to think that a killer struck in that hall? That whoever did it might come back? That you could have been walking into danger?'

'I just wanted to understand the layout. How someone could have got in and out without us seeing them.'

'And did you work it out?'

'Yes, actually. The storage room hatch, the electric ladder, the back door–'

'Which *we* already knew about.' Dave's voice was level but tight.

'Well, *we* didn't.'

'The police are investigating this case properly, Ellie. With forensics and evidence and proper procedure. We don't need you climbing around in lofts.'

She opened her mouth to argue, then closed it again. He was right. Sort of.

'First the ladder re-enactment with Belle,' he continued, 'now this. Do you have any idea how it looked? First responders arriving to find an intruder, and it turns out to be my wife?'

'Who called the police?'

'A concerned neighbour said they'd seen someone creeping about and breaking in.'

'With a key? Were their binoculars not in focus?'

'They were simply doing their duty. There's no need to mock.'

He pulled up at a red light and turned to look at her properly. 'I'm glad you're safe. But I'm the SIO on this case. And when I arrive at the scene of a reported break-in... and find my wife...' He rubbed his face with one hand. 'It's embarrassing. For me, for you, for the whole team.'

The light turned green. They drove on.

Ellie bit her lip, trying to stay serious. Trying to feel appropriately chastened. But something about the whole situation – the uniformed officers shouting up at the loft, Dave's face when she'd poked her head through the hatch – struck her as absurd.

A small giggle escaped.

Dave glanced at her sharply. 'This isn't funny.'

'I know. I'm sorry.' She pressed her lips together, but her shoulders were shaking. 'It's just... your face when you saw me...'

'Ellie.'

'Two police officers and a detective for little old me. In the loft. My head sticking out of the hatch like a bewildered meerkat.'

Another giggle burst out, then another. She knew she was making it worse, knew Dave was genuinely upset, but the wine from earlier and the exhaustion of the day had caught up with her. Everything suddenly seemed ridiculous.

'I'm sorry,' she gasped between giggles. 'I'm really sorry. It's not funny. I know it's not funny.'

'Then why are you laughing?'

'I don't know. I'm exhausted. It's been a very strange day.' She wiped her eyes, trying to get control of herself.

He said nothing. Just drove, cheek twitching, clearly not amused.

By the time they pulled into Thimble Lane, Ellie had managed to stop laughing, though her stomach still ached from it. She felt simultaneously guilty and slightly giddy, like a schoolchild who'd been told off but couldn't quite take it seriously.

Dave parked outside Stream Cottage and killed the engine.

They sat in the dark car for a moment.

'I am sorry,' Ellie said quietly. 'But I did work out the route the killer took. That has to count for something.'

Dave sighed. 'We'll talk about this tomorrow. When you've stopped giggling and I'm less...' He trailed off, clearly searching for a word that wouldn't make things worse.

'Annoyed?' she suggested.

'Frustrated,' he corrected.

They got out of the car and walked up the path to the cottage. The lights were on inside, warm and welcoming. Dave unlocked the door and pushed it open.

The scene that greeted them was carnage.

The lounge curtains – the nice cream ones that the landlord had put up especially for Ellie when they'd moved in – lay in heaps on the floor. One was wrapped around something that wriggled and yapped. The other was being enthusiastically mauled by Rebus, who had his front paws planted on the fabric and a substantial portion hanging from his mouth like a hunting trophy.

Marple emerged from her curtain cocoon, tail wagging madly, trailing cream fabric behind her.

'Oh no,' Ellie said.

Dave stood in the doorway, taking in the destruction. The curtain pole hung at an angle, one bracket torn from the wall. Cream fabric was scattered across the sofa, the coffee table, the rug. Both dogs looked immensely pleased with themselves.

'Zoe must have left her,' Ellie said weakly. 'I didn't know she was dropping Marple off.'

'Perhaps she texted while you were climbing around in the loft...'

Ellie checked her phone. Sure enough there was a message from Zoe.

Got invited to a talk on river conservation. Have left Marple with Reeby. Will collect in morning. X

Dave looked at the curtains. At the dogs. At the bracket dangling from the wall. At Rebus, who'd managed to get his head stuck in a fold of fabric and was staggering around like a confused ghost.

He turned to Ellie.

'That's it. I've had quite enough of today,' he said firmly but without heat. 'I love you to bits, Ellie. But I'm going to bed.' He walked over, kissed her forehead, and headed for the stairs.

'Dave–'

He lifted a hand for quiet.

She heard his footsteps on the stairs, the bedroom door closing with a decisive click.

Ellie stood in the wreckage of the lounge, surrounded by destroyed curtains and two very proud dogs. Rebus had finally freed himself from the fabric and was now sitting beside Marple, both of them panting happily.

'Well,' she said to them. 'I hope you're pleased with yourselves...'

Marple barked in agreement.

Ellie gathered up armfuls of cream fabric, assessing the damage. The curtains were beyond saving. The bracket would need fixing. And Dave was upstairs, no doubt lying in bed wondering what he'd done to deserve a wife and dogs who caused mayhem.

Hopefully by the morning he would have forgiven her. And them.

Chapter 24
WEDNESDAY

The next morning, Ellie was up and out early for a dog walk with Jo. The panto cast and crew were meeting at the hall at 8.30am. It was the only time they could agree on when most of them could be there.

It was crisp and bright, the kind of winter day that made everything sparkle.

Ellie still had Marple. They walked a loop round Bramhurst, the dogs charging through snow drifts and chasing each other with boundless energy.

'Can we stop by the chapel?' Ellie asked as they walked along Thimble Lane, Rebus and Lily trotting ahead, Marple a little tired. 'I'd love to show you the steel frame. It went in yesterday.'

'I'd like that,' Jo said.

The chapel sat just beyond Stream Cottage, its post-Norman stone walls solid and reassuring. The large arched window had been reinstated, the glass back in place, sealing the building from the elements again.

Ellie unlocked the heavy wooden door and pushed it open. The interior was cold but bright, winter sun streaming through the stained glass windows. The coloured light – ruby red, sapphire blue, emerald green – fell in jewelled patterns across the stone floor and the new steel structure.

The frame rose up through the centre of the space, clean industrial lines against the ornate Gothic architecture. The sections were bolted together now, creating the skeleton of a first floor that would eventually hold bedrooms and a bathroom.

'Oh, Ellie,' Jo breathed. 'It's going to be beautiful.'

Piles of floorboards were stacked along the chapel wall, pale and clean. They seemed solid and homely, waiting to be fitted into place.

'You think so?' Ellie looked up at the steel beams, already imagining the finished space. 'Sometimes I worry it's too modern for a building like this.'

'No. It's perfect. Old and new together. History and future.' Jo walked around the perimeter, Lily padding beside her, both of them careful on the uneven stone floor. 'The light through these windows... it's going to be spectacular.'

Rebus sniffed at the steel uprights with interest, tail wagging slowly.

'The staircase will go here,' Ellie said, pointing. 'That's arriving in a day or so. And the stud walls will section off the bedrooms and bathroom. Dave's convinced it'll be done by summer.'

'He's an optimist,' Jo said with a smile.

'True. But it finally feels like it's happening. *Finally* feels real.'

They stood for a moment in the coloured light, listening to the silence. The chapel felt peaceful, despite the building work. Sacred, still.

'Come on,' Ellie said. 'Let's get our coffees and see how Belle's doing.' She checked her watch. There was half an hour before the meeting.

They stepped back outside, locking the door behind them. As Ellie turned the key, a robin landed on the wrought iron handrail that ran beside the stone steps down from the main entrance.

It perched there, head cocked, watching them with bright black eyes. Its red breast was vivid against the grey stone and white snow.

Jo smiled. 'It's a good omen when a robin adopts your home.'

Fifteen minutes later, they were outside the Hop Picker's Rest, tucking into thick slices of stollen from one of the market stalls and sipping cappuccinos. The dogs panted happily, while Belle balanced on her ladder, reindeer horns in place, cleaning the upper windows.

'I gather you've been upsetting the dancing detective even more, Ells,' Belle teased affectionately. She wiped her squeegee across the glass in smooth strokes.

'Don't,' replied Ellie. 'The ladder re-enactment, he understood. Sort of. But the hall was a step too far...' She summarised what'd happened.

Jo was keeping a firm grip on Lily's lead. The red setter was eyeing a squirrel which was foraging around a nearby tree. Rebus and Marple were play-wrestling on the tarmac.

'Is he speaking to you this morning?' Belle asked with a grin.

She chuckled. 'I made him a cuppa and apologised again. He managed a smile.'

Ellie took a sip from her coffee.

'Poor Dave,' said Jo. 'We all love him. And your private investigation is incredible, Ells. But it's got to be a nightmare for him, having the Blix women digging around in the cases he's investigating.'

'Unfortunately, it didn't end at the hall. You should have seen his face when we got home last night. The curtains were in shreds. Marple had wrapped herself up in one like a sausage roll...'

'He sent Phil a photo of the curtain rail.'

Jo chortled.

'And Reeby had the other one in his mouth, looking enormously pleased with himself. Dave just stood there, looked at the carnage, and said "I've had enough of today".'

Belle, reindeer horns dancing on her head, laughed so hard she nearly dropped her squeegee. 'Poor Dave. The man's having a week.'

'Rebus isn't usually a chewer, but I think having Marple there, the two of them just couldn't resist. They would have been better off in the kitchen. Nothing to chew in there.'

They were all still laughing when Dave's Audi pulled into the car park.

Ellie's smile faded slightly. 'Oh. I wonder what they're here for.'

Dave got out, followed by DS Carmichael. Both had their professional faces on.

Something was wrong.

Belle must have sensed it too. She paused mid-wipe, looking down at them. 'Uh-oh.'

Dave walked over, his expression serious. 'Belle, would you mind stepping down from the ladder, please?'

Belle shot a worried glance at Ellie, who shrugged. She descended the ladder, squeegee still in hand, antlers still wobbling. 'What's this about? Have you come to breathalyse me?'

'Belle Kersey, I'm arresting you on suspicion of the murder of Neville Snipe.' Dave's voice was formal, official. 'You do not have to say anything, but it may harm your defence if you do not mention when questioned something which you later rely on in court. Anything you do say may be given in evidence.'

The world seemed to tilt.

'What?' Belle stared at him. 'You're joking. Is this to get us back for the ladder re-enactment and drinking?'

'We will escort you to the station.'

'Dave,' Ellie said, finding her voice and jumping to Belle's side. 'You must have made a mistake. This is Belle. She didn't–'

'Ellie, please.' Dave's tone was gentle but firm.

'But she was with me in the hall. She couldn't have–'

'Mrs Blix.' DS Carmichael stepped forward. 'We need you to step back, please.'

Belle had gone very pale. 'What evidence are you basing this on?'

'We'll discuss that at the station,' Dave said. 'We need you to come with us now.'

'But I haven't done anything.' Belle's voice rose. 'This is ridiculous.'

Ellie felt sick.

'This is insane,' Jo said, her hand on Lily's collar. 'Belle wouldn't hurt a fly.'

'Can one of you call Phil?' Belle asked. 'Let him know.'

'Course,' Ellie and Jo chimed.

DS Carmichael touched Belle's elbow. 'If you'll come with us, please.'

'My ladder,' Belle said dazedly. 'I need to bring it d–.'

'We'll take care of it,' Darren called from the pub doorway, having emerged to see what was happening.

Belle looked at Ellie, her eyes wide with shock and fear. 'I didn't do this. You know I didn't.'

Ellie trusted Dave. He wouldn't have arrested Belle without sufficient cause to suspect her. What that evidence was, she didn't know yet. But Dave had integrity. He would question her fairly. He would interrogate the evidence rigorously. She, Sylvia and Zoe *had* to do the same.

'Leave it to us,' she said calmly. 'We'll sort this out.'

Dave's eyes closed briefly in irritation and his jaw tightened.

He and DS Carmichael walked Belle to the Audi. She moved like someone in a dream, or a nightmare.

DS Carmichael gestured to the antlers. 'You might want to remove them?'

Belle slid them off her head and seemed to hesitate for a few moments, as though she didn't know what to do with them.

Ellie jumped forward, hand outstretched. 'I'll take them.'

They settled her in the back seat, DS Carmichael beside her.

Dave paused before getting in the driver's side, looking at Ellie. His expression said everything he couldn't say out loud: I'm sorry. I have to do my job. Please don't make this harder.

Then he got in the car and drove away, taking Belle with him.

Ellie stood frozen, watching the Audi disappear down the lane.

'This is wrong,' she said. 'Completely wrong.'

'What evidence could they possibly have?' Jo asked.

'I don't know. But whatever it is, we need to find out and debunk it. The police have twenty-four hours to hold her.

Then they need either to charge her or release her.' Ellie pulled out her phone with shaking hands.

'There must have been some mistake. Got her confused with someone else perhaps.'

'I'm calling an emergency meeting with Sylvia and Zoe. Straight after the meeting with the cast and crew.'

'Do you want an extra one? Another brain?'

'Thank you. That would be useful. You've lived here for much longer than me and know more about the history of the place. Of Bramhurst Players. Shall we meet at Stream Cottage? We can go straight from the hall.'

'Yes. Shall we drop the dogs home now and go onto the hall in a minute?'

'Good idea. I'll contact Sylvia and Zo about meeting afterwards.'

Ellie's fingers flew across the phone screen, texting both women: *Emergency meeting. Stream Cottage 9.30am. Belle's been arrested.*

The replies came immediately.

Sylvia: *Righto.*

Zoe: *WHAT?? Need to transfer a fox from my van to Kieran's. Then coming.*

Ellie looked at Jo. 'This wasn't the start to the morning that I expected.'

Chapter 25

Ellie and Jo left the Hop Picker's Rest in a daze, shuffling through the snow with the dogs towards their respective homes on the way to the church hall. The shock of Belle's arrest echoed between them, and silence alternated with animated discussion.

'We can't cancel this cast and crew meeting, can we?' asked Jo.

'No. We need all the information we can get. I should've got everyone together sooner really, but there's been so much to do.'

Jo nodded.

'I'd offer to have Lily at my house with Reeby and Marple,' Ellie told her, 'but after the curtain catastrophe last night, I won't risk it.'

They dropped Rebus and Marple off at Stream Cottage and Lily at the rectory.

'As Ellie walked, she checked her email and messages for who was coming, ticking off the cast and crew in her mind. 'I've not heard from Daphne, our fairy godmother. Have you?'

'No.' Jo had been helping her chase people up.

'I guess we'll just have to wait and see if she turns up. Might be a bit soon for her.'

'Yes. I've just had a text from Gideon. He and Rory are coming together. They've just left the garden centre. Been getting a Christmas tree for Daphne to cheer her up.'

They were Prince Charming and Buttons. Ellie had visions of them arriving with Daphne's fir tree on their roof rack.

'Frances hasn't replied,' said Ellie.

Their Cinderella.

'Margaret's already at the hall,' said Jo. 'Bless her. She's made some mince pies to cheer us all up.'

She ran the wool shop and was an ex-dressmaker. With a little help from Ellie and Sylvia, she'd created all the costumes. Some had been altered from previous productions. Others had been acquired from charity shops.

'No idea about Phil now Belle's with the police,' said Ellie. 'And I'm not about to chase him. Chloe was going to come but she might be with her dad.' She switched from

WhatsApp to email. 'Hopefully Paul will make it. I've not heard from him. Have you?'

Phil and Paul were the ugly sisters, the only two men in the village game enough to wear drag for the production. Dave had said an immediate no.

'Hang on.' Jo stopped walking. 'Text from Marie-Hélène. She and Paul are both on their way with some *pains au chocolat* from the bakery.'

Marie-Hélène was the wicked stepmother.

'Dee rang me last night,' said Jo. 'She and Mel are coming.'

She was their Baron Hardup in drag and Mel was their stage manager.

When they arrived at the hall, Mike was outside on his phone, discussing interest rates and payment plans. He gestured that he'd be in in a second. Perhaps he was negotiating a big contract given he was discussing payment terms.

Rory and Gideon were parking.

Inside, glum faces greeted them. The lights were off and they were all standing at the stage in the dull light.

Mike joined them. 'Is it true about Belle?' He stuffed his phone in his pocket and checked first Ellie's face for information, then Jo's.

Ellie switched on the lights.

Paul and Marie-Hélène followed them in.

Mel and Dee hadn't arrived, but they had to start.

'OK, listen up, folks.' Ellie explained that Belle had been arrested. 'We need anything you know that might help her. Whether about Belle herself or about anything to do with Neville. Anyone who had a grudge against him.'

Jo explained about Belle having been in the hall with Ellie.

'We were literally in this room,' Ellie told them, 'inspecting the set for what to store while Neville was being killed.'

'Oh, Ellie,' said Marie-Hélène. 'That's very unsettling. Poor Neville. And Belle. She can't be guilty, surely? She's one of us. And if she was with you, how could she have killed Neville?'

Ellie gave a huge shrug. 'This is the thing. What evidence do the police have to suspect her of murder?'

'And you can't think of anything?' asked Marie-Hélène.

'No. Nothing. It doesn't make sense. Except – obviously my husband is the officer in charge, and I know he'll have evidence. They cannot arrest someone without it. So, they must have something on Belle that we don't know about.'

'I know this isn't the priority at the moment but is it impossible that we might find another director?' asked Paul.

'It's very short notice,' Gideon replied. 'Most jobbing directors will be in the middle of rehearsals.'

As Gideon spoke, an idea occurred to Ellie. She'd discuss it with Jo later.

Jo was checking her phone. 'I handle the hall bookings. The stage here was booked for the panto so you can leave the set up. See if you can find someone.'

'If you don't mind that,' said Mike. 'It was a tricky beast to set up as it's so large, so I don't want to dismantle it and reassemble it unless we have to.'

'No problem. I'll keep the booking in place. Ells? Do you want to say anything about Neville or Belle?'

'Neville was a cruel man.' Rory spoke quickly. 'He used my mother when she was vulnerable to get into Bramhurst Players and then ditched us because Whitstable Playhouse would've been more advantageous.'

'How is she?' asked Ellie.

'Embarrassed. Angry. Upset.' Rory flicked his hand in frustration. 'But in a strange way, it's helping her knowing how many other people he's treated badly. Lauren. Chloe. Patricia. Frances too probably.'

'Hopefully it'll feel less personal,' Ellie told him.

Rory nodded. 'He's also commissioned professional services from a number of people locally and not paid them.'

'Geoff, for one,' said Mike. 'He did the electrics for the panto and some rewiring work in Neville's house. Neville hasn't paid him for either.'

Gideon sucked in air.

'We're talking a lot of money.'

Mel bowled in with a kind smile. She had a snood over a messy bun.

Dee followed her, the usual tornado of noise and movement. 'Sorry we're late,' she said, her purple hair and earrings catching the light. 'Had a couple of punters in the shop, looking at Mel's pottery.' She smiled at everyone. 'What can we do to help?'

'Don't suppose Neville owed you money too,' asked Rory.

'As a matter of fact, no. But he owed Geoff quite a bit–'

'Funnily enough, we were just talking about that,' Ellie told them.

'It's poor show, especially at this time of year,' Mike added. 'I really feel for Geoff. It's going to be a lean Christmas for Sadie and me too.'

The double doors opened and Frances arrived in a green uniform. The hall went silent.

'I can't stay long,' she said. Her long, blonde hair was in a scrunchie. 'I've got to get to work. I wasn't sure whether to come at all but having heard you all running Neville down, I'm glad I have.'

Ellie glanced at Jo.

'I know he behaved badly with some of you but I want you to know that he's always been kind to me.' She sniffed and patted her tummy beneath her coat. 'I'm pregnant. We were going to have a baby together and now... now it'll be just me.'

Chapter 26

After the meeting in the spacious hall, Stream Cottage felt even smaller than usual with four women, two dogs, and a crisis packed into it.

The cottage was a typical two-up-two-down, compact and cosy with small rooms. Downstairs was open-plan with a small extension, housing a kitchen and bathroom.

Ellie had the log burner going, flames crackling cheerfully behind the glass door, throwing warm light across the space where the destroyed curtains had hung.

The dangling curtain rail had been taken down, leaving holes in the wall. The torn fabric had been bundled into bin bags. The window looked oddly naked, so Ellie had switched on the fairy lights and hung a heart in the empty space.

Sylvia arrived first, carrying a tin of millionaire's shortbread and a bag of marshmallows. 'For the hot chocolate,' she said, setting them on the kitchen counter. 'Crisis management requires proper provisions.'

Zoe arrived moments later.

Marple, who hadn't seen her "mum" since the night before, immediately launched herself at Zoe in a frenzy of puppy excitement. The two dogs eventually settled by the fire, Marple flopping across Rebus like he was a comfortable cushion.

Jo came last, bringing a bottle of Prosecco. 'For when Belle's released.'

Ellie made hot chocolate whilst Sylvia cut the shortbread into generous squares. The smell of caramel and chocolate filled the cottage.

'I'll pay half for the curtains and the rail,' Zoe said, eyeing the empty window. 'Marple was clearly the instigator.'

'Don't worry, lovey,' Ellie said. 'These things happen.' She knew Zoe didn't earn much and it wouldn't be an expensive fix. Just slightly annoying. 'I'm hoping your dad will fix the rail.'

They settled around the small dining table, mugs steaming, marshmallows within easy reach. Outside, snow had started falling again, soft flakes drifting past the bare window.

'Right,' Ellie said. 'Belle's arrest. We need to work out why.'

'What does it take to arrest someone?' Zoe asked. 'Legally, I mean.'

'I've just googled it,' Jo said, pulling out her phone. 'Police need "reasonable grounds" to suspect them of a criminal offence. Not proof, just reasonable suspicion.'

'Dave would have that,' Ellie said firmly. 'I have one hundred per cent confidence in his professionalism. He wouldn't arrest Belle unless the evidence justified it.'

'So, what evidence could they have?' Sylvia bit into her shortbread thoughtfully.

Ellie had been racking her brain ever since the arrest. 'I told Dave that Belle went to the loo while I was in the main hall,' she said quietly. 'It was only a few minutes but it's a gap in her alibi, I suppose.'

'You don't seriously think Belle did it?' Zoe looked appalled.

'No. Of course not. I'm just trying to think of what the police might be working with.'

Zoe stared at her mum.

'That gap exists, and Dave's working with evidence, not personal feelings.'

'Except just as it creates a gap in Belle's alibi,' Sylvia added, 'it also creates one for you and they haven't arrested you.'

'Very true,' said Ellie. 'So, it either cannot be that or they've got something additional.'

'But Belle wouldn't hurt a soul,' Jo said. 'I've known her for years. She's a bit hot-headed but she's kind, patient, devoted to Chloe. Murder? It's absurd.'

'Agreed,' Sylvia said. 'But the police don't know Belle like we do. Like Ellie says, they're working from evidence and we need to figure out what they might have.' She counted on her fingers. 'They'll have checked four main sources. One: CCTV. Two: crime scene evidence. Three: Neville's communications data – texts, emails, calls. Four: house-to-house inquiries.'

'CCTV will show Belle entering the hall with her ladder,' Ellie said. 'She *did* enter. With *me*. That's not incriminating.'

'Unless a camera caught her somewhere she shouldn't have been,' Zoe suggested. 'Near the storage room? The back door?'

'Possible. But Belle went to the hall legitimately.' Ellie was starting to feel guilty for mentioning that Belle went to the toilet. 'Her ladder, her equipment. She had every reason to be there. She was helping Neville out, for goodness' sake.'

'You said she was at the hall when you arrived,' said Sylvia. 'Could she have been seen doing something before you got there?'

'Possibly. Like what?'

'I don't know. All we can do is hypothesise until we hit on something.'

'What about the crime scene evidence?' Jo asked.

'Ah,' said Zoe. 'I looked this up after you rang me.' She brought up a list on her phone. 'Crime scene evidence covers a wide range of things, most of which we, as sleuths, cannot check. Biology. That includes DNA, hair, bodily fluids. Then fingerprints. Next there's trace evidence, like fibres, soil. Then footwear. Then digital and electronic evidence. Then weapons and lastly, scene context, which is about the position and pattern of things.'

'Well done, lovey,' said Ellie. 'Shall we go through each category in turn?'

'Yes,' said Sylvia. 'The CSIs will probably have found Belle's DNA and hair, maybe saliva around the ladder, as she set it up for Neville and it's the ladder she uses every day. Same with her fingerprints.'

'Yup,' Ellie said. 'She positioned it, checked it, made sure it was secure.'

'And that's not evidence of murder,' Sylvia stated. 'That's evidence of her doing exactly what she was there to do.'

'One of the key issues is that when we got to Neville,' said Ellie, 'the ladder was semi-retracted and the two bolts were both drawn back.'

Sylvia spoke again. 'If Belle checked it was secure, that would've meant the bolts were in place. Perhaps the police think she's lying about locking the ladder and sabotaged it.'

Jo said slowly. 'Belle knows ladders inside out. She'd know how to make one fail. I'm not suggesting she did, but the police might think it's possible she did. If there's other evidence against her too...'

A heavy silence fell. The fire popped and Ellie added a couple of logs.

'She didn't sabotage the ladder,' Ellie said firmly. 'But yes, they might think she had the technical knowledge.'

'Let's keep going through the list. Like with the other categories, trace evidence could've transferred from Belle to the ladder, and possibly from the ladder to Neville. Like jumper fibres, mud, paint. You've only got to touch something and evidence transfers. Again, it's not proof of anything except that Belle touched the ladder before Neville used it.'

'Next it's electronic evidence,' said Jo. 'We've got no way of knowing what's on Neville's devices.'

'We didn't see any weapons,' said Ellie. 'I didn't think it was that sort of death.'

'Hmm,' said Sylvia. 'True. Oh dear. We're not getting very far, are we?'

'We haven't considered the crime scene context,' said Zoe. 'Did you notice anything about the positioning of Neville's body? Of the ladder?'

Ellie frowned. She hadn't. There'd been too much going on. The door slamming. She shook her head. 'Don't think so.'

'What about the police evidence from house-to-house inquiries?' Sylvia continued.

'That would confirm what CCTV evidence would've told them,' Ellie said. 'That Belle entered the hall. Maybe someone saw her van earlier? Or later?'

'Or – I'm just playing devil's advocate here,' said Jo. 'Maybe someone saw Belle doing something else before you arrived, Ells? Something incriminating we don't know about?'

'Possible. But I think...' Ellie wrapped her hands around her mug. 'I think another option is Neville's communications data. Texts, emails.'

'Like what?' Zoe asked.

'I don't know. Something that establishes motive and intent on Belle's part perhaps?'

Sylvia nodded slowly. 'That would do it. Threatening texts plus opportunity plus technical knowledge equal reasonable grounds for arrest.'

'So, we need to find out if Belle sent anything to Neville,' Ellie said. 'And if she did, what it actually meant. Context matters.'

'And to talk to Phil and Chloe,' Jo suggested. 'They'd know if Belle was in contact with Neville. If there were any arguments.'

'Good idea.' Ellie pulled out her phone to check the time. 'Phil might have gone to the police station. If he's at work, when does he finish?'

'Depends on the jobs,' Jo said. 'Chimney sweeps work to their own schedule. Could be afternoon, could be evening.' She checked her watch. 'We should try and speak to Phil now. Catch him between appointments if we can. I've got the carol singers' lunch at the rectory at 1pm, so this morning's better for me.'

'I'll come with you,' Ellie said. 'Sylvia, Zoe – can you two talk to Chloe?'

'Where is she?' Sylvia asked.

'Belle's house, probably. Or the stables. I'll text Phil.'

His reply came within a minute: *Chloe's at stables. Devastated. What's happening? Why have they arrested Belle?*

We're trying to find out, Ellie re-plied. *Can Jo and I come & see you this morning?*

I'm in Bram until noon. Meet me at the house after?

We'll come now and catch you between jobs. It's urgent.

Alright. I'm at Mr Patterson's at 59 School House Lane. Give me twenty minutes.

Ellie showed the others. 'Phil's working locally. We can catch him soon.'

'I'll meet you at the stables at eleven,' Sylvia said to Zoe. 'Talk to Chloe then.'

'I need to collect a cormorant first,' Zoe said apologetically. 'Member of the public found it along the Stour in Canterbury looking sleepy. I'm taking it to the vet, then I'll head to the stables. Should make eleven easily.'

'A cormorant?' Jo looked fascinated despite the circumstances.

'Yes. Beautiful bird. They fish on the quiet sections. Hopefully just eaten something dodgy.'

They finished their hot chocolate and gathered their things. The dogs were reluctant to leave the fire, but eventually allowed themselves to be coaxed into movement.

'Before we go, shall we compile our list of suspects?' said Ellie. 'The killer has to be someone who is familiar with the layout of the village hall and knows there's a loft hatch in the storeroom...'

'... and can get up a loft ladder,' Sylvia added. 'With a motive and opportunity.'

'Half of Bramhurst?' said Jo.

'Ugh,' said Ellie. 'Yes.'

'Well, we haven't found any answers yet,' Sylvia observed, pulling on her coat. 'But we have a plan of action. To find something that proves Belle's innocent.'

'She *is* innocent,' Jo said firmly. 'We just need to prove it to the police. And if they don't release her, we can protest outside the police station.'

'Good grief, no,' said Ellie, half-laughing. 'I think Dave would see that as grounds for divorce.' She changed the subject. 'We should be OK to go and speak to Patricia today. Enough time has elapsed. Let's do that this afternoon. And we also need to speak to the electrician, don't we? Sylvia, can you do that?'

'Yes.'

They filed out into the snow. Marple went with Zoe.

Ellie locked the cottage and turned to Jo. 'OK,' she said. 'Let's go and see what Phil can tell us.'

Just as they were heading up the lane to the jeep, a van passed them and pulled up outside Stream Cottage.

'Hang on. That's Mike.'

He wound down the window. 'That was good timing. Your husband rang me about a job. I've come to put your curtain rail back up.'

Chapter 27

Ellie got Mike settled in the lounge, made him a coffee and set off for School House Lane with Jo.

The tiny street wound through a part of Bramhurst which Ellie had only been to once when Rebus took off after a rabbit, and led her through a hedge and across two fields. It was on the outskirts of the village and a little more rural.

They drove along the narrow lane, lined with Victorian terraces. The snow was thicker here and less disturbed, and Ellie was grateful for the jeep's four-wheel drive.

She turned down the car radio. 'Do you mind if I put some carols on? I need cheering up.'

'Please do.'

She switched to Radio 2, where *"Good King Wenceslas"* was playing. They sang along half-heartedly, the familiar words a comfort.

'What time is the family crib service on Saturday?' Ellie asked as they pulled up behind Phil's van, which had "Kersey Chimney Sweep" painted on the side in red letters.

'It's at 2pm. We've got the children's nativity group doing the tableau, and carols in the morning. You should come.'

'I will. Normal life. Good to forget about murder investigations.'

Jo smiled. 'That's the idea.'

They got out of the car just as shouting erupted from the house.

'... absolutely outrageous. Look at this mess.'

The front door was already open and a man stormed out, his face puce with rage, coat flapping behind him.

'You can forget about payment,' he yelled back at the house. 'And I'll be leaving a review telling everyone to avoid your *services*, if you can call them that.'

Phil appeared in the doorway, soot-stained and looking miserable. His face and hands were black, his work clothes covered in fine dust.

'Mr Patterson, please, let me explain–'

'What is there to explain? There's a cloud of soot all over our cream carpet. Our lovely new cream suite. Our cream curtains.' Mr Patterson noticed Ellie and Jo standing by the car. 'Are you contemplating using this buffoon? Professional chimney sweep, he calls himself.'

'What happened?' Ellie asked Phil.

'I'll tell you what happened,' Mr Patterson replied. 'He shoved his rod down our chimney and brought half a ton of soot into our living room, that's what happened.'

Phil ran a dirty hand through his hair and took a long, slow breath. 'With respect, your chimney hasn't been swept in over ten years. I did warn you there could be a build-up of hardened soot.' He turned to Ellie and Belle. 'The rod loosened a large lump, which fell down, hit the hearth, and sent up a cloud of dust.'

He then faced Mr Patterson again. 'You simply cannot hold me responsible when–'

'*Responsible*? It's your job to prevent things like this.'

'I did advise you of the risks, to have protective sheeting down, and you said your wife didn't want ground sheets on the carpet–'

'Don't you *dare* blame my wife.' Mr Patterson jabbed a finger at Phil. 'You're not getting a penny. Not one penny. And everyone in Bramhurst is going to hear about this.' He stormed off down the street, still muttering furiously.

Phil slumped against the doorframe. 'That's me ruined, then. Word of mouth is everything in this business.'

'I'm sure you can sort it out,' Jo said gently.

'Where's he going?' asked Ellie.

Phil gave a sheepish shrug. 'Probably to set up the stocks on the village green...'

Ellie smiled at the image created in her mind by Phil's remark.

'Mrs Patterson's in tears inside. The carpet's covered. The walls, the furniture, everything.' Phil looked at them properly for the first time. 'You wanted to talk about Belle, didn't you?'

'Yes, but we can see–'

Phil's face tightened with concern. 'I can't stop now. I've got to try and salvage this situation.'

'Where can we meet you?' Jo asked.

'The bookshop café? Give me half an hour or so to clean up as much as I can and resolve things with Mrs Patterson while her husband's out.' He looked back at the house. 'Blimey, what a morning.'

'We'll wait for you,' Ellie said. 'Belle needs our help.'

'Oh, I know that. I'll see you shortly.' He strode back towards the front door.

The bookshop café was quiet mid-morning, just a few customers browsing the shelves and two women with yoga mats having coffee and bagels by the window. Ellie and Jo claimed a corner table and ordered cappuccinos.

Phil arrived forty-five minutes later, soot still all over his face, around his hairline and under his nails.

'How did it go?' Jo asked as he sat down, passing him a coffee.

'Mrs Patterson's calmed down a bit. She admitted I warned them of the risks and that she said no to the protective sheets. I've arranged for the room to be cleaned professionally, including the carpet.'

'That's good of you.' Ellie was wondering what she would've done in the situation.

'*Mr* Patterson's still furious and determined to ruin my reputation, but hopefully he'll calm down.' He rubbed his eyes tiredly. 'They've only just moved into the village so hopefully not too many people will listen to him'

'I'm sorry,' Ellie said.

'It can't be helped. Very occasionally these things happen. And when you try and cut corners, it's more likely. Ten years without sweeping, what did they expect? They didn't like my dust sheets as they said they were dirty. I offered to buy new ones but said I'd need to add the cost to the bill. They said no. They didn't want *any* dust sheets on their new carpet.' He looked at them both. 'With hindsight, I should've refused to do it without sheets. However...' He sighed. 'What do you want to know about Belle?'

'We're trying to understand why the police arrested her so we can prove their evidence false. Do you have any idea what reason they might have?' Ellie was direct with him.

Phil stared into his coffee. 'I... er... don't know.'

But his hesitation, and tone, suggested otherwise. Ellie exchanged glances with Jo.

'Did anything happen between Belle and Neville in the weeks before he died?'

'Not really.'

'Phil,' Jo said gently, 'time is critical. They could charge Belle at any moment. The more we understand about what the police might have, the better we can challenge it and help her.'

Ellie explained about "reasonable grounds". 'They won't just have arrested her on suspicion of murder because she was at the hall. If that was the case, they'd have arrested me too.'

'I... I don't want to make things worse.'

'You won't,' Ellie said. 'But we need to know the truth. All of it.'

Phil was quiet for a long moment. When he spoke, his voice was soft. Resigned. 'Belle had a huge bust-up with Neville. About him sacking Chloe and giving her role to that Frances woman.'

'What sort of bust-up?' Ellie leaned forward. 'Do you mean *physical*?'

'No. Not physical.' Phil's jaw clenched. 'But... er... not good. You know what Belle's like. Heart of gold, but fiery. And fiercely protective of Chloe.'

'What happened?'

'I wasn't there. Belle told me about it later.' He still wouldn't meet their eyes. 'She was furious. Said things she shouldn't have said.'

'What *things*?'

He shook his head.

'The best way to protect Belle is to help us understand what the police might have found,' Jo said firmly. 'We *have* to be able to counter that evidence and produce alternative explanations. We can't do that with evidence we don't know about.'

'She was protecting Chloe. Any mother would do the same.'

'Of course,' Ellie said. 'We're not judging Belle. What happened?'

Phil's hands tightened around his coffee cup. 'What if I tell you, and it makes things worse for her?'

This was the second time a witness had expressed this sentiment. It struck Ellie how awful it must be to potentially know something about a crime and be scared to mention it.

'Listen to me,' said Jo in her vicar-giving-a-sermon voice. 'Belle could be charged. How much worse could it get?'

Ellie kept her comments steady, persuasive. 'Belle needs our help.'

He looked up finally, his eyes tired and frightened. 'She confronted him at his house. Told him he was a cruel, manipulative–' He stopped. 'She was really angry. Said Chloe was devastated, that he'd destroyed her confidence for nothing. That replacing her with his fancy woman was disgusting.'

'When was this?' asked Ellie.

'A week or so before he died.'

Ellie's stomach sank. A confrontation at Neville's house, not long before his death. That would definitely interest the police.

'Was anyone else there?' Jo asked. 'Any witnesses?'

Ellie had been thinking about Patricia and their daughters. Talia perhaps.

'I don't know. Belle just said she'd gone round to tell him what she thought of him.' Phil met Ellie's eyes finally. 'But there's something else. I get the impression there's something she hasn't told me.'

'Oh, crikey,' said Jo.

'What do you mean?'

'I asked her what exactly happened at Neville's house, what she said to him. She got defensive, said it didn't matter, that she'd just told him he was out of order. But she was lying. I know when Belle's lying. She gets huffy.' His voice cracked slightly. 'She's keeping something back. Hiding something. And I don't know what.'

Ellie sat back, her mind racing. Belle confronting Neville, angry and protective. Something happening that she wouldn't tell Phil about.

And now Belle was under arrest, and whatever that secret was, it might be the evidence that had put her there.

Chapter 28

The riding yard was tucked down a lane behind Belle and Phil's house, a small collection of stables where local horse owners kept their animals. The snow had been cleared from the concrete paths, piled in slushy grey heaps against the fence.

Wham's *"Last Christmas"* drifted from the tack room.

Sylvia and Zoe found Chloe in one of the stables, mucking out. She was bundled in layers – thick jumper, gilet, wellies – and wielding a fork. A stocky bay horse stood tied in the corner, peacefully pulling hay tufts from a net.

'Chloe,' Zoe called from the stable door. 'Can we talk to you for a minute?'

Chloe looked up, her face pale and tired. 'About Mum?'

'Yes. And a little bit about Neville, if that's alright.'

'Come in. I need to keep working though. Bramble needs riding and I'm already behind schedule.'

They stepped into the stable, the smell of horse and straw strong in the enclosed space. Sylvia leaned against the doorframe whilst Zoe perched on an upturned bucket.

Chloe gave a weak smile and returned to forking soiled bedding into a wheelbarrow. 'Fire away.'

Zoe explained what they needed. 'You told Mum and Gran about Neville sacking you. Sorry to raise it again. You mentioned him saying Frances was a better fit. Did he say anything else that indicated why he'd done it? What might've been in his mind?'

Chloe stood for a moment, shaking her head sadly. Then seemed to remember something. 'Actually, now I think about it, he did say something a bit odd. It sort-of registered at the time but not fully.'

'What?' Sylvia straightened.

'He switched. From being unkind and insulting to... seeming to feel bad. He said "Look, it's not you, it's me".' Chloe made air quotes with her fingers. 'Like people do when they're breaking up with someone.'

Sylvia glanced at Zoe. That was a classic line, meant to soften the blow. A cliché designed to make the rejected person feel better. 'People say that to try and lessen the hurt,' Sylvia said carefully. 'It doesn't always mean anything.'

'I know. But...' Chloe frowned, seemingly trying to connect with the exact moment. 'I got the impression he meant it. Wasn't just saying it to be kind. He looked... I don't know. Uncomfortable? Like he was genuinely trying to explain something but couldn't give me all the details. And he rattled the sentence off, like it embarrassed him to say it.'

'What do you think he meant?' Zoe asked.

'I don't know. At the time I was too upset to think about it properly.' Chloe picked up the wheelbarrow handles. 'Look, I really need to get on. Bramble needs tacking up and I want to ride before it gets too cold.'

She wheeled the barrow out of the stable, Sylvia and Zoe following.

They watched Chloe push the wheelbarrow steadily, wheel squeaking slightly, heading towards the large heap of waste piled up by the fence.

'We forgot to ask about her mum and Neville,' said Sylvia. 'We can't really go after her now. We'll have to hope Phil's able to help.'

Zoe nodded. 'What d'you reckon about the "it's not you, it's me" thing? Do you think Frances might've been hassling Neville to allow her to play Cinderella?'

Chapter 29

The house in Rough Common was modern and detached with a double garage and a tidy front garden.

Zoe had joined her mum.

Talia answered the door quickly, as if she'd been waiting. Her eyes were pink and a bit bloodshot, and she looked like she hadn't slept.

'Thanks for coming,' she said quietly. 'Mum's in the barn. Getting logs.'

'How is she?' Ellie asked.

'Not good. Crying a lot. Angry. Confused.' Talia led them through the house and out the back door. 'I haven't told her you were coming.'

The garden was long and well-maintained, even in winter. At the far end stood a wooden barn, its doors open. A woman was inside, sitting on a stool, elbows on her legs and leaning forward, head in her hands. Her shoulders were shaking.

'Mum?' Talia called softly.

Patricia straightened, wiping her face with her sleeve. She was a slight woman in her fifties, with short brown hair and the same dark eyes as Talia. Those eyes were swollen now, her face pale and blotchy.

'These ladies are Ellie and Zoe Blix. They're private detectives. I've asked them to help us find out who killed Dad.'

Patricia looked at them without warmth.

'We're also back-stage crew for Bramhurst Players,' said Ellie. 'We're very sorry about your husband's death.'

'Thank you. I don't know what you think I can tell you.'

'We're trying to put together a picture of what happened that morning,' Ellie said gently. 'A witness saw you arrive at the village hall around eight forty-five.'

Patricia's gaze snapped to Talia, sharp and questioning.

'Tell them, Mum,' Talia said quietly.

Patricia brushed wood chips from her jeans. 'You want to know why I went there.'

'Please.'

'Alright.' Patricia's voice was tight with emotion. 'Neville and I had been arguing for months. Talia's probably told you. Years, really. I wanted a divorce.

He didn't. Or rather, he liked the convenience and respectability of having a wife and family.'

'What were you arguing about?' Zoe asked.

'Everything. His affairs – and yes, there were multiple. His debts. The way he used people, manipulated them, threw them away when they were no longer useful.' Patricia's hands clenched. 'That morning, first thing, a man came to the house. Geoff, an electrician. Demanding money Neville owed him. Shouting on our doorstep.'

'We know about Geoff,' Ellie said.

'Then you know what kind of man my husband was. Took services, didn't pay for them. Made promises, broke them. All while acting like the victim.' Patricia's voice cracked slightly. 'It was wrong. And so embarrassing. I saw red. Watched Neville fob this man off, make more excuses, more promises he had no intention of keeping. And I thought: enough. I'm done.'

'So, you followed him to the hall,' Ellie said.

'I did. The night of that last row, he'd pleaded with me to give him time, to be patient. Having Geoff turn up, I knew with a certainty I'd not felt before that I wasn't prepared to stand by him any longer. To turn a blind eye while he was ripping people off.'

'What happened?'

'I went to tell him that I wanted a divorce immediately. That I didn't care about his career or his reputation or whatever excuse he'd make.' She looked down at her hands. 'But as I sat in the car outside the hall, I realised something.'

Ellie waited.

'I didn't need to announce my intentions. I didn't need his agreement, or to argue about it, or to give him one more chance to manipulate me. I could simply file the papers and start the process. He couldn't stop me.' Patricia's laugh was bitter. 'So, I left. Didn't go in.'

'What did you do?'

'I rang my lawyer and asked him to submit an application on my behalf to divorce Neville. He asked if I was sure and I said one hundred per cent.'

'Do you mind me asking which law firm?'

'Caspar & Green in Canterbury. I can forward you the follow-up email I sent them confirming my request.'

'Thank you.'

'I also asked them to tell him I wanted him to move out of the family home within the week.'

'And then?'

'I drove to the Magical Glade instead and walked for an hour, clearing my head. Even had a quick skate.'

The glade was popular with families and walkers. Hopefully, easy enough to verify if she'd been there.

'Did you see anyone there?' Zoe asked.

'A few people. Dog walkers, mostly. It was still quite early. I don't know if they'd remember me.'

Ellie believed her. The story had the ring of truth – the sudden realisation, the decision to take control rather than confront.

'Who did Neville have rows with before he died?' Ellie asked.

Patricia counted on her fingers. 'Geoff, obviously. Belle Kersey – she was furious about what he did to her daughter. Chloe herself. Daphne. Not sure what that was about. Lauren Blackwell at the Whitstable production.' She paused. 'Reverend Jo. I think that was more a professional disagreement than personal.' Her eyes took on an even more pained expression. 'You know about Frances, don't you? His latest fancy woman.'

Ellie nodded. 'Was his relationship with Frances serious?' They knew Frances was pregnant – or said she was. Not that that necessarily meant it was serious on Neville's part.

Patricia shrugged. 'If you mean, was he thinking of marrying her, I doubt it. But I'm sure he was making out he was serious. It's how he manipulates them all.'

'So, who do *you* think killed him?' Ellie asked softly. She got out her phone to take Patricia's email address.

The answer came immediately and without hesitation. 'Belle Kersey.'

Ellie felt her stomach drop. 'Why Belle?'

'Because she came round here and threatened to kill him.'

Chapter 30

The high street was busy with Christmas shoppers, people bundled in coats and scarves, carrier bags swinging. Above the street, the Christmas lights hung in swooping garlands from lamppost to lamppost, currently blazing even though it wasn't dark yet.

A van was parked nearby, 'Fleming Electrical' painted on the side.

'That's Geoff,' Sylvia said to Leonard, who was always happy to help the Blixes with their investigations.

Geoff Fleming stood steady on the top rung of a ladder propped against one of the shops, fiddling with a control box. He was a well-built man with a tool belt round his waist. He had the sort of confidence that forty years in the trade gave you, and was focused on a panel of wires.

They watched as he opened the timer unit, examined it carefully, then pulled out a replacement from his tool belt.

Within minutes, he'd swapped the units, tested the new one, and was descending the ladder.

'Efficient,' Leonard observed.

'And someone else who's familiar with ladders,' Sylvia whispered.

Geoff had the ladder down and was sliding it onto his van's roof rack when they approached.

'Mr Fleming?' Sylvia called.

He turned, wary. 'Yes?'

'I'm Sylvia. This is Leonard, my husband.'

Sylvia noticed Geoff clocking Leonard's dog collar.

'Gets me nervous when someone calls me Mr Fleming.' He rubbed his beard.

'We're looking into Neville Snipe's death on behalf of his daughter,' Sylvia said. 'We're private investigators. Could we have a word?'

Geoff's expression hardened. 'The police already questioned me.'

'I know. We're also trying to help a friend who's been wrongly arrested, we believe. Belle Kersey.'

'*Belle?*' Geoff looked surprised. 'They think Belle did it?'

'They've arrested her.'

'That's mad. Belle's a good person.' He secured the ladder with ropes. 'What do you want to know?'

'Listen, could we buy you a coffee?' Leonard suggested. 'The pub's just there. You look cold and it's a bit more private.'

Geoff glanced at the Hop Picker's Rest, its windows glowing warmly. 'Alright. I could do with a hot drink. Nippy up that ladder. Not as young as I was and my hands feel the cold these days. Can't be long though. I'm helping Mike out with a job shortly.'

Inside, the pub was festive and welcoming. Christmas songs played softly – Bing Crosby crooning about a white Christmas – and the tree in the corner twinkled with lights. The fire roared in the centre of the bar, open at either side of the chimney breast. Several tables were occupied by Christmas shoppers taking a break and eagerly reviewing their purchases.

Rory was playing pool with a young woman. Long chestnut hair, dungarees and a hoodie saying BBC Radio Kent on the back.

She looked a bit younger than Zoe. '... shadowing the breakfast show producer this week,' she told Rory as she took a shot at the ball.

Geoff waved at her. 'Alright, Sadie?'

'Who's that?' asked Leonard.

'Mike's daughter.'

They found a quiet corner. Leonard went to the bar whilst Sylvia and Geoff settled into chairs.

'Terrible business,' Geoff said, rubbing his hands. 'I didn't like Neville much, but I wouldn't wish that on anyone.'

'Yes. Now, we gather Neville owed you money,' Sylvia said.

Geoff frowned. 'He did. Over £6,000. I rewired the ground floor of his house and did the electrics for the panto.'

This confirmed what they'd been told.

'Where were you between 8.30 and 9am?'

'I was at my job in the village. Got there around 8.15.'

'You didn't pass the alley and stop for a few minutes?'

He shook his head. 'From Rough Common, I didn't go that way. I did an emergency job at the bakery in the high street.'

'You mean: Pain au Bramhurst?' asked Leonard.

'Correct. Their consumer unit kept tripping, and they needed to use the ovens.'

Sylvia made a note. Consumer units were big jobs. They'd had to have a new one installed at the rectory. 'Now, talking about Rough Common,' said Sylvia, 'we understand you went to Neville's house the morning he died.'

'I did. At 8am. Asked him for the money he owed me.' Geoff's jaw tightened. 'I'd invoiced him, as agreed, sent reminders, he kept fobbing me off.'

'Why do you think he withheld payment?' asked Sylvia. 'Is he struggling financially?'

Geoff snorted. 'You've gotta be kidding. He's directed in London for years. And you've seen the size of his house, right?'

'Why then?'

'Because he could. Because he enjoyed wielding power over people.' Geoff accepted a coffee and a chocolate brownie from Leonard with a nod of thanks. 'He had the money. I know he did. He just deliberately messed people about.'

'Was it ego?' Sylvia asked. 'Why do you think he was like that? Withholding payment, manipulating people?'

'Ego and power, like I said. Some people are just wired that way. They get off on controlling others, making them desperate.' Geoff wrapped his hands around the coffee mug. 'As for wanting the money for something else... well, there were rumours about affairs.'

'We've heard,' Leonard said carefully.

'Then you know about Frances?'

Sylvia nodded. 'Ellie's spoken to Patricia.' She was wondering what Neville might have been using his money for.

Geoff sipped his coffee. 'The only thing I can think of is maybe he was supporting Frances. New girlfriend, expensive tastes, who knows? Perhaps she was pregnant?'

Sylvia and Leonard shared a look, both equally shocked. Did he know about the baby or was he simply speculating?

'All I know is he had my money and wouldn't pay it.'

Geoff set down his mug. 'Look, I hope you can help Belle. She doesn't deserve this. But I can't tell you who killed Neville. I don't know.' He stood up, pulling on his jacket. 'I've got another job to get to.'

Chapter 31

After Geoff left, Sylvia and Leonard sat by the fire in the Hop Picker's Rest, warming their hands on fresh coffees that Leonard had insisted on buying. Outside, the Christmas lights blazed cheerfully, now properly timed thanks to Geoff's work.

'What do you think Christmas will be like?' Sylvia asked quietly. 'If the police haven't caught Neville's killer by then?'

'Tense,' Leonard said. 'Everyone looking at each other sideways. Wondering.'

'Belle could still be in custody.'

'Yes.' He stirred sugar into his coffee. 'Though if we can prove she didn't do it–'

'We need evidence. Actual evidence, not just people's word.' Sylvia stared into the fire, thinking. 'There has to be something we're missing.'

Leonard was quiet for a moment, then sat up straighter. 'All that talk about the back of the hall. I'd forgotten.'

'What about it?'

'I parked there once when I was doing an event at the hall – some community policing presentation. There's rear access into the building from the road and the high street.'

'Yes.' Sylvia's mind raced. 'Belle and Ellie saw a man leaving the hall. I don't know if they got as far as finding out where the path leads. The killer could've arrived and left from the road.'

'Possible,' agreed Leonard. 'More discreet than the front entrance, especially if you're trying not to be seen.'

'When Ellie was at the hall doing her reconnaissance last night, it was dark. And she was intercepted by the police before she could explore properly. She probably didn't check the path then either.' Sylvia got up. 'Come on. Let's go and look.'

'Look for what?'

'Anything that can help us identify the killer and link them to the murder.'

They left the warmth of the pub and headed up the high street on foot. The village hall was only a few minutes' walk, and the cold air helped focus Sylvia's thoughts.

The path ran along the back of several buildings, including the hall. It was narrow, barely wide enough for a car, with high fences on either side. Snow had drifted against these, and the path itself was churned up with footprints – delivery drivers, probably, and the occasional resident taking a shortcut.

'This way,' Leonard said, leading her past a holly bush that stuck out.

They moved carefully, eyes scanning the ground. The snow made everything harder to see – white on white.

'What exactly are we looking for?' Leonard asked, steadying himself on the fence.

'I don't know. Dropped evidence. Something the killer might have left behind in their hurry.'

They searched methodically, Leonard taking one side of the path, Sylvia the other. As they progressed, the snow was deeper, untouched except for their own footprints and a few older tracks that had frozen solid.

Leonard's foot caught on something hidden beneath the snow. He stumbled, his arms like a windmill, and nearly went down.

'Careful.' Sylvia grabbed his arm, steadying him.

'I'm alright. Just–' He looked down at what he'd tripped over. A bicycle tyre and a small pile of frozen rubbish, half-buried. 'Nothing. Just debris.'

They continued searching. The fence here was weathered wood, gaps showing through to gardens beyond.

Sylvia almost walked past it. A dark shape caught in the bottom of the fence, partially hidden by a drift of snow. She crouched down, pulling on her gloves, and carefully extracted it. A beanie. Dark blue, the wool a bit bobbly. A "Peter Storm" logo. Snow had got inside it.

'Leonard, look at this.'

He came over, peering at the hat. 'Could have been there for ages.'

'Or dropped recently and covered by fresh snow.' Sylvia turned it carefully in her hands. 'Ellie and Belle said the person they saw leaving the hall was wearing a beanie.' She peered at Leonard, excitement bubbling. 'We need to get this to Dave's team for testing.'

Chapter 32

The garden centre was heaving when Ellie arrived. Sylvia had texted about the hat they'd found in the alley, and Ellie was wondering who it might belong to. She'd put a post on the Bramhurst Facebook page, asking if anyone had lost a dark blue beanie. Hopefully, they'd get some responses on that.

She left the jeep in the overflow car park and was about to get out when her phone rang. She glanced at the screen: Talia Snipe.

'Talia? Is everything alright?'

'I need to tell you something about Belle.' Talia's voice was shaky. 'About what she said to my dad.'

Ellie swung her legs back in and shut the door. 'Go ahead.'

'After you spoke to Mum, I kept thinking about Belle being arrested.' Talia took a breath. 'I was there when she threatened to kill my father.'

Ellie felt the tickle of excitement. *'You were there?'*

'I was upstairs in my room, supposed to be studying. Belle arrived and I heard raised voices, so I came to the top of the stairs. She and Dad were in the hall below. Belle was furious about what Dad had done to Chloe.'

'What exactly did she say?'

'She was shouting about how cruel he'd been, how he'd humiliated Chloe for no reason except to make room for his girlfriend. Mum was there too, trying to calm everyone down. But Belle was beyond calming.' Talia paused. 'The thing is, I got the impression it was frustration and anger speaking. And feeling Chloe's pain. Not that Belle actually intended to kill Dad. It was motherly protection, you know? Like when parents say "Oh, I could kill you" to their kids when they break something, but don't mean it literally.'

'I understand. But what were her exact words?'

Talia was quiet for a moment, remembering. 'She said: "If you do one further thing to upset my daughter, you'll have me to reckon with. And I will kill you".'

Ellie thanked Talia and sat in her seat for a few minutes. If this was what the police had arrested Belle for, surely she'd have told them how she'd meant the phrase? She texted the information to Dave.

Time to speak to Frances.

Christmas trees of every size lined the entrance, their piney scent mixing with the smell of cinnamon from the café. Families browsed festive garden ornaments – light-up reindeer, inflatable snowmen, strings of outdoor fairy lights. A loudspeaker system played *"Jingle Bell Rock"*.

Ellie navigated the crowds, scanning for Frances. She'd tracked down her employment through Jo, who was on the Bramhurst Players committee, and had Frances' surname and workplace on the cast records. Frances Carmody, assistant manager at Bramhurst Garden Centre.

Ellie was heading towards the till area when she spotted a familiar figure already there, talking to a young woman in a green work uniform.

Rory Henderson and Frances.

Ellie approached them. 'Hello, you two.'

Rory turned, and his expression was not welcoming. 'Ellie? What are you doing here?'

'Same as you, I suspect. Wanting to talk to Frances. Have you been here long?'

Rory's jaw tightened, irritated to be joined. 'No. Literally just arrived.'

Frances looked first at Rory then Ellie, confused. Her long blonde hair was tied with a scrunchie, and she had a name badge pinned to her fleece. Pretty in a quiet way, and with eyes which were tired and red-rimmed.

'I'm investigating Neville's death on beha...' Ellie changed her mind about mentioning Talia.

Frances' face fell and her hand went to her belly. 'Look, I've already spoken to the police. I don't want to keep going over everything.'

'We won't take much of your time,' Ellie said gently, deciding she might as well try and facilitate a quick chat for Rory and herself. 'But we'd appreciate a few minutes. Can you take a break?'

Frances glanced at her watch. 'I haven't had lunch yet so I can take ten minutes now. But that's it. We're swamped today.'

She led them to a quiet corner of the café, away from the main rush. They sat at a small table surrounded by potted poinsettias, the Christmas music slightly muted here.

'Why are *you* investigating?' Frances asked, wrapping her hands around a bottle of water. 'Aren't the police doing it?'

'Yes,' Rory said. 'I'm helping my mum and Ellie is–'

'... helping a friend who's been arrested,' Ellie finished. 'Belle Kersey.'

'She's a nice woman,' said Frances. 'Was always kind to me at rehearsals, despite me taking over from her daughter.' She paused, gathering her thoughts perhaps. 'I'm sorry about my bombshell news at the meeting earlier. I… I'm so fed up with everyone…' She stopped there. 'There's no point me repeating myself. I want people to know that Neville and I were serious.'

'We're trying to understand what happened to him,' said Ellie. 'Belle is innocent.'

'We're all sorry for your loss,' Rory added, his tone softening slightly.

Frances' eyes filled with tears. 'We were in love. He was going to leave his wife for me. We had plans.' She stroked her belly.

Ellie felt a pang of sympathy mixed with anger. Neville had told Frances he was leaving Patricia. But Patricia had said Neville didn't want a divorce. Someone was being lied to. Probably both of them.

'How long had you been together?' Ellie asked.

'Four months. We met before he cast Cinderella.' She bristled. 'I know what people think – that I'm some home-wrecker, that I stole someone's role.' Frances wiped her eyes. 'But it wasn't like that. Neville said Chloe wasn't right for the part and he'd made a mistake. That I embodied what he wanted for the character.'

Or he wanted you in the role so he could spend more time with you, Ellie thought, but didn't say.

'Did he talk about his financial situation?' Rory asked.

'Sometimes. He said money was tight, that his wife controlled everything and was constantly spending. That once they divorced, he'd be free.' Frances looked at Ellie with what seemed like genuine sadness in her eyes. 'I know people probably call me a gold digger. But I never took a penny from Neville. Not one penny. He offered to help with my rent, to buy me things, but I refused. I wanted him for *him*, not for what he could give me.'

Crikey. That was unexpected. Like a few of the panto group probably, Ellie had assumed Neville was supporting Frances, that his debts to people might have been because he was spending money on his new girlfriend. But if Frances was telling the truth, that wasn't the case.

'Did he seem worried about anything before he died?' Ellie asked. 'Threatened by anyone?'

'Yes. He was stressed. The cancelled panto, the arguments with people, Patricia refusing to give him a divorce...'

Frances was pregnant and Ellie didn't want to upset her by challenging the narrative. She'd let the police do that with trained officers to support her.

'Did you know about the panto in Whitstable that he was directing?'

'No-o.' Her eyes welled up with tears as implications dawned on her. 'Is that why he cancelled ours?'

Ellie frowned, noticing that Frances had said "ours". 'I was about to ask if you knew why he cancelled Cinderella.'

'He told me he was cancelling it because the vicar's health and safety concerns were crazy. "PC gone mad", he said.'

Ellie waited a moment while Frances absorbed the news that Neville hadn't been truthful with her. Then asked, 'Did he tell you anything else?'

'That a few people in Bramhurst were giving him trouble, but he wouldn't say who.' Frances' voice broke. 'I got the impression one was a woman.' She sniffed. 'If I'd known he was in danger, if I'd asked more questions...'

'This isn't your fault, Frances,' Rory said firmly, kindly. 'Whatever happened to Neville, it's not on you.'

A voice called over the loudspeaker: 'Manager to the tills, please. Customer waiting.'

Frances stood, wiping her eyes and tucking her hair behind her ears, trying to compose herself. 'I have to go. I'm sorry I couldn't help more.'

They watched her hurry away, disappearing into the crowds of Christmas shoppers.

Outside, in the car park, Ellie turned to Rory. 'I thought you were working on a different case.'

'I am. But my mum asked me to look into Neville's death too.'

Ellie was curious as to why. 'Is she OK? She was very upset about Neville's death when we spoke to her at the Magical Glade.'

Rory's expression was closed. 'She will be.'

'Has she said anything about Belle having been arrested?'

'I don't feel comfortable discussing her personal business. You'll have to speak to her yourself.'

'OK... but Belle's in custody. If your mum knows something–'

'She doesn't,' corrected Rory. 'She just... she's worried. About how everything looks. About who might be blamed.'

'Someone *has* been blamed. *Belle*.'

Rory pulled out his car keys. 'Look, I can't tell you more than that. She's my mum. I'm just trying to help her. If she tells me anything that helps Belle, I'll let you know. I promise.'

'Thank you. How do you know Mike's daughter, by the way?'

'Oh, Sadie. When she was doing her journalism degree, she got in touch with me about TikTok and podcasting as we both have Kent connections.'

'Nice.'

'She's had her heart set on working for the BBC since she was a child. Developed into a determined, resilient young woman. She's interning at BBC Radio Kent. She lives in Tunbridge Wells but comes to see her dad at weekends sometimes. He's recently been made redundant. Which is a bit tricky as he usually helps her with her rent.'

Ellie was thinking about Talia's mother. 'Where's her mum?'

'She lives in Yorkshire. They're divorced. Sadie and Mike are very close.'

Rory got into his car and drove away, leaving Ellie standing in the car park, turning Rory's words over in her mind.

She's worried about who might be blamed.

Who did Daphne think was going to be blamed?

Ellie shuffled over to the jeep and got in. Started the engine. She pulled out of the car park and headed back to Bramhurst, mind racing with possibilities.

Chapter 33

After finding the beanie in the alley behind the hall, Ellie and Sylvia met to knock on some of the doors in the vicinity to find out who saw what. Ellie had wanted to do it sooner but the investigation's twists had kept shifting her focus.

The houses in this part of the village were a mix of Victorian terraces and large detached residences with drives and garages, most with views of either the main entrance or the alley that ran behind.

Ellie and Sylvia started at the front, armed with determination and a photograph of the beanie on Sylvia's phone.

'Let's see how many doors we can knock on in an hour,' Ellie said. 'Someone must have seen something.'

'Let's hope they're willing to talk about it and that someone has CCTV,' replied Sylvia, waving her mobile.

The first house was number forty-five, Church Lane, a neat terrace with a holly wreath on a white door. A woman in her sixties answered, a shiny, red bauble in her hand, still singing *"Away in a Manger"* which drifted from inside. Through the doorway, Ellie saw a half-decorated tree in the hall behind her.

'Sorry to interrupt,' Ellie said. 'We're private detectives and are investigating the death of Neville Snipe. We're asking residents living near the hall about the morning he died. Did you see anything unusual?'

The woman's face lit up. 'Oh, you're *investigating*. How exciting. Like Miss Marple.'

It wasn't quite the reaction Ellie was expecting.

'Did you see anything?' Sylvia prompted.

'Well, I saw the ambulance arrive, of course. And all those police cars. Terrible business.' She whispered conspiratorially, 'I heard it was murder.'

'We're trying to establish what happened,' Ellie said. 'Did you see anyone around the hall that morning? Before the emergency services arrived?'

'I saw Belle Kersey's van. She does my windows. Such a shame about the arrest.' The woman shook her head. 'Did *she* do it? Did Belle kill him?'

'She *most definitely* did not kill Neville,' said Ellie, trying not to sound too terse. 'Belle and I had arranged to meet him at the hall. So, people will have seen Belle and her van there because she was.'

Sylvia moved on. 'Did you see anything unusual?'

'No. Just regular comings and goings.'

'If you don't mind – what and who are those?' Ellie was thinking these people might also have seen something useful.

'The postman. Next door leaving for work. They're away at the moment. Got the builder in. The students in the lane. Six of them in that house, you know.' She rolled her eyes in horror. 'Then there were the children at forty-six going to school with their mum. The dad going to work...'

'Did any of them go over to the hall?'

She shook her head.

They thanked her and continued to the next house, number forty-six, but no-one was in. Number forty-seven was answered by a man in paint-splattered overalls, holding a roller. He looked harassed and uninterested.

'Not flippin' Jehovah's Witnesses again,' he said with a groan.

'We're private investigators actually,' Sylvia said with a prim smile. She mentioned the incident at the village hall.

'Oh? The murder? What about it?'

'Did you see anything that morning?'

'I was at work. Eight 'til six. Saw nothing, know nothing.' He started to close the door. 'Try next door. Mrs Gibson's got nothing better to do. Always peering out of her window, she is.' His last remark dripped with contempt.

The door shut firmly.

His van said: 'DAVIS DECORATORS'.

'Well,' Ellie said. 'That was to-the-point. I shan't be getting Mr Davis to quote when we need the chapel decorating.'

As they approached number forty-eight, the curtain dropped back into place. Mrs Gibson was a tiny, elderly woman with an apron. She invited them in, leading them to a front room with a perfect view of the entrance to the village hall.

'Oh, yes, dear. I saw *everything*,' she said proudly, brushing her apron down with her hands. 'I always do.' She settled into an armchair by the window. 'Have a seat.'

They perched on the sofa whilst Mrs Gibson straightened the covers on the arm rests of her chair.

'Could you run through what you saw?' Ellie asked, anticipation bubbling.

'Belle Kersey's van arrived just after half past eight. Then a jeep about fifteen minutes later. Then Mr Snipe's car about five minutes after that. Then the ambulance and police putting up the crime scene tape. Very dramatic.'

There was nothing new there.

'Did you see anyone else? Anyone walking near the hall?'

Mrs Gibson thought carefully. 'Lots of other vehicles went past. Church Lane is a cut through to the high street. At that time, it's usually mums going to-and-from school, and builders.'

'Did you recognise any of them? Did anyone stop?'

'A van driver slowed down, as though deciding about parking. I wonder if he was your killer.'

Ellie's pulse quickened. 'What time was this?'

'Before the other vehicles. Maybe... eight thirty? The driver slowed down and sped up. I remember thinking they were in a hurry or had something on their mind.'

As the woman spoke, Ellie imagined her standing at the window, curtains parted slightly, taking it all in and chewing over the implications.

'Can you describe the man? Or the van?'

'Not really. Difficult when someone's driving.' Mrs Gibson frowned. 'I'll let you know if anything comes to me.'

'Was he wearing a beanie?' asked Sylvia.

She didn't know what that was, so they showed her the photo of the one Sylvia had found. Mrs Gibson couldn't say if the man had been wearing one similar. After thanking her for the information, they moved to the houses on Luck Lane.

Number twelve had a view straight down the alley. It was a large, detached property with an unkept front garden. Two bicycles were at the door next to a large recycling box full of empty bottles. Ellie pressed the bell but didn't hear any sound inside and knocked.

A young man answered. Hair wet, towel in hand. Scruffy clothes and barefoot.

'Alright?' He towelled his hair.

'We're asking about the morning of the incident at the village hall,' Ellie began.

He frowned. 'Monday?'

'Yes.'

'Oh. I was on a run.'

A young woman came up behind him. 'Who is it?' She peered round the young man. 'Is this about the murder?' Her eyes danced. 'I'm Alice. *I* was here.'

She seemed more promising.

Ellie introduced herself and Sylvia. She repeated their questions.

'There was a bloke in a beanie with dark clothes. He went up the alley at 8.30am and... er... came out again about half an hour later.'

'Have you started curtain twitching like old Mrs Gibson?' her friend teased.

She smiled. 'No. I had a delivery booked for between eight and ten.' She explained the relevance of this to Ellie. 'Our bell doesn't work – the landlord's rubbish at fixing things – so we have to keep watch at the window. This was a Christmas present for my mum, and I didn't want the hassle of it being returned to the depot or delivered to a neighbour–'

'Of course,' said Ellie, who had herself spent several days tracking down a parcel which a courier claimed had been handed to her. 'Did you hesitate just then when you mentioned the beanie man the second time?'

Alice nodded. 'At first, I wasn't sure it was him when he came out of the alley as he wasn't wearing the beanie. But the clothes *were* the same. It was definitely the same guy. Navy cargo-style trousers with pockets. Navy fleece.' She frowned. 'Think it had some sort of logo or image on the back.'

Finally – a breakthrough?

'Did you recognise the man? Seen him before?'

Alice frowned. 'I think he has a dog. I work on the hot chocolate stall at the Magical Glade. I think I've seen him there with one.'

'What breed?'

Alice looked blank. 'Sorry. I don't know. Let me have a think. See if I can remember anything.'

Ellie thanked her and asked for her telephone number. And they moved onto number thirteen.

Here they got a surprise when the door was opened.

'Sylvia,' said Geoff the electrician, his eyebrows shooting up. He had a length of plastic cable in his hand. 'Long time no see.'

'Oh, hi.' She blushed. 'I'm not stalking you, I promise.' She explained what they were doing and finished with, '... trying to help Belle.'

Geoff showed them into an open plan lounge. The radio played Christmas songs. In areas, floorboards were up with cables carefully positioned. In one corner, Mike was sawing lengths of wood on a work bench next to alcoves where he was putting in cupboards.

'How's it going?' asked Mike.

Ellie knew Sylvia had only just spoken to Geoff so she initiated the questions. 'Were you two working here on Monday morning?'

'*I* was,' said Geoff. 'Not Mike.'

'What time did you get here?'

'I got to my first job about 8.15am.' He gestured to Sylvia, who he'd given the details to. 'The bakery. Then arrived here around 10am. Had to come round the back way as the police had the hall cordoned off.'

'And I was working at the rectory on Monday morning,' said Mike. 'Doing Jo's storage.'

That was right. Ellie had seen him there.

They said goodbye and left.

'Two more houses,' said Sylvia.

She was about to open the gate at number fourteen when a young woman, called over, 'Can I help you?' from the pavement by a white Mini. She had the rear door open and was undoing the seatbelt on a toddler.

They waited for her to get her daughter out and lock the car. Then Sylvia explained what they were doing. 'We're trying to piece together who was about,' she said diplomatically.

'I'm Emily and this is Sasha.'

The little girl clutched her furry zebra to her mouth, grinning. 'Mama,' she said, waving her hands about.

Emily gave one hand a squeeze. 'I did see someone. I've told the police but will share it with you too. He was in dark clothes, and running down the alley, like he was late for something or...' She paused. 'Or running *away* from something.'

'Definitely running down the alley towards the road...?'

'Yes.'

'And you've said "he"?' The two other witnesses had said the person they'd seen was male.

'Yep. It was definitely a man. The way he ran.'

'Which direction was he going?'

'Onto the road and towards the high street, away from the hall.' Emily steered Sasha up the path. 'I didn't think much of it at the time. People use that alley as a shortcut. The students are always running everywhere. Late for lectures. Late to get home, y'know? But when I heard about the murder, I contacted the police.' She looked from Ellie to Sylvia. 'Do you think he was the killer?'

'We don't know.' Ellie smiled gratefully. 'Can I check how you're so certain about the time?'

'Sure. I dropped this one at her day care and when I got home, I was listening to Radio 4, and they gave the time. It was nine o'clock and they announced the next guest. Some politician bloke.'

The final house, number fifteen, belonged to a couple who looked around Sylvia's age. The woman answered the door with suspicion. 'If this is about that business at the hall,' she said, clinging to the door handle, 'we've already told the police everything we know.' Her voice was timid.

It always amused Ellie that responses varied so much when they knocked on doors. Just today, they'd encountered the Miss Marple fan, the local curtain twitcher, the students and… now, this lady who looked terrified.

‘Who is it, Phyllis?’ came a man’s voice from behind her.

‘It’s alright, darling,’ she called back to him. ‘They’re just leaving.’ She faced Ellie and Sylvia again.

‘We won’t keep you,’ said Ellie. We’re just following up.’ She gave what she hoped was a reassuring smile. ‘Did you see anything that morning?’

Phyllis’ husband appeared behind her. He had a stick in his left hand.

‘I was putting the rubbish in the bin,’ the woman said, ‘and saw Belle Kersey going down the alley and–’

‘I-I-I think we should leave it to the police, love,’ said the husband. ‘They know what they’re doing.’

‘Hmm. OK. Sorry.’

They thanked the couple and left, walking back towards Sylvia’s car.

‘I wonder what she was going to tell us,’ Ellie said once they were out of earshot.

They sat in the car for a few moments, discussing what they’d learnt, engine running, heater blasting warm air.

‘Phil might know if Belle went down the alley,’ said Sylvia.

But while Ellie also was worried about her friend, she was preoccupied with a different question. Who was the man in dark clothes and a beanie that several of them had seen at the rear of the hall?

Chapter 34

Sylvia had never been particularly interested in social media, but watching Rory Henderson set up his phone for a TikTok live was rather fascinating in its way. He'd positioned himself outside the village hall, the building a suitably dramatic backdrop, with Zoe standing beside him adjusting the angle. Ellie had gone home and Zoe had roped her grandmother in to be their helper.

'Right,' Rory said, checking the frame. 'Sylvia, can you see yourself in shot?'

Sylvia peered at the phone screen he'd propped on a small tripod. 'Just about. I don't want to put my glasses on. They make me look–' She stopped there.

'Oh Gran-n,' said Zoe with an exaggerated eye roll. 'There are lots of old people on TikTok.'

'Thanks very much,' Sylvia replied indignantly. The fact was: she felt like a fish out of water. 'Are you sure this is a good idea?'

'Trust me,' said Rory. 'TikTok is where the eyeballs are. If anyone local saw something, they'll be watching when I go live.' He adjusted his collar. 'Zo, you ready?'

'Yup.' Zoe had plaited her hair and was wearing a warm fleece. She looked young and earnest, exactly the sort of person people would relate to and want to help.

'Are you clear about the information we're asking for?' Rory asked, fingers hovering over the "Go Live" button.

Sylvia tapped her notebook. 'All here in case I forget.'

'Great.' Rory pressed the Live button and immediately his face appeared on the screen, viewer count coming straight up and immediately climbing. 'Hey everyone, Rory Henderson here, AKA Criminally Curious, your favourite true crime podcaster.'

Sylvia didn't know where he got his confidence from.

'I'm outside Bramhurst Village Hall in Kent, where local theatre director Neville Snipe died in suspicious circumstances on Monday 15th December.'

The viewer count jumped to fifty, then eighty.

'With me today is Zoe Blix and Sylvia from Blix Investigators, both locals.' Rory's voice was professional, warm, engaging. 'And we're asking for your help. If you have any information about Neville Snipe's death, now's the time to share it.' He glanced at Zoe, checking she was ready. 'Hey, Sadie. Zo,' he said into the camera. 'I've made you both admins so we can keep the live happy and legal.'

Sylvia wasn't sure what that meant. They weren't doing anything illegal, were they?

Usernames were displayed briefly when people joined the live. Or at least that's what Sylvia thought they were. She couldn't see properly without her glasses. And people used such strange names.

Zoe smiled into the lens next to a graphic showing the contact number for Kent Police and Dave's name as the senior investigating officer. 'If you have any information, please contact the police via the number on the screen... or us, if you'd prefer, and we can pass on your information.'

'Tell them what on,' Sylvia hissed.

'We're particularly interested,' Zoe explained, 'in anyone who saw something unusual that morning, Monday December 15th, around 8am to 9am. Did you see anyone near the village hall? Anyone acting suspiciously? Did you notice anything unusual afterwards? People acting out of character.'

The comments started flooding in. Sylvia watched them scroll past on Rory's phone, a rapid-fire stream of emojis, questions, and speculation.

omg is this the panto murder???

I heard it was the ladder lady

my mum lives in bramhurst

where's branhirst im in USA

this is wild

Rory read out the useful, local comments.

Sylvia found them hard to read without punctuation. Perhaps you got used to it.

'Okay,' said Rory, 'we've got someone saying their neighbour saw a person in a beanie running down Luck Lane that morning. Can you contact me directly with details? We've got someone else saying Neville owed money all over the area. Anyone got specifics on that?'

Zoe was keeping an eye on her phone in her hand and Sylvia assumed that meant she was watching the live stream. Every now and then Zoe screenshot the feed, presumably when she saw an interesting remark.

More comments poured in. The viewer count hit three hundred. Three-eighty. Five hundred. Crikey.

my dad did work for Snipe and never got paid

he was having an affair

I'll ask me mate he knows

the whole village hated him tbh

'This is good,' Zoe murmured to her gran. 'People are engaging... and they're local. I've seen them on previous lives of Rory's.'

Sylvia watched the comments with growing interest. She couldn't believe how fast they moved. Social media was rather effective, in its chaotic, gossipy way. It was both international *and* local at the same time. People were sharing theories, tagging friends who lived locally, promising to ask their relatives.

wait didn't they arrest someone?

yeah window cleaner

she didn't do it though everyone knows that

An admin pinned a post to the top of the timeline, saying: *ALL INFO PLS TO KENT POLICE DCI DAVE BLIX*

'Thanks, Sadie,' said Rory.

'Some of you will know Belle Kersey has been arrested,' Rory said to camera, responding to comments, 'so we're trying to establish what actually happened that morning because Belle has a solid alibi.'

The viewer count passed a thousand. Someone had shared the live to a true crime group. The comments were coming too fast to read now.

Zoe spoke again. 'Expanding a little on what we're looking for, we want to know if anyone has information about Neville Snipe that might explain his death. Anyone had a disagreement with him.'

'We're getting a lot of engagement,' Rory said, excited. 'Someone's messaging me saying they saw a guy in the alley behind the hall early that morning.'

'Just adding to this,' said Zoe, 'in person witnesses have told us that the man they saw in the alley was wearing a dark blue beanie. If this tallies with what you saw, let us know.'

Sylvia's phone buzzed. A text from Ellie: *Dave's just called me. He's in the high street & he's seen Rory's live stream. He's furious.*

Rory continued, oblivious. 'Keep the info coming, guys.'

Sylvia received another text from Ellie: *please save a recording of the live so we can see what people said x*

More comments:

Geezer in beany has a dog

'@miss_marple, is this the man in the alley?' asked Rory.

Zoe pressed the buttons on the side of her phone again, presumably taking another screenshot.

Yeh mate, said @miss_marple

'Thanks. And to repeat: if you know Belle Kersey and have information that might help clear her name, please reach out to the police. Sadie has posted the details up-thread. To repeat: Belle Kersey has an alibi for the time in question.'

'Oh dear,' Sylvia said, trying to catch Zoe's attention below the level of the camera lens.

Another text from Ellie: *Dave's in the village, he's on his way.*

Zoe was still reading comments, answering questions. Suddenly she saw Sylvia's face and her eyes widened. 'What?'

Sylvia jumped off-camera. 'Your dad's seen the live,' she hissed.

'So what?' Zoe said dismissively. A look Sylvia had seen before flashed over Zoe's face. 'We're not doing anything wrong. All we're sharing is information that's in the public domain. We're not interfering with anything.'

But as she spoke, a familiar Audi screeched to a halt on the snowy tarmac outside the church hall. Dave got out, his expression thunderous.

'Switch that off, please,' he shouted over.

'Dad.' Zoe turned, smile fading. 'We're jus–'

Dave strode towards them. 'Rory, switch that off right now, please.'

'We're getting some really useful information, Mr Blix,' Rory protested.

Comments flooded the screen on Rory's phone.

whos that bloke?

who's he?

gotta be a copper attitude like that

'I don't care,' Dave told Rory. 'This is a police investigation, not entertainment for TikTok.'

see – copper told ya

arrest him

this is going to be fun

Dave's voice was tight with controlled anger. 'You're interfering with a murder investigation.'

not happy is he?

ive seen him on the news Blinx or something

'We're helping,' Rory's own temper flared. 'People are telling us things they might not have told the police. This is how investigations work now.'

Oh dear. Dave wasn't going to like that.

'*Investigations,*' Dave enunciated the word slowly, 'work by following proper police procedure, and by gathering evidence in accordance with the law.' He got his warrant out of his pocket. 'Not broadcasting sensitive information to hundreds of people online.' Dave pointed at the phone. 'END. THE. LIVE. NOW.'

The viewer count was now over three thousand. The comments were going wild.

arrest them all

real life just got realer

hope someone's screen recording this

i am

'We're not doing any harm,' Rory said stubbornly. 'We're just asking questions.'

'You're compromising the integrity of the investigation. Any information you gather this way could be inadmissible in court.' Dave turned to his daughter. 'Zoe. Mum. You should know better.'

'We're trying to help Belle–'

'By making a spectacle of a murder investigation?' Dave's voice rose slightly. 'This isn't a game. This is serious police work.'

'But it's taking too long,' Zoe shot back. 'Belle's in custody for something she didn't do while you lot follow your procedures.'

'Those procedures are there for a reason–'

'To let the *actual* killer get away?' Rory interjected. 'Because that's what's happening while you're busy arresting innocent people.'

Dave's face went very still. 'Rory, I'm giving you ten seconds to end the live stream before I arrest you.'

'On what grounds?'

'Interfering with a police investigation. Potentially contaminating evidence. Take your pick.' Dave pulled out his phone, his jaw tense. 'I can have a patrol car here in two minutes.'

Rory held Dave's gaze for a long moment, then reached over and ended the stream. The viewer count vanished. The comments stopped.

'There. Happy?'

'Of course not.' Dave turned to Sylvia. 'What were you thinking?'

'Ellie said can you save a recording of the live?' she whispered to Rory. Then said to Dave, 'That we might get useful information from local residents,' Sylvia said calmly. 'Which we did, actually. Several people mentioned seeing things that morning.'

'We need those people to come forward and give proper witness statements. We need their names and addresses.' Dave rubbed his face. 'Now that they've written comments on TikTok, they might think they don't need to do anything.'

Ah. That was a possibility.

'Do you have any idea how much this could compromise things?' Dave's eyes flashed with anger.

Sylvia put her notebook away, now feeling a bit guilty. 'We displayed the number for the incident room and gave your name. A couple of times actually.'

'Well, that's something, I suppose.'

'It's investigating,' Zoe said firmly. 'Which is what *you* should be doing instead of arresting our friends.'

'Actually,' said Dave, 'Belle was arrested on instructions from my superior officer, and on evidence–'

'Wrong evidence in that case,' Rory interrupted. 'Because the real killer is still out there while you're focused on the wrong person.'

Dave's jaw clenched. 'You don't know that.'

'Yes, we do. Everyone in Bramhurst knows Belle didn't kill Neville. Except apparently the police.' Rory packed up his tripod. 'I'm trying to help my mum. She asked me to look into this, and I'm doing it. With or without police approval.'

'Your mother–' Dave stopped himself. 'Never mind. Just stay away from my investigation. All of you.'

'It's not just *your* investigation,' Zoe said quietly. 'Belle is our friend. The village is our community. We have every right to ask questions and try to help.'

'I'm not discussing it any further.' Dave looked at his daughter, his mother, and Rory, all three of them united against him. His expression was somewhere between fury and exhaustion.

His phone pinged.

'I can't investigate a murder while my family is running around playing detective on social media.'

'We're not *playing*,' Sylvia said, a little more sharply than she'd intended.

Dave's phone pinged again. He lifted a hand for pause as he read the message, then returned his attention to the group. 'Stay out of it. That's not a request. And I'll need a copy of your live.' He stomped off and got back into his car, leaving the three of them standing outside the village hall in the December cold.

'We've well and truly annoyed your dad,' Rory said after a moment. 'But we've got some great information to follow up.'

'And,' said Sylvia, 'several more people have reported seeing a man that sounds like the one Ellie and Belle saw leaving the hall.'

'... who has a dog,' added Zoe. 'Let's find the dog.'

Chapter 35

After traipsing about in the snow for an hour, Ellie's bones were aching with cold by the time she got home, and she could barely feel her feet. Dave was out so she said hello to Rebus, hung up her coat and headed straight for the bathroom. She ran the bath, adding a few drops of lavender oil and climbed in before it was even full. The warm water wrapped around her like an invisible blanket. Her head rested back on a folded towel on the bath rim. She let her eyes close. She was dying to look at the recording of Rory's TikTok live, but didn't have the energy.

What a day. Belle's arrest. Frances' pregnancy. The information they'd got from knocking on doors.

Her mind had just drifted when her phone beeped. Ellie reached over the side of the bath, dried her hands on a towel and picked up her phone. On the lockscreen she saw the preview of the text. It was from Dave.

Belle has been

Oh, no. Please, don't let her have been charged. She swiped the screen to see the full message.

Belle has been released. NFA. Phil's taken her home.

Ellie squealed.

"NFA" meant no further action. Quite right too.

Rebus came running, wondering what the commotion was.

She tapped out *thanks x* to Dave and sent it.

She'd get dressed and head over to the Kersey's.

Half an hour later, Ellie was at their door.

Once Chloe had got over her mum being released and was prepared to let her out of her sight for a few moments, Ellie and Belle escaped into the summer house in the garden.

Belle plugged in the oil filled radiator and switched it on. Ellie pulled up a chair one side of it, Belle the other.

'Did they tell you why they'd arrested you?' asked Ellie, handing Belle her fluffy antlers. They'd heard what Patricia had said, and Talia had confirmed the context, but she wanted to hear it from her friend.

Belle put her antlers straight on. 'Thanks, Ells.' She turned up the heater. 'They didn't state explicitly why, but I could pretty much figure it out from their questions. Main thing seems to be me going round to see Neville at the family home and getting frustrated with his lack of concern for Chloe.' She met Ellie's gaze and scrunched up her face in embarrassment. 'I'd completely forgotten I'd told him I'd kill him if he hurt or upset Chloe again.'

Ellie touched her arm comfortingly. This was what Patricia and Talia had heard.

'Also, they'd got my prints, hair, saliva on the ladder and on the bolts either side of the ladder where you lock it when it's extended. *Of course.*' She tutted. 'And a witness saw me going up the alley before you arrived. Which I did, as I was trying to figure out whether it was best to bring my ladder in the front way or round the back.'

'Hmm.'

'Plus, I went to the loo, and that apparently gave me enough time to unlock the ladder so that Neville would fall when he came down.'

'Ah. Sorry. I mentioned that you went to the loo. Dave asked and–'

'That's fine. I heard him. You did nothing wrong.'

'Were the police OK with you?'

Belle nodded. 'I got the impression it was someone over Dave who'd demanded I be arrested. Means, motive and opportunity. Dave had to review the evidence.'

Ellie updated Belle on developments in the investigation, and they switched off the radiator and returned to the house.

Chloe was waiting for them at the door, fingers pulling at her mouth, face creased with worry.

'Y'alright, sweets?' Belle asked.

Chloe shook her head. 'I texted Rory to find out what everyone talked about at the meeting of the cast and crew this morning...'

Belle put her arm round Chloe.

'He said one of the tradesmen was talking about Neville owing money to someone who did work for him. Do you know about that?'

Belle looked at Ellie, having not been there herself.

'That's right,' said Ellie. 'It's Geoff. He did some work at Neville's house and did the electrics for the panto. He went round to see Neville and said he wanted his money.'

Chloe released a deep sigh. 'That's OK. I wasn't sure if you knew. I just want the real killer caught. I'm scared Mum's going to be arrested again.'

'Don't worry,' said Ellie. 'We won't let that happen. And thanks for checking.' She gave Chloe a hug and left. Her bath wouldn't still be warm but that didn't matter. The main thing was that Belle was home safely with no further action needed.

Chapter 36
THURSDAY

Overnight there had been heavy snow.

Dave had a late start as he'd agreed, long before Neville's death, to be Santa in the grotto at the Magical Glade.

He and Ellie had just finished breakfast when his phone rang.

'Hey Mike. What's up?'

Dave listened.

'Yikes. Just what we need.'

He listened again.

'Would you be able to do that? What time are you due at the uni?'

Dave was quiet.

'Oh, crikey, mate. That's terrible. Really sorry to hear that. Dreadful time of year to happen too.'

Dave continued to listen.

'That would be really kind. Thank you.' He explained about the Santa job, thanked Mike and rang off.

'What's happened?' asked Ellie.

'The lorry carrying the staircase for the chapel has got stuck in the snow in Thimble Lane. Mike's going to see to it.'

'That's kind of him. What did he say that's "terrible"?'

'He's been made redundant, poor chap.'

Ellie remembered now: Rory had mentioned this and she hadn't taken it in.

'All the maintenance guys have been laid off, not just the carpenters. The electricians, plumbers, the lot. The university have decided to outsource the work to an agency in an attempt to cut costs.'

'That explains it,' said Ellie. 'I wondered why he was doing so much work in the village. Everywhere I went, he seemed to be doing a job.'

Half an hour later, Ellie and Dave were at the Magical Glade. A corner of the café area had been transformed into something from a storybook. Fairy lights wound through the bare branches overhead, casting a warm glow in the soft morning light. A wooden grotto stood at the centre, painted red and green, with fake snow dusted across its roof. Christmas music played from hidden speakers, drifting through the cold air.

A queue of excited children snaked along the path, parents clinging to them firmly as they bounced with anticipation. Volunteers dressed as elves guided them forward, whilst someone in an enormous reindeer costume posed for photos near Santa's sleigh.

Ellie stood near the sleigh handing out pencils and paper for children to write their name on, and their Christmas wishes. She watched Dave in full Santa regalia, pride fluttering in her. They hadn't lived in Bramhurst long and they already felt part of the village. The red suit was snug around Dave's middle (padding, he'd insisted, not mince pies). The white beard suited him, and the black boots made him bow-legged. But his ho-ho-ho was convincing, and the children loved him.

Rory stood to one side with a professional camera, capturing each child's moment with Santa. Not the best timing, right after the TikTok live the night before, but Ellie had warned Dave that Rory was going to be doing the photography and the two men gave each other a terse nod when they met.

Santa had seen ten children so far.

'Next,' called one of the elves.

A small boy scrambled onto Santa's knee, eyes wide.

Ellie noticed Dave shift slightly in his chair as though he was uncomfortable.

'Well, hello there,' Dave said in his jolly Santa voice. 'And what's your name?'

'Thomas. How... how fast are your reindeer?' The little boy went pink.

'The fastest is Dasher,' Dave told him. 'But only when someone opens the biscuit tin.'

Thomas' parents laughed at Dave's joke. The boy grinned, unsure what to say.

'Have you been kind to your friends and family this year?' Dave asked him, his shoulder twitching.

Ellie moved closer, trying to see what he was doing.

The boy launched into a long explanation involving his sister, who'd taken his LEGO. Dave nodded patiently, continually shifting position, pressing his back against the chair in a way that suggested he was trying to scratch.

After Thomas left, clutching his present, Ellie approached quickly. 'Are you alright? You look a bit red round your beard.'

'This costume,' Dave muttered, tugging at the collar. 'It's making me itch. Everywhere. I think it's the dust or the fabric or…' He scratched vigorously at his shoulder. 'How long do I have to do this?'

'Forty-five minutes.'

His expression was tragic beneath the white beard.

'Next.'

Ellie retreated to her station. Dave plastered on his Santa smile as a tiny girl approached, though his eyes were watering now and he looked distinctly uncomfortable.

The event continued, and Ellie watched her husband valiantly attempt stoicism whilst clearly suffering. He'd scratch frantically between children, then compose himself when the next one approached. At one point she saw him doing subtle shoulder rolls, pressing against the chair back, tugging at his collar.

'You're doing brilliantly,' she whispered during one gap.

'I'm dying,' Dave whispered back, scratching frantically at his wrist. 'This is torture.'

'Perhaps previous Santas were less allergic.'

'Or less alive.' He scratched his neck again, wincing. 'If I survive this, I'm burning this costume.'

Ellie pressed her lips together to keep from laughing. DCI Dave Blix, who could face down criminals without flinching, was being defeated by a dusty Santa suit.

'Next.'

A girl of about eight approached, confident and cheerful. She climbed onto Dave's knee and he wriggled, clearly uncomfortable as the suit rubbed against what must be increasingly irritated skin.

'Hello. And who are you?' Dave managed, voice slightly strained.

'Emma.'

'What a lovely name. Have you been helping at home this year?'

She nodded enthusiastically. 'I helped Grandad with his work sometimes, passing him tools and things.'

Dave changed position again. Ellie couldn't tell if he was scratching or was aching from sitting.

'That *is* helpful. And what would you like for Christmas?'

Emma listed pencils, a book about horses, and roller skates. Reasonable requests. Dave reached for the present sack, and Ellie saw him scratch his wrist subtly on the coarse hessian.

'Excellent choices. Have you finished your Christmas shopping? Got presents for your family?'

'Almost. I still need something for Mummy. I got Grandad a new beanie. He lost his old one recently and was quite upset about it.' Emma beamed. 'It's his work one, you know. For when it's cold. He's an electrician.'

She spoke with pride, eyes shining with love for her grandfather.

Ellie froze and looked at Dave. She saw the exact moment he processed what Emma had said.

His hand stopped on the present sack, the itching apparently forgotten. 'You must be Emma Fleming then.'

Geoff's granddaughter. Geoff, who was owed £6,000 by Neville. Geoff, who'd lost his beanie recently.

Possibly the beanie Sylvia and Leonard had found in the alley.

'That's a very thoughtful gesture,' Dave said, his Santa voice steady now despite everything. He handed Emma her present. 'Your grandad is lucky to have such a caring granddaughter. Merry Christmas.'

Emma hopped down, clutching her gift, and ran back to her grandfather – Geoff – who waited near the sleigh. The older man waved at Santa, smiling, completely unaware.

Ellie was about to send the next child in when Dave started scratching his neck frantically, then descended into a coughing and sneezing fit.

Chapter 37

Dave lasted another five minutes as Santa and, with mutterings about 'anaphylactic shock' and 'antihistamines', he announced that Santa needed to take a break. And with that he strode off to the men's toilets, changed back into his work clothes and said he was going to the police station via the chemist.

The drive to Rough Common took Ellie ten minutes. Ever since she woke up, she'd been unable to dismiss a nagging question about something Patricia had said, and it wouldn't leave her alone. She needed to clarify it with her, to understand properly.

She had just turned into the village when her phone rang.

'Ellie Blix speaking.'

'Oh, hi, Mrs Blix. This is Alice, one of the students you spoke to yesterday.'

Excitement nipped at Ellie.

'I remembered what the image was on the guy's top. It was an acorn.'

'An *acorn*?' Ellie's mind was spinning.

'Yeah. I'm an artist. I had to draw it to figure out what I saw. An acorn in a circle.'

'Thank you.'

In the morning light, the Snipe's house looked different from the cottages in Bramhurst.

Ellie realised what it was as she approached: no Christmas tree in the window. No lights, no wreath, no decorations at all. Every other house on the street blazed with festive cheer, but Patricia's remained dark and bare. Not surprising in itself – Patricia had just lost her husband.

And the front door was ajar.

Ellie crept up the steps and paused on the doorstep. 'Patricia? It's Ellie Blix.'

Perhaps Talia's mother hadn't realised it wasn't shut. Ellie had done that before. She rang the bell. Knocked. No answer. She pushed the door wider and stepped into the hallway.

The house felt hollow, sad. Post lay scattered on the mat, unopened. Christmas cards, by the look of the envelopes. A coat hung on the banister, one sleeve trailing on the floor as if it had been tossed there in a hurry and forgotten. In the living room, the curtains were still shut. A mug sat on the coffee table next to a bowl. The whole place had the air of someone barely functioning, just getting through each day.

'Patricia?'

Silence.

Ellie moved through to the kitchen. There were unwashed dishes in the sink from the night before. A calendar on the wall, December's page showing family appointments that would never be kept. The back door was closed.

She checked upstairs quickly. Empty. The bed unmade, Patricia's dressing gown draped over a chair. Everything spoke of grief and exhaustion.

Downstairs again, Ellie went to the back door and opened it. The garden stretched before her, lawn sloping down to a fence.

'Patricia?'

Still nothing. Maybe she was in the barn, fetching logs like she had been last time.

Ellie walked across the patio and down the garden path. The barn doors were closed. She pulled them open.

Just stacked logs and garden tools.

She turned back towards the house, scanning the garden properly now. That's when she saw the stone steps running down the side of the house.

And at the bottom, a crumpled shape.

'Oh crikey, no.' Ellie ran towards the steps, already knowing what she'd find.

Patricia lay at the bottom, completely still. Her hair was matted with blood around the hood of her jacket. A dark pool had spread across the paving stones and snow. One wellie boot was half off.

Ellie dropped to her knees, pressing shaking fingers against the woman's neck.

Nothing. The skin was cool. The blood had dried. She'd been dead for a while.

Ellie pulled out her phone with trembling hands and dialled Dave.

Poor Patricia. She'd wanted to escape. What had happened?

Chapter 38

Ellie waited for the first responders at the top of the steps so she could wave them over. Instinct made her look around for signs of a struggle; for evidence of what had happened. She knew that as soon as the police arrived, the scene would be secured and she would be moved.

From where she stood, the garden spread below in hushed white. On either side, the flower beds rose in snowy banks, their outlines soft. Clumps of hellebores pushed pale blossoms through the snow. Early snowdrops pricked the drifts with green shoots. The wiry stems of pruned lavender and rosemary. The skeletal roses waited patiently, while the evergreen yew at the back held its dignified shape beneath the weight of snow.

At the foot of the steps lay a broken angel statue, its stone form half-buried under the white carpet, as though it had stumbled into some silent drama. The trail of disturbed snow down the steps drew Ellie's eye. The only footmarks, hers.

In no time, the police arrived with an ambulance, and the Snipe family home became a crime scene.

It didn't take Ellie long to tell DS Carmichael what she'd seen when she arrived. Dave gave the all-clear, and Ellie left.

In the jeep, her mind was reeling. Before setting off, she tapped out texts to both Sylvia and Zoe: *Can you meet me in 15 mins? Hot choc cabin in market? Patricia dead.*

The main question was whether Patricia had fallen accidentally or been pushed?

It was a bit of a coincidence that Neville had also had a fall. But coincidences *did* occur, and sometimes they were meaningful and sometimes not.

Ellie's temples were beginning to throb.

She hadn't noticed anything confirming murder and Dave, unsurprisingly, had refused to tell her what his view was.

There were endless motives and possible suspects for Neville's death, but what reason could anyone have for wanting to kill Patricia?

Ellie drove slowly along the lanes, shock echoing through her. The fresh snow looked achingly beautiful, so at odds with the news of another death in their community.

Sylvia and Zoe were already at the hot chocolate stall in the Christmas market when Ellie arrived. *"Jingle Bell Rock"* tinkled from speakers. A female sales assistant was dancing along, tinsel in her hair. Her male counterparts were wearing Christmas jumpers and reindeer horns. It was jarring. It all felt too jolly, too bright, too cheerful.

She slid onto a stool round a giant wooden barrel under an awning.

'Mum?' Zoe's expression was full of concern. 'What's happened?'

Sylvia pushed a steaming cup of velvet-rich hot chocolate towards Ellie. It was crowned with whipped cream and curls of chocolate.

Ellie filled them in on the death.

Sylvia let out a low moan and sat back on her stool.

To their left, one machine was roasting cocoa beans. Another separated nibs from shells.

'Poor Patricia,' said Zoe. 'She seemed a nice lady. And to have put up with Neville all that time.'

'Any word on what happened?' asked Sylvia. 'Was it an accident or...?'

Ellie shook her head. 'I scanned the area as much as I could before the police arrived. The first responders called Dave.'

All three of them knew that meant the police believed the death was suspicious.

She told them about the statue.

Zoe was immediately on her phone, googling photos of the Snipe's garden. 'Here we go. Old Rightmove listing from when they bought the house.' She scrolled. 'This is the best view of that part of the garden. See. Two angel statues at the top of the steps.'

'How did you find that?' asked Sylvia, eyes twinkling.

'Magic, Gran.' Zoe showed them her screen.

'The steps look pretty wide,' said Ellie, recoiling slightly at the image of where she'd just seen a dead body.

'Yes,' said Zoe. 'This is what CSIs call "scene context". It's about the relative position of one thing to another in the crime scene. Angles and all that.'

Ellie was keen to hear what her daughter had to say.

'I listened to a podcast on it the other day while I was waiting for a fox to come round from an anaesthetic.' Zoe pointed at her screen. 'If you look at the image on Rightmove, there's quite a distance between the two statues at the top of the steps. Two people on their own could fit between them easily if they were walking side-by-side and not carrying anything. One person: also easily.'

Ellie thought back to what she'd seen. 'Apart from the broken statue, I didn't see anything beside her. She had wellies on and her jacket – the same one she was wearing when we visited her – so presumably she was already outside.'

'No bags of compost or broken plant pots?' asked Zoe.

'Not that I saw.' Ellie tried to visualise what would happen to a bag of compost if you dropped it or fell while carrying it down the Snipe's steps. 'That sort of bag is heavy. I carried a couple through to the back garden at Stream Cottage. Reeby got in the way at one point, and the bag slid to my feet in the lounge.'

'Your point being?' said Zoe.

Sylvia elbowed her.

'That if Patricia had been carrying something like that, it would likely have been visible at the top of the steps or on the path down. And a pot would probably have smashed.'

'Hmm.' Zoe sat back for a moment. 'Perhaps she wasn't feeling well and stumbled onto the statue, knocking it over and falling.'

Ellie shrugged. 'Perfectly possible.'

'What's also possible,' said Sylvia in a solemn voice, 'is that there was a struggle with another person or someone pushed her.'

Silence fell over the three women.

'Yes,' Ellie said finally. 'But I hope not.'

"Silent Night" started up.

Tears gathered in Ellie's eyes and she swallowed, sniffing.

'Drink your hot chocolate.' Zoe put her arm round her mum. 'It'll warm you up and give you a sugar fix.'

They chatted for a few minutes about the stall and all the chocolate paraphernalia. The mouth-watering aroma.

After a few minutes, Zoe whispered, 'I can't stop thinking about Talia.'

Ellie nodded. 'Dave sent specialist officers to collect her and her sister. They're both going to stay with their aunt for a few days.'

Sylvia patted her chest. 'Thank goodness.'

'At least Belle's out of the frame on this one,' said Ellie. 'I saw her last night when she got home.' She brought them up-to-date with their friend's time in custody.

'What are we going to do?' asked Zoe. 'We don't seem to be getting anywhere with this investigation and now someone else has died.'

Zoe's question mirrored how Ellie had been feeling.

'Ditto to that,' said Sylvia.

'We need a different approach.' Ellie sipped her drink. 'First, I think we should concentrate on Neville's death as we know that was murder. Two, because so many people have grudges against Neville, there are too many possible suspects. I wonder if a better angle might be to consider *opportunity* rather than motive.'

'That's a good idea,' said Sylvia. 'We're drowning in motives, aren't we?'

'As for means,' said Zoe, 'the killer needs to have been able to get up a ladder into the loft and back down again, and been able to pull back the bolts on the ladder.'

'And make a swift exit,' Sylvia added.

Ellie fished out her phone and tapped out a text to Belle: *are the bolts on your ladder stiff? Easy to operate?*

'So, we're not looking at someone elderly and frail,' said Zoe. 'Could Daphne get up a ladder?

'Oh, yes,' said Sylvia indignantly. 'She's very sprightly. Similar age to me.'

'Shall we go through all our suspects and consider whether they might've had the opportunity to kill Neville?' said Ellie, weariness swooping over her.

'We need another hot chocolate each though,' said Zoe.

'I'll go for coffee,' said Sylvia. 'The one I had was delicious, but I now feel like I've got about a kilo of sugar shooting around in my bloodstream.'

Ellie laughed. 'I'll have a coffee too. Anyone want to share a piece of *Apfel strudel*?' She felt a little uncomfortable tucking into cake when Patricia lay dead. As though it was disrespectful somehow. But she was feeling lightheaded and wanted something in her stomach that wasn't liquid.

'I'd like my own piece,' said Sylvia. 'I forgot to eat before I came out.'

'What about your blood sugar, Gran?' said Zoe cheekily.

'The coffee will soon dilute it,' Sylvia replied stiffly, sliding off her stool, poised to go over to the counter with her purse.

'I'll share some apple strudel with you, Mum.'

'That's two strudels, two coffees and another hot chocolate.' Sylvia went to order.

Ellie got out an envelope from her jacket pocket. 'Stick your hand in your gran's bag, Zoe, lovey. See if she's got a pen in there.'

Ten minutes later, the three of them were stuffing apple strudel and whipped cream.

'The pastry's perfect,' said Sylvia. 'Just the right consistency for filo.'

'I like the combo of sweet and spicy,' said Zoe.

'OK,' said Ellie. 'Possible suspects. Shall we name them all and evaluate them as we go?'

Sylvia nodded, finishing her last mouthful of pie. She swallowed. 'If we're just going to consider Neville's murder, I had Patricia as a possible suspect for that.'

'Right,' said Ellie. 'Suspects: Patricia. Daphne.' She added their names to the list on her envelope. 'Chloe? Lauren?'

'Geoff, the electrician,' said Zoe.

'Wait. Are we seriously going to consider Chloe a suspect?' asked Sylvia.

Ellie waited to see what Zoe said as she didn't want to bias her daughter's reasoning. 'We've got to evaluate everyone against the same criteria, whether they're our friends or not.'

'Gran and I spoke to Chloe together,' said Zoe. 'I don't see her murdering anyone. Do you?' She peered at her grandmother.

Sylvia shook her head. 'Absolutely not. But we're looking at *opportunity* here, don't forget. Where was she at 8.30am on Monday?'

'Belle said she has to be at the stables by 8am,' replied Ellie.

'OK,' said Sylvia. 'Let's rule her out then. Lauren?'

'I don't see her as a killer either,' said Ellie. 'She said she was at home at that time, and her Facetime friend is her alibi.' Ellie crossed out Chloe and Lauren's names on her paper. 'Patricia and Daphne have both admitted being at the hall just before Neville was killed. In my view, they both had means, motive and opportunity.'

'I agree,' said Sylvia.

'What about Frances?' said Ellie.

'She said she was at the garden centre,' said Zoe. 'That gives her an alibi. Geoff?'

'According to Geoff's granddaughter,' said Ellie, 'he's lost his beanie and Leonard found one in the alley. Plus – a couple of residents said they saw a man in a beanie running down the alley.'

Zoe faced them both. 'So did a couple of people on Rory's TikTok live. Based on opportunity and means, our main suspects are Daphne, Patricia and Geoff.'

'What would Daphne's motive have been?' asked Sylvia. 'I don't feel clear.'

'Feeling slighted and used by Neville,' Zoe replied. 'Wanting to let him know how much he'd hurt her. She might've wanted Patricia dead too.'

It was an unsettling thought.

'Hmm,' said Ellie. 'I've got two things that aren't consistent with Daphne being our killer. Or Patricia, for that matter. I don't see either of them wearing a beanie. And – they've both got small frames. I wouldn't describe the person Belle and I saw fleeing from the back of the hall as having been small.'

'If that person *was* the killer,' said Sylvia. 'We still don't know.'

But something else was niggling at the back of Ellie's mind and she couldn't put her finger on what it was. It was something from yesterday.

'I need a bit of a think,' she said. 'I'm going to take Reeby to the Magical Glade. See if the woods will help me to clear my head.'

Her phone beeped with a reply from Belle: *The ladder locks are stiff, always getting wet, need a bit of a wiggle and a yank.*

Ellie relayed the information.

'I understand what Mum says about there being build differences with Daphne and Patricia,' said Zoe, 'and that may rule them out. But from the point of view of just the bolts being stiff, people who are busy and capable like Patricia and Daphne, they'll be used to bolts that get stuck.'

'That's true, you know,' said Ellie. 'I've been climbing with Daphne. Marie-Hélène took us once. Daphne was like spider woman. I've never seen someone hook and unhook ropes so efficiently, and tie knots.'

'What d'you want us to do, Mum?' asked Zoe.

'I've got a few calls to make and a bit of information to chase up. Can you keep your phones handy?'

Chapter 39

It didn't take Ellie long to pick up Rebus and drive to the glade in the village. She deliberately kept the radio off, allowing her brain time to decompress after seeing Patricia dead in the snow.

Once out of the jeep, she and Rebus walked amongst the trees. She tried to allow the woods to soothe her. To bask in the winter birdsong. The high-pitched chatter of the tits, as they moved through the branches restlessly. The "tseeps" of the thrushes as they hunted fallen berries amongst the snow. In the background, doves and pigeons cooed, and a distant woodpecker tap-tap-tapped.

Patricia kept slipping into Ellie's mind, not just because she'd just died, but also because she'd come here to the glade after instructing her solicitor to submit her divorce application.

Realising she'd forgotten to check whether Patricia had forwarded the promised email, Ellie opened her inbox and there it was, dated Monday 15th December at 9.12am, from her to William Green at Caspar & Green:

Dear William,

As discussed on the phone just now, this is to confirm that I would like you to 1) submit my application to divorce Neville, and 2) tell him I want him to move out of the family home within 7 days, after which time I will change the locks. If he hasn't left, and taken what he wants by then, I will arrange for everything to be disposed of.

Regards,

Patricia

Ellie read it a couple of times. One thought hit her before any other. Given Talia's mother had begun divorce proceedings, she clearly wanted to be able to enjoy her life free of Neville. Why would she then kill a man she'd finally decided to divorce? Or – put another way: if she'd been planning to bump him off, why go to the bother of instructing a solicitor? It didn't make sense. As long as Patricia had been straight with them, she hadn't wanted revenge on Neville. She'd wanted *freedom* from him.

At that point, Ellie was reminded of something Sylvia had said once: that murder wasn't meant to make sense to other people. The only person it made sense to was *the killer*. To them, it felt not just necessary but the *only* solution to whatever problem they perceived.

As Ellie watched locals skating on the ice rink, she rang the garden centre where Frances worked. 'Yes, hi,' she said to the young man who answered. 'A very nice lady helped me carry some items to my car first thing on Monday morning, around 8.45am. Struggling with my back at the moment. I wanted to leave a review on Google. Fiona? Freya?'

'That would've been Frances, one of our managers,' said a young male voice.

'She was definitely in on Monday, was she?'

'Sure was. I'm Toby. I worked the same shift. We put out a new range of Christmas wreaths together.'

'Excellent. Thank you.'

Ellie rang off. Her thoughts shifted to a question she, Sylvia and Zoe had often discussed: whether the murder location was significant. Sylvia had always said it revealed information on the offender's characteristics, and on the victim-offender relationship. Choosing to kill Neville at the church hall when Ellie and Belle were there was a *particular* crime. It suggested the culprit knew Neville was going to be there. That either meant a connection with Bramhurst Players – someone who'd been at the rehearsal on Sunday night and heard Neville cancel the panto and say he'd be at the hall the following morning to collect his property – or someone close to Neville.

But killing Neville at the hall, when people were in the room next-door, or downstairs, was high risk. It suggested that the killer had perhaps succumbed to desperation and impatience. Whatever they'd wanted to do, they wanted it done. Over with.

She let her imagination sift through the other culprit qualities they'd identified.

Familiarity with the village hall layout.

Knowledge of the storeroom hatch.

Familiarity with multi-section ladders.

Ability to operate stiff bolts.

Ability to get into the loft and back down – either using Belle's ladder or the electronic one.

Knowledge of electronics – storeroom control.

Alibis? She wondered if there was something here. The only person who had a solid alibi was Frances. The garden centre had confirmed she'd been on site for her whole shift. Whereas Daphne and Patricia had only been able to give their *own* word that they'd been at the hall very briefly and not gone in. Geoff had said he was at a job at 8.15am.

She reviewed the motives of their suspects. They'd teased Zoe when she'd told them a while back about "motive pressure" – the term criminologists use for the amount of force behind a motive. However, it was a useful construct, and there was something about the motive pressure which didn't feel equal amongst their suspects. And there was something about killing a person when others were close by that suggested the drive was strong.

Given Daphne seemed to still have feelings for Neville, would she really have felt driven to kill him? However bizarre it seemed, it was as if Daphne had got stuck in – or reverted to – an earlier phase of her life, and had been half-hoping Neville would realise he was in love with her and "pick" her. Had the illusion shattered, anger might've resulted. But – poor Daphne didn't seem to have reached that point yet.

Or was Ellie grasping at straws? Would Patricia and Geoff have had stronger motives?

In her mind, she ran through what their motives might be.

Jealousy.

Revenge.

Hurt and rage.

Pressure and stress.

She needed to talk to Sylvia. She was good at the psychology side of things from her social work career. She dialled.

Sylvia answered quickly. 'Ells?'

"Hark the Herald" was on the radio at the rectory.

'I need to tap into your knowledge. I've been thinking about motives. How do we evaluate one motive over another?' She listed the ones she'd thought of.

The carols stopped. 'That's better,' said Sylvia. 'Can hear you now.'

Ellie heard footsteps.

'In my experience, it's usually about the importance of the motive to each person.'

'You mean how strongly they feel what they're feeling?'

'Exactly. The feeling strength drives behaviour and buffers the person from the potential consequences of their crime. I always describe it as being like a temporary madness.'

A temporary madness.

That was so apt.

She thanked Sylvia and rang off, returning to her deliberations.

She turned now to the means and opportunity of each suspect. Patricia and Daphne had been at the hall before the murder took place. Geoff said he'd been at an emergency job at 8.15am.

No. The key was in the motive, Ellie was sure of it. And the murder location. What did the church hall represent to the killer?

Seeing the huts with their lanterns and fairy lights, she was reminded of Belle's daughter, Chloe, saying Neville owed one of the tradesmen money: Geoff. Was *he* their killer? £6,000 was a lot of money.

She bought a hot dog and a coffee from one of the huts and sat down by a fire pit. A couple of kids were heating marshmallows and giggling while their parents sipped coffee.

While warming herself by the fire, she moved onto the next thing she wanted to check: Rory's TikTok live from the night before. She scrolled through the recording he'd sent her, reading the comments. She was interested in the ones Zoe had given her screenshots of. In particular, those by someone called "@miss_marple" who'd mentioned that she'd seen a man at or near the hall wearing a dark beanie. And that he had a dog. It was unclear whether he'd had the dog in the alley.

They knew Geoff had lost his beanie as his granddaughter had told them. Did Geoff have a dog? She didn't know.

Then there was the comment from someone whose father had done work for Snipe and not been paid.

She rang Zoe.

'Mum? D'you know who did it?'

'Hi, lovey. Not yet. How do I find out the identities of the people commenting on Rory's live?'

'It's like Instagram and Facebook. It depends how they're registered and whether they want people to know who they are. We need to set you up with your own TikTok so you can–'

'Good grief, no.' She told Zoe about the two users she was interested in.

'The person saying their dad was fleeced by Neville is called "@littleacorn". I don't know who they are. I'm pretty sure "@miss_marple" is Rory's mum.'

'You're kidding?'

'Nope. She has an account to watch Rory's live sometimes. You know what she's like for neighbourhood crime.'

'Miss Marple. Of course. That fits.' Ellie was trying to think and talk.

'Rory's never admitted it but a few times I've seen comments that can only be from her, and he's called her "Mum" on lives.'

'Except – does she really say "yeh mate" and call people "geezers"?'

Zoe laughed. 'She copies it from other users. Thinks people won't know it's her if she uses that sort of language.

It's all a bit ridiculous, especially when Rory calls her "Mum" when he's not thinking.'

Clearly TikTok was a whole other world, Ellie thought, pleased she had Zoe to navigate it for her. It was rather scary what people could do from behind a keyboard.

'So, Daphne saw the beanie wearer at the hall the morning Neville was killed.'

'Seems so.'

'She didn't tell us that at the glade, did she?'

'No. Before you go, there are a few interesting comments on your Facebook post about the blue beanie. One is from a woman saying she saw a chap in a beanie in the hardware store at 9am on Monday.'

'Brilliant.'

'I've asked for more details. I'll keep you posted.'

'Thanks. I'll go into the hardware store now and see if they know who that was.'

'We're getting close, aren't we?' asked Zoe.

'Definitely.'

Ellie thanked her daughter for her help and left the Magical Glade and headed for the high street.

Like all the shops, the hardware store was busy. Here, people were buying plastic toboggans, shovels, firewood and kindling, and fairy lights.

She'd screenshot an image of Geoff from his Facebook page. It was bothering her that they only had his word for it that he'd been at his jobs on Monday morning. What if he'd crept off, gone to the church hall and murdered Neville? It wasn't any crazier than thinking Daphne or Patricia had done this.

She picked up a box of firelighters and headed for the woman on the till and explained she was a private investigator.

'We understand a man in a beanie was in here first thing on Monday morning?'

The woman frowned. 'You mean Geoff? He's often in here.'

So, he'd lied.

'What time did he get here?'

'Just as we opened. Nine o'clock.'

Right after Neville was killed.

'Thanks. What did he buy?'

'A small can of WD40.' She picked one up from a box by the till. All displaying a pink sticker saying: £2.89. 'Everyone's buying them for their locks and car battery terminals. Works a treat in this cold weather.'

Ellie snapped a picture of the cans, paid for her firelighters and left. All she could think about was: if Geoff had lied about where he was, what else might he have lied about?

Next, she checked Facebook. She stood in the shop doorway, inspecting first Neville's page, then Daphne's. Then Geoff Fleming's. His wife, their children and grandchildren, the family dog.

And it was then that the final few pieces of the puzzle fell into place.

The dog.

Rory's TikTok live.

Witness evidence.

Local knowledge.

Motive pressure. It was all about the motive and the murder location.

Ellie was sure now who Neville's killer was.

She selected Dave's number from her call log and dialled. Then, when she'd filled him in, she did the same with Sylvia and Zoe.

Chapter 40

The bookshop café wasn't too busy when Ellie and Sylvia arrived. Quite a few of their friends and neighbours were already there. Zoe was at a table with Rory, Daphne and Marie-Hélène. Belle and Reverend Jo were in a corner, playing cards with Leonard and Janine.

Ellie had a quiet word with Rebecca as she ordered a pot of tea for Sylvia and herself. 'OK to have a quick chat with Geoff about our electrics?'

'No problem,' Rebecca replied. 'I was about to take them over a cuppa actually.'

'I can do that for you,' Ellie told her.

Dave slid in the door with DS Carmichael. He made sure Ellie had seen him. Flipped the shop sign to CLOSED and sat down at the table by the entrance.

Sylvia collected their tray of tea things and took them over to a table near Zoe.

Rebecca handed Ellie coffees for the two workmen.

'Handy catching you here, Geoff,' said Ellie as she approached with their drinks. 'I wanted to ask what's involved with an electric loft hatch like the one in the storeroom at the village hall...'

A couple were showing each other home décor books. The woman stirred her tea absently.

'Oh, right?' said Geoff, taking the mugs and putting one down for Mike. 'What do you need to know?'

Ellie sat down at a table. 'Does it involve you going into much of the loft as ours isn't boarded.' This wasn't a lie.

'Depends where the electricity supply is up there. Easy enough to tread on the joists. Not stuck my foot through anyone's ceiling yet...' He gave a nervous chuckle. 'There could always be a first time, I suppose.' He gave Ellie a wink. 'But given I'm retiring in a few months, I'd quite like to leave without having done that.'

'Wish we had nice loft boarding like the hall,' said Ellie. 'That was your handiwork, wasn't it, Mike?'

'Eh, what?' Mike lifted his head. Ellie watched him reach into his tool bag and dig around amongst the items in there for a tape measure. 'Yeah. It doesn't have to cost a fortune though. Bit of boarding across the joists works a treat.'

'Actually, I probably need to talk to you too then. You installed the wooden hatch in the storeroom as well, didn't you?'

'He did it all, Ellie,' said Geoff helpfully. 'He even laid a lot of the cables. All I did was connect up the electricity.'

'It's an impressive system,' said Ellie. 'I went up there a couple of days ago. Wanted to see how easy it would be.'

Mike smiled. 'Thank you.'

In the picture book section of the bookshop, children's voices rose and fell.

'Not many people know about the second hatch in that room. I didn't until Belle mentioned it.'

'Really?' said Mike.

'Convenient too, isn't it?' said Ellie. 'Especially given the hatch in the main corridor doesn't have a ladder.'

'Yeah. Think there are plans to put one in, but you know what committees are like at making decisions...' Mike rolled his eyes and measured the area where he was working.

'It's also convenient because the back door leads straight onto the alley that takes you down to the road.' Ellie looked at Sylvia, making sure she'd caught her signal. 'In case you want to bring stuff in or out.'

Geoff's features crunched into a puzzled frown. 'Are you planning on setting up a marijuana operation up there, or something?' He chuckled. 'What would you want to bring in the back way and secrete into the loft?'

Ellie forced a small laugh and went along with the joke. 'I'm thinking more of bringing production costumes and set equipment along the alley.'

On hearing the signal word – alley – from Ellie, Sylvia came over. 'My husband nearly disappeared into a snow drift on that path the other day. Must be the wind that blows stuff down there. We found all sorts.' She called over at Leonard. 'What colour was the beanie we found, love?'

'Navy blue. Someone must have a cold head in this weather.' He attempted a laugh. 'Got a photo of the thing on my phone here somewhere. Hang on.' He swiped the screen and scrolled for a few moments. 'Roof slates to show the diocesan advisory committee... nativity rehearsal photos... the rectory cat... Mrs Chapman asleep on the sof–'

'We don't need that, thank you,' snapped Sylvia, blushing.

'Ah. Here we are. Dark blue beanie. Peter Storm label. That's Millets. I bought my walking boots there.'

Sylvia glanced round. 'Anyone missing a nice warm beanie from Millets?'

'Didn't you lose yours?' Mike said to Geoff.

Geoff frowned. 'No. Where d'you get that from?'

Mike blushed. 'Er...' He looked round the café. 'Oh.'

'Actually, I heard that at Santa's Grotto,' said Ellie. 'Your granddaughter, Emma, told my husband when she was talking about Christmas presents.' This was true and Ellie said it deliberately.

'My wife must've told her I'd lost mine to help her with prezzie ideas,' said Geoff, shrugging. His jacket hung over the back of a chair, and he reached into a pocket, producing a red, woollen hat with a cream lining. 'This is mine.'

Ellie glanced round the room. 'I wonder whose the blue one is then.' She paused. 'Oh well. The police have it...'

'We do,' said Dave from his seat.

'... so if it's related to the murder of Neville Snipe,' Ellie continued, 'that'll come up in their forensic analyses. Hair and skin cells. Saliva, if there is any. Trace evidence...'

The mention of murder and Neville's name caught the attention of two women who were having coffee and discussing the latest celebrity cookbook. Ellie recognised the younger of the two from St Millie's film club. The woman put the book on the arm of her chair and started whispering across the table at her friend.

'Zoe, lovey, what did you find on the blue beanie?'

Zoe got up and joined her mum. 'I followed up some of the comments we had on Mum's Facebook post.' Her voice was quiet to start with, but it quickly increased in volume and authority. 'I know we all sneer at social media, but it can be incredibly useful when it comes to solving crimes.'

Dave gave his daughter a proud nod.

'When Mum told me about your granddaughter's comment, Geoff, I had a look on your Facebook page...'

Ellie studied the two workmen while Zoe was asking questions.

Geoff's face clouded over and he threw an irritated look first at Ellie then Zoe.

'Don't worry. As you've shown us, your beanie is red...'

Geoff released a sigh and surveyed the room in relief.

'I was interested in one of the photos on your timeline though,' Zoe continued. 'This one, dated November 5th 2025.' She held up her phone for Geoff to look at. 'What do you see there?'

Geoff's face went white. 'It's... er... It was on bonfire night. At the fireworks display on the village green.'

'And who's in the photo with you?' asked Zoe.

Ellie shuffled over a few steps so she was standing next to Zoe.

'Mike.' Geoff's reply faltered.

'And what's Mike got on his head?'

'Er...' Geoff shot a nervous look at his friend. 'It's a...' He raised his hands in a gesture of defeat. 'Mate, d'you wanna answer this?'

Zoe fixed her gaze on the carpenter, holding out the image.

He bent closer for a quick look, then went straight back to his work.

'The hat you're wearing in this photo. Is it yours?' She waited a few moments. 'We didn't have time to print out the image but it's a–'

'Dark blue beanie from Millets. Yeah, it's mine.' Mike's expression was tight and his eyes had changed. Much smaller now. 'I dropped it somewhere and didn't know where. Mystery solved.'

'Why didn't you say it was yours when Reverend Chapman mentioned finding it?'

Mike gave a hurried shrug. 'Worried I was going to be accused of something, I guess. I've had a tricky few months, what with being laid off at the university. I... I dunno. Sorry.'

Ellie put her hand on Zoe's arm, signalling she was going to take over. 'It must've been a very worrying time for you, getting made redundant. Your own bills to pay without your usual income...'

'Well, it was a shock, but I've been able to pick up quite a bit of work locally. People know me and trust me.' His voice cracked as he said this. 'Fortunately, I'm handy on the tools so I can do quite a few things that aren't strictly carpentry and joinery.' He gave a sad smile.

'A witness mentioned that you very kindly help your daughter with her rent too while she's doing her internship with the BBC.' She didn't want to name Rory. The police could obtain a statement from him.

He nodded. 'Sadie's wanted to work in radio for years. Ever since she was a child, she's had this seed of an idea about working for the Beeb.'

Ellie felt his love for his daughter.

'But it's so difficult to break in. These companies expect youngsters to do these unpaid internships, to learn the ropes and prove their commitment. But how are they supposed to live when they're not earning any money?'

Ellie gave him a sympathetic smile.

'I don't know why I'm telling you all this really, except that it's been nerve-wracking watching Sadie carry this tiny dream inside her since childhood, knowing how competitive the industry is. Seeing her nurture it in the hope it'll grow...'

'A bit like an acorn, you mean?'

Mike nodded. 'Exactly.'

'Neville's daughter, Talia, has been doing voluntary work with Zoe's wildlife rescue charity,' Ellie told him, 'in order to boost her employment opportunities and CV...'

He gave a sad smile.

'The reason I used the word "acorn" is because we saw a comment that someone posted on a TikTok live recently, saying that their dad had done some work for Neville and never got paid. The username was "@littleacorn". That's your daughter, isn't it?'

'Er...'

'It's OK. We know it is. And we know from that comment that Neville owes you money. My point is it made us realise what an impact Neville not paying you has had on you.'

Mike was silent but nodded.

'And we understand. Losing your job cannot have come at a more difficult time.' Ellie didn't want to pry into whether Sadie's mother could help. Unfortunately, she was now going to have to.

'Tell us about the set you built for Bramhurst Players. Everyone's commented on what a fantastic job you did on it.'

'Thank you.'

'It must've cost you a lot to make. Planning it. The materials. Several days of joinery. Paint and painting.'

Ellie herself had been shocked by the amount when she researched it. 'We looked online. Somewhere in the region of £2,000 to £2,500?'

'That'd be about right.'

'Have you been paid for that?'

Mike shook his head, his nostrils flaring a little. 'No. I haven't.'

Ellie had discussed with Sylvia how to broach this in order to be sensitive. 'Can you explain to us what your arrangement was with Neville over the set?'

Mike sank down onto a chair with a thump.

The home décor couple started whispering and moved their chairs closer together.

'That man was a conman and a thief. I wish I'd never agreed to do the work for him. If it weren't for the fact I'd lost my job, and needed to honour my commitments, I would've told him no.' He swallowed, seeming to gather his thoughts.

Everyone in the room tensed, keen to hear what Mike was about to share.

'Neville agreed to pay my costs. I wasn't looking to make a profit from the Players. I simply said if I was going to spend time building the set, it was time I couldn't spend on paid jobs. I told him how long it would take. Four days' carpentry – £1,200. Two days' painting – £200. Materials, including paint and brushes, and fixings – £600. Two grand in total. It actually cost me a bit more than that as some of the materials had gone up and I wanted to pay Chloe something for helping.'

'And he did,' said Belle.

'I emailed Neville the costs and asked him to confirm he would pay me when the set was complete. He said he would. He said he'd got the green light from the Players' committee, and that they would give him the money and he would pass it on to me.'

'We *did* pay him,' came a woman's voice. Marie-Hélène. 'I do the accounts for the bakery, and do Bramhurst Players' too. We agreed the amount. I transferred it into Neville's account so he could pay you. We had no idea he hadn't.'

'In that case,' said Mike in a sad tone, 'his behaviour is even more irritating and inexcusable. The set was complete over two months ago.'

'I agree,' said Marie-Hélène.

'I always build them quickly so the cast can get used to acting around the real set. The proper dimensions and so on.' He took a deep breath and shook his head in disbelief. 'I sent my invoice to Neville, followed by a couple of polite requests for payment. I rang him. He wouldn't take my calls or phone me back…' Mike's narration of events ground to a halt.

Ellie waited.

'What happened then?'

'I went round to his house. His wife answered. I explained why I'd come. She fetched him. He was furious I'd had the "cheek" to turn up at his house, "hounding him for money".' Mike's gaze dropped to his hands on his lap. 'I said *I* was furious he'd had the cheek to confirm payment terms and not pay me. I said I needed the money to pay bills. That I was hoping to use the set for Cinderella to build a portfolio so I could pitch for other set design and construction work. And he said he was going to put the word out in the acting community that I was difficult to work with, unreliable and threatening over money.'

'What happened the fortnight before he died?'

'What d'you mean? Nothing.'

'Was that the last communication you've had with him? The time you went to the house?'

'Well. I saw him on Sunday 14th at the hall with the rest of the crew and cast. One of the hinges was a bit tight so I came along to loosen it a bit.'

'When were you in the alley behind the hall? To lose your beanie?'

'Er...' he pursed his lips. 'Not sure. I use it quite a bit to park in. That weekend probably.'

'You see, Belle and I saw a man leaving the hall via the back door and running down the alley towards the road just after Neville fell to the ground.'

Mike's eyebrows rose and he shrugged. 'You've lost me.'

'The man was wearing dark clothes like yours, and a dark beanie.'

He shook his head.

'And then Sylvia and Leonard found a blue beanie in the alley – the item you've now admitted is yours.'

Mike stared at Ellie.

'You're not suggesting that was me, are you? That I killed Neville?'

'Was it? Did you?'

Dave got to his feet and blocked the door.

The home décor couple were now rapt, nudging each other and muttering comments.

'No. It was not. Don't be ridiculous. As if I'd kill Neville...'

'In addition... a couple of residents have reported seeing a man in dark clothes with a dark beanie in the alley behind the hall just before Neville was killed. Was *that* you?'

'No-o.'

'One of them has described the logo they saw on the man's clothes.' She said the next sentence slowly. 'A round logo... with an acorn in the centre...' She watched as Mike's face coloured, a fleeting frown crossing it before fear took hold. 'Isn't your business called "Acorn Joinery"?'

He nodded.

'Isn't your logo round with an acorn?'

'Yeah,' he said begrudgingly.

'Was that you then that we all saw? Leaving the hall via the alley once you'd killed Neville?'

'No.'

Ellie signalled to Sylvia to take over. They weren't done yet. Just changing tack.

'Can you tell us about your history with Neville Snipe?' Sylvia asked. 'Have you done work for him before?'

Mike snorted. 'As I explained, I should've known better. Had I not been in need of money...'

'I'd appreciate it if you could elaborate, please?'

'Around a year ago, he asked me to do some set designs for him. I'd done a course on using computer-aided software, and was building up my reputation for good designs. However, I was a bit naive. I know now to watermark everything on paper. And digitally on the computer. In short, I did some designs for Neville. He stole them and claimed they were his. He then used them for a production at the Gulbenkian Theatre at the university. As soon as I tried to challenge his claims, he started telling the Gulbenkian staff I was a pretender; that I had issues and was unstable.'

Marie-Hélène gasped. 'That's dreadful.'

'I was an unknown,' said Mike, sadness seeping into his voice. 'Neville had more power than me and he used it to abuse me. I should've told him to stick it. Why didn't I?'

Sylvia waited for Mike to finish and said gently, 'I can see it must've been infuriating when he abused you again. Took advantage of you a second time.'

'It was.'

'Did you want revenge?'

'No. Not really.'

'Not *really*?'

'Not *at all*.'

'What did you want?'

'I wanted my money and I wanted him to never again be able to take advantage of someone the way he had done with me.'

'So, what did you do to achieve those two things?'

'Nothing. As I said, he had all the power.'

'You see,' said Sylvia, 'as much as it saddens me to say it, and for everyone to hear it, I think you went to the village hall on Monday morning before Ellie and Belle arrived. You knew what time their meeting had been arranged for.'

'No.'

'You followed Neville up into the loft. Had some sort of argument with him. Came down, unlocked the bolts on the ladder so it would collapse, and Neville would likely fall to his death. And then you left.'

'No.'

'You told him what you thought of him. You told him he was never, ever going to treat anyone again the way he'd treated you.'

Mike shook his head. 'I don't know where you're getting this from.'

Ellie took over again. 'Until literally a couple of hours ago you hadn't come up on our radar as a suspect. We were thinking Geoff had... er...'

Geoff's face was thunderous.

'But a few things made me realise we needed to shift our attention to you. You mentioned that you and Sadie were going to have a slim Christmas. You were here, there and everywhere, doing jobs. Sadie mentioned you getting a lodger. You were careful to slip in comments about Neville's bad behaviour towards Chloe and Geoff. And – you were on the phone discussing interest rates and payment plans when I got to the hall yesterday morning.

Initially, I thought you were negotiating a big contract. Was it for a bank loan?'

Mike's face was expressionless. 'So what if it is? I've been made redundant.'

'Listen,' said Ellie. 'No shade there. We've all got to pay bills and put food on the table. But sabotaging a ladder so someone will hurt themselves?'

Silence.

'You will be on CCTV. And unless you wore gloves, the CSIs will have your fingerprints on Belle's ladder.' Ellie waited for him to absorb these two pieces of information. 'Furthermore, one of the witnesses recognised you through your dog.'

Mike's eyes narrowed.

Ellie showed him a screenshot of one of his Facebook posts, showing a photograph of Sadie and him with a black-and-white collie. It was the man and collie that the archdeacon had encountered.

'No, no. It's all a misunderstanding.'

'It's not, I'm afraid,' said Ellie. 'We have you at the hall on Monday morning, just before nine o'clock. You knew about the loft hatch and back door in the storeroom. You're fit and healthy. Getting up into the loft and back down wouldn't have been a problem for you. You have a strong motive for wanting to hurt Neville. The game's up. You killed him, didn't you?'

He shook his head.

'I was sure it was you, Mike, when three things came together. First, our witness describing the acorn logo. Only you use that symbol. Second, your daughter's TikTok comment about her father being cheated by Neville. The username 'littleacorn' was too specific and it emphasised how traumatic the knock-back had been. Third, and most telling, you made a mistake just now. When you mentioned Geoff losing his beanie, it was an odd thing to say. Geoff himself said he hadn't lost it. Only the killer would say that, because he'd lost his own.'

Mike sat motionless.

'That's why you said *I'd* lost my hat,' said Geoff, his voice heavy with disappointment. 'You were deflecting attention from yourself.'

Mike lowered his head.

'We'll leave you to discuss with the police when exactly you decided to kill Neville,' said Sylvia. 'We can see how desperate you must've been feeling with your regular income having disappeared overnight. Christmas around the corner. Your daughter needing your help...'

'Her landlord threatened to give her notice if she didn't pay what she owed by the new year.' His voice was a whisper. 'I was hoping the panto money would cover it...'

'I'm sorry for her situation,' Sylvia said carefully.

'I should never have gone to the hall.' Mike's voice was still quiet, his face partially covered by his hand. 'I had no intention of killing Neville. I went to plead with him to at least give me enough money to pay Sadie's rent. I waited in the storeroom until he arrived. Heard Belle set up the ladder in the main corridor. Heard Neville go up into the loft. I went up after him via the storeroom ladder. Confronted him about my money. Begged him to pay up.' He shook his head. 'But Neville has this way of talking to people. Full of contempt. Sneering. Dismissive. I said I'd start legal proceedings and he laughed at me. Said given I had no money, I wouldn't be able to. It enraged me, literally, and my anger got the better of me.' He removed his hand from his face now. 'All I could think about was that my daughter was going to struggle because of him. I went back down via the ladder in the storeroom, quickly unlocked the bolts on Belle's ladder, fuelled by the knowledge he'd never rip anyone off again. Once I heard Neville fall, I left via the back door and down the alley, and went over to Jo's house to do her storage.'

Dave got up and shifted from one foot to the other.

It was a tragic story. And unlocking the bolts showed intention and premeditation. With the ladder collapsing beneath Neville, he would've fallen fast.

'Tell us about Patricia. Did she say she was going to inform the police about your visit to the house, demanding money?'

Mike rubbed his chin. 'Yes. I couldn't have that, could I? I had to stop her. And just my luck, the day I went to see Neville at the house, their neighbours almost lost their Christmas tree on the corner of the lane. I helped them get the tree up the drive, and I'm on their doorbell-cam. Not doing anything wrong, but it's evidence I was at the Snipe's that day.'

And there it was, just as Sylvia had explained: a motive that made Mike's actions feel essential. They made sense to him – a temporary madness.

Dave strode over. 'Mike Daniel Edwards, I am arresting you on suspicion of the manslaughter of Neville and Patricia Snipe. You do not have to say anything. But it may harm your defence if you do not mention, when questioned, something which you later rely on in court. Anything you do say may be given in evidence.'

Chapter 41
SATURDAY

It was two days after Mike's arrest and Ellie and Dave were up early and at the chapel with Reeby.

The robin was waiting for them as they approached the building, perching on the railings at the front door again, like it had been when Ellie had been here with Jo. It cocked its head at them with familiar bright-eyed curiosity, and Ellie felt her heart lift.

'There's our friend,' she said softly, balancing the thermos of coffee while Dave carried the bag of warm, foil-wrapped muffins. Their smell was making her stomach rumble.

Dave whistled for Rebus, who'd disappeared off after a rabbit. He unlocked the chapel door, and they stepped into the beautiful space. The steel framework soared above them, creating the bones of their home-to-be. Where once there had been just empty air beneath the vaulted ceiling, now a proper first floor stretched across the building, and partitions were going up.

'Look at those stairs,' Ellie said, setting down the thermos to admire the wood. The new staircase curved gracefully up to the first floor. 'It's really happening, isn't it?'

Dave wrapped his arms around her from behind, resting his chin on her shoulder. 'Our home,' he murmured.

After a few moments, they climbed the stairs together, Rebus, leading the way, their footsteps echoing in the empty space. At the top, they could see out through the Gothic windows across the village. The morning sun kissed the snowy fields.

The contractors had only put up a few walls so far, but Ellie could already imagine windows with curtains, and a comfortable sofa positioned to catch the morning sun.

'Perfect picnic spot,' Dave said, settling cross-legged on the plywood flooring.

Rebus immediately claimed the space between them, tail wagging hopefully at the smell of food.

Dave tapped at his phone screen a few times and *"Away in a Manger"* drifted up to the rafters, the melody filling the ancient silence.

Ellie unpacked their breakfast: two toasted muffins, stuffed with fried eggs and pigs-in-blanket. She passed Dave his, slathered with brown sauce, keeping hers – with tomato ketchup.

'Heaven,' Dave said after his first bite, brown sauce dripping down his chin.

The coffee was steaming hot from the thermos, and they sat in comfortable silence for a while, watching their breath mist slightly in the cool air and listening to the sounds of the village waking up. Church bells. Cows at the farm. A blackbird singing from somewhere in the trees. A car door slamming. A dog barking. Life carrying on.

Ellie reached into her bag and pulled out a small white candle in a jam jar. She lit it with the lighter she'd brought.

'For the Snipe and Edwards families,' she said quietly holding the candle between them, 'and their friends and loved ones.'

They sat watching the candle flame.

Ellie leaned against his shoulder, feeling the solid warmth of him, the steady rhythm of his breathing. 'We're lucky,' she said. 'To have each other and our family. To have this chance to build something new. To wake up together and share egg-and-bacon muffins with ketchup.'

'I think you mean brown sauce.'

They laughed.

The candle burned steadily between them, a small bright point in the vast space that would become their home. Outside, the robin sang its song from the railings, and somewhere in the distance, a cock crowed.

'We should probably head back,' Dave said eventually, though neither of them moved. 'We've got to collect our meat from the butcher's this morning. And then, are we still going to decorate the tree?'

They were a bit late this year, but that didn't matter. It was a job they both loved.

'Yes. Five more minutes,' Ellie said. 'I want to remember this exactly as it is. The way the light comes through those windows, the smell of the old stone, the sound of the village waking up.'

Dave put his arm around her, and she rested her head on it. After a few moments, he said, 'Oh, by the way. Mum mentioned something last night and I said I'd talk to you.'

Ellie's stomach sank.

'It's Finn. She's heard he's coming home for Christmas.'

Ellie gasped. 'You're kidding?'

'Not confirmed,' Dave continued, 'and we haven't said anything to Zoe yet. The question is: do we?'

'Why can't he stay in flipping Scandinavia? He can't break her heart and come back...'

Dave shrugged.

'We can't let her bump into him,' said Ellie. 'She'd never forgive us. If there's a chance he's coming home, we need to tell her. At least then she'll be forewarned.'

He nodded. 'I agree.'

Later that day, in the afternoon light, St Mildred's glowed, candlelight flickering in every window. Ellie and Dave walked up the path together. Around them, the village was gathering.

Belle and Phil arrived with Chloe between them, Belle's arm linked through her daughter's. Sylvia and Leonard stood near the entrance with Zoe, all bundled in coats and scarves. Leonard had been "asked" to hold his carol service at a different time so they could both attend St Millie's.

Rory held the door open for his mother. Daphne looked better than she had when they'd seen her in the glade, though her gaze was still low.

Inside, the church was beautiful. Every pew end held a candle in a glass holder, flames steady and bright. The ancient stone walls seemed to hold the light, reflecting it back in soft golden tones. At the front, the nativity scene had been set up. Mary and Joseph, the baby Jesus, shepherds and wise men were all arranged around the manger.

The smell of incense hung in the air, sweet and solemn. Reverend Jo stood near the altar in her vestments, the thurible in her hand, waiting for the service to begin.

Ellie slid into a pew beside Belle and Phil. Dave sat on her other side, his hand finding hers. Around them, locals filed into the church.

Janine arrived with her mother Hattie, both women looking around with quiet sympathy. Gideon took his usual spot near the pillar, as he liked to watch the vicar's expressions as she talked. Marie-Hélène and Paul were in a row with Dee and Mel. Geoff and his family sat at the back.

The pews filled slowly, people greeting each other in hushed voices. Some hugged. Some just nodded, acknowledging the weight of the past week without words.

Two families wouldn't be attending carols today. Mike and his daughter Sadie. The Snipes – what remained of them. Their absence was felt like a gap in the congregation, a reminder of what had been lost. Hopefully, Frances would be with her family somewhere.

Jo began to swing the thurible, the silver ball moving in steady arcs. Incense smoke rose, curling toward the ancient beams above. The scent intensified – myrrh and frankincense, traditional and comforting.

'Let us begin,' Jo said, her voice carrying clearly. 'We gather this afternoon in candlelight, in community, in hope. We gather after darkness, seeking light. After despair, seeking faith.'

The congregation settled, silent now.

'This past week has tested us,' Jo continued. 'We've seen tragedy. We've questioned each other. We've doubted. We've grieved... and we've loved.' She paused, looking out at the familiar faces. 'But we're still here. Still together. Still a community.'

Someone – Ellie thought it was Daphne – made a small sound of agreement.

'Tonight, we light candles for those we've lost,' Jo said. 'For Neville Snipe, whose death shook our village. For Patricia, taken too soon. For the Snipe family and friends, grieving far from here.'

She lit a large candle at the altar, the flame catching and growing strong.

'We light candles for those who've struggled,' Jo went on. 'For Mike, whose desperation led him down a dark path. For his daughter Sadie, who bears no blame but will carry the ghost of her father's choices.'

Another candle lit.

'And we light candles for ourselves,' Jo said softly. 'For our ability to forgive, to heal, to move forward together.

For our faith in each other, even when that faith has been tested.'

A third candle joined the others.

The organ began to play – softly at first, then building. The opening notes of *"Once in Royal David's City"* filled the stone space and the solo chorister began. The congregation rose for the second verse and began to sing. Voices blended, some strong, some wavering, some barely whispers. Leonard's rich baritone was a beautiful complement to Chloe's bright soprano.

They moved through the familiar carols. *"Silent Night"* with its gentle promise of peace. *"In the Bleak Midwinter"* acknowledging the cold and dark. Ellie's favourite, *"Hark! The Herald Angels Sing"* with its burst of joy.

A tear crept down Ellie's cheek during *"O Little Town of Bethlehem"*. She wasn't quite sure why. Relief? Comfort? The beauty of the service?

Dave squeezed her hand.

After the final carol, Jo stood before them again. The candlelight caught her face, showing both sorrow and strength.

'We cannot undo what has happened,' she said. 'We cannot bring back the dead or erase the pain. But we can choose how we move forward.' She took in her congregation and gestured to the nativity scene. 'This story we celebrate – it begins in darkness, in a stable, in difficult circumstances. But it's also a story of hope. Of light coming into darkness. Of new beginnings.'

The church was quiet and still.

'Bramhurst has always been a community that supports its own,' Jo said. 'That comes together in crisis. That finds ways to heal and grow.' She smiled. 'And I'm delighted to share some good news with you. Something which will hopefully be a bridge to better times.'

Ellie felt Dave shift beside her, curious.

'The Christmas pantomime,' Jo said, and a ripple went through the church – surprise, interest, confusion. 'Many of us were disappointed when Cinderella was cancelled. Cast, crew, those of us who bought tickets.'

Chloe sat up straight and grinned at her mum.

'But Ellie and Daphne have worked miracles behind the scenes,' Jo continued. 'They've arranged for a new director to take over. Someone wonderful, someone committed to bringing joy back to our village stage... so that Cinderella *can* go to the ball.'

A cheer went up. People turned to look at Ellie, who felt her face flush. Some were in on the secret, some guessed, others were curious.

'I won't spoil the surprise of who it is,' Jo said, her eyes twinkling. 'Cinderella opens this evening, yes, this *very evening*, folks. Six forty-five for a seven o'clock curtain. And there will be performances tonight, Sunday, Monday and Tuesday, which is the day before Christmas Eve. And we very much hope you'll all come to support it.'

Excited whispers spread through the pews.

'All tickets have been reimbursed. The website is open so book whichever tickets you'd like. Two quick things: one, if tonight sells out and you particularly want to come this evening, simply turn up and as long as we keep the fire exits clear, we'll try and accommodate everyone. Geoff's collected extra chairs. Two, if the website crashes, don't blame me.' She gave a warm smile. 'Come and discover who'll be leading Bramhurst Players forward. Come and be part of something joyful again.'

Belle was crying now, but smiling through her tears. Chloe clutched her mother's hand, hope written across her young face.

'Let us go forth in peace,' Jo said, beginning the blessing. 'Let us go forth in hope. Let us go forth in community, supporting one another, believing in one another, choosing light over darkness.'

'Amen,' the congregation responded.

As people filed out into the cold December night, there was warmth in their voices. Plans being made. Speculation about the new director. Children asking parents if they could go to the panto. Parents agreeing.

Ellie stood outside the church with Dave, watching the village disperse and head home to warmth and safety.

'You arranged a new director,' Dave said quietly. 'When did you manage that?'

'It was all Daphne,' Ellie said. 'We decided we needed something to bring us together again. Something to heal with.'

'Who is it?'

Ellie grinned. 'You'll find out this evening. Zoe's helping with the sound, but she's already bought you, me, your mum and Leonard a ticket.'

'You, Mrs Blix are a wonder. An utter pain on occasions, but the best partner in crime a man could hope for.'

'Talia texted me,' Ellie told him. 'She and her sister are going to stay with their aunt until the new year. They're pleased to be together. They're both going to do bereavement counselling once the funerals are over.'

'Good,' said Dave. 'Rory's spoken to Sadie, who's at her mum's.'

'You and Rory are talking, are you?'

Dave smiled. 'Sadie wants to set up a campaign to raise the awareness of the impact of financial pressure and shock redundancy. To help prevent future tragedies. She knows she can't undo what her father did, but hopes that greater support and information might stop someone else from reaching desperation.'

Chapter 42

The village hall car park was packed well before 6.45pm. Families streamed through the entrance, stamping snow off their boots, unwrapping scarves, their faces bright with anticipation.

Reverend Jo stood by the door, greeting everyone with warmth. 'Welcome, welcome. Find your seats, it's going to be wonderful.'

Inside, the set stood exactly as it had been left the weekend before, the painted cottage with its cheerful yellow door, the ballroom backdrop with Belle's daughter's beautiful work. Chairs filled the space, arranged in neat rows facing the stage, with overflow seating at the side and back. Christmas lights twinkled along the edge of the stage.

Ellie found seats for herself, Dave, Sylvia and Leonard near the middle. Around them, the village settled in –

excited children bouncing in their seats, parents shushing them gently, grandparents smiling in anticipation. Zoe was at the back of the hall with Geoff, on the sound desk.

Belle had arrived early and sat with several family members, her face glowing. She waved at Ellie. This was what they'd worked for. This was why the set had been built, the lines learned, the costumes made.

Some people were in their seats, ready. Others stood in huddles, chatting, hugging and smiling.

At seven o'clock on the dot, the lights dimmed. A hush fell over the audience.

Two women walked onto the stage in the dark. When the lights came up, the room saw Janine and Lauren Blackwell. Janine wore jeans with a Christmas sweater. Beside her, Lauren was in a red jumper dress.

'Good evening,' Janine said, her voice carrying clearly. 'No-one is more surprised than Lauren and me to be up here on this stage. We are, however, delighted to be stepping in as co-directors... so that Cinderella *can* go to the ball.'

Applause erupted, warm and genuine. Someone whistled. Janine smiled.

'When Ellie and Daphne asked if we would help out, and save the pantomime,' Janine continued, 'we didn't hesitate. This village supported me for many years. You welcomed my productions, applauded our efforts, became part of our theatre family. It's an honour to give something back.'

Lauren stepped forward. 'We've had just two days to finish rehearsals, so please forgive any wobbles. The cast and crew have worked incredibly hard, and have created something magical. So, without further ado...' She gestured to the wings. 'Let us present: Cinderella.'

The lights broadened out. Music began. The cottage scene revealed Chloe centre stage, dressed in rags, sweeping the floor with weary movements.

Tears pricked Ellie's eyes. Chloe was playing Cinderella after all.

The ugly sisters burst onto the stage, and the audience roared with laughter. Phil in an outrageous orange wig and padded costume, Paul from the bakery in shocking pink, both hamming it up magnificently. Their bickering was perfectly timed, their physical comedy spot-on.

'You can't wear *that* to the ball, Grimelda.'

'I most certainly can, Berylina. And you can't stop me.'

They chased each other around the stage, nearly knocking over furniture, whilst Chloe rolled her eyes in perfect comic exasperation.

Marie-Hélène swept on as the stepmother, all haughtiness and cruelty. 'Cinderella. Stop that daydreaming and fetch my shawl.'

Baron Hardup appeared next – Dee in full drag with a magnificent false moustache. 'My dear wife, perhaps we could be kinder to the child?'

'Nonsense. She's lucky to have a roof over her head.'

The transformation scene arrived. The stage went dark except for a single spotlight. Daphne walked on wearing a glittering silver gown, a wand in her hand, a crown on her head.

The fairy godmother.

She looked radiant, confident.

'Cinderella, my dear child,' Daphne said gently. 'Dry your tears. You *shall* go to the ball.'

Magic happened. Lights shone. Music swelled. Chloe's rags transformed into a beautiful ball gown, and she twirled, delighted.

The ball scene showcased Rory as Prince Charming, resplendent in a blue velvet jacket and moving with surprising grace.

'May I have this dance?' he asked Chloe, bowing low.

'You may, your Highness.'

They waltzed across the stage, and the audience sighed collectively. Young love, poignantly portrayed.

Gideon appeared as Buttons, the servant in love with Cinderella. His timing was perfect, his devotion to Chloe's character both funny and touching.

'I'd do anything for her,' he confided to the audience. 'Even if she never notices me.'

'Oh, we notice you, Buttons,' someone shouted from the audience, and laughter rippled through the hall.

The clock struck midnight. Chloe fled the stage, losing a glittering slipper. Rory clutched it dramatically.

'I'll search the kingdom,' he declared. 'I'll find her, no matter how long it takes.'

The search scene had the ugly sisters trying desperately to fit into the tiny slipper, their feet comically oversized, their attempts increasingly ridiculous. Children in the audience shrieked with laughter.

Finally, the slipper found its rightful owner. Chloe slipped it on, and the transformation occurred again – rags to riches, servant to princess.

'It's you,' Rory breathed. 'It was you all along.'

They embraced. The music built to a crescendo. The cast gathered for the finale, everyone singing together.

'And they all lived happily ever after,' said Buttons.

The audience leapt to their feet, applauding wildly. Chloe took her bow, tears streaming down her face. Belle was crying too, clapping so hard her hands must've hurt.

Phil and Paul curtsied elaborately as the ugly sisters, still in character. Daphne waved her wand, smiling. Rory bowed deeply, looking pleased with himself.

The applause continued.

Janine and Lauren came back on stage, and the noise grew even louder. They'd done it. In two days, they'd saved the pantomime.

As the clapping began to subside, Ellie slipped out of her seat to join Reverend Jo on stage with the new directors. The two friends walked on, beaming.

'What a wonderful evening,' Jo said, her voice warm, looking out at the audience of familiar faces, neighbours, friends. 'What a gift you've all given us,' she said, gesturing to the Blackwells and the cast.

Janine dabbed at her eyes with a tissue from her pocket.

Ellie stepped forward. 'Thank you to Janine and Lauren for saving our pantomime. Thank you to our incredible cast and crew. And thank you to all of you for coming tonight, for supporting the panto, for believing in Bramhurst.' She glanced round the hall, taking in the faces of her friends and neighbours. Her family.

Jo raised her hand in blessing. 'Go forth in joy. Go forth in peace. And from all of us here tonight...'

The cast joined in, their voices ringing out together, 'Happy Christmas.'

The audience echoed it back, followed by cheers, warmth and hope filling the village hall.

In a few months, Ellie and Dave would be in their new home, with their adopted robin and Reeby, laying down roots and deepening connections. Belonging was not just a gift here. It was the ground beneath their feet and the people around them.

Outside, the snow fell thicker now, muffling the village in quiet mystery. And though tonight – and Christmas – were for joy and peace, Ellie knew that Bramhurst's secrets waited, patient as ever, to lead the way to the next investigation.

The End

If you enjoyed Ellie, Dave, Sylvia and Zoe's story in this book, you can follow their adventures in the next one, *Murder in the Summer House*, which is available on Amazon here.

This is the blurb...

MURDER IN THE SUMMER HOUSE.

When neighbourly squabbles turn deadly...

Spring has arrived in Bramhurst and Ellie Blix longs to savour her final weeks at Stream Cottage. Wisteria trails the rear wall, tulips bob in the breeze, and peonies unfold.

But village peace is shattered by neighbours' squabbles over fences, hedges and trees.

And when Ellie discovers Prudence Dragg dead in her summer house, with the word "PALING" scrawled across the window, it's a chilling echo of Prudence's eerie predictions.

As gossip ripples through the village, Ellie is drawn into a tangle of tarot cards, disputed maps and secrets potions. The Blix women must untangle the mystery... before another neighbour pays the price.

Order *Murder in the Summer House* here.

A note from the author

Dear reader,

Thank you so much for reading this book. It has been a pleasure to write. Without you, however, it would simply be words in a document on my hard drive.

If you'd like to receive news on my writing, the best way to keep in touch is to join my newsletter. This is where I share news first, including exclusive offers, early reads, 'behind the scenes' & giveaways. You can join here.

Supporting the series

You can do this in three ways:

a) telling your friends, family, book clubs, and online groups. Word of mouth is one of the best forms of marketing.

b) leaving a quick, written review on Amazon. A few lines saying what you liked about the story helps other readers to know what the book is like.

c) pre-ordering the next book in the series, which you can do here.

Please note: I am a British writer and I write using British English. This story is set in an English village and the manuscript has been edited and proofread by British professionals. A few spellings, terms and words may, therefore, be different for some readers. I've tried to ensure, however, that the meaning is clear for everyone. In addition, the stories are intended to be lighthearted reads. They aren't police procedurals and genre norms mean that the sleuths do things detectives aren't allowed to do. This is intentional and is meant to be part of the fun of a cosy mystery.

Bramhurst isn't a real place. Sorry. It is a fictional village which I've created by borrowing elements of many of the villages outside Canterbury, mixing them up and fictionalising them. If you try to plot places, you may find I've moved them, changed them and given them different names!

Finally, writing a novel is a team effort. I come up with the plot and characters, and write the words, and other people contribute at various stages. Without their input and magic, this story would not have made it into print.

I owe massive thanks to the following people for their editing and proofreading. In no particular order: Amy Sinclair, Doug Collins, Pete Jones, Trudy Cairns. Thanks, too, to Ian Rankin, whose crime novels I've devoured for years. The name of Ellie's dog is a tribute to Ian's detective. I must, also, mention Agatha Christie, as I've used the name of her sleuth for Zoe's puppy. Finally, to all my early and beta readers – thank you.

Sincere apologies to anyone I've forgotten.

About the author

Izzie Harper is the pen name of British writer, teacher & story coach, Vicky Newham. Vicky lives on the south coast of England.

As Izzie Harper, she writes cozy mysteries.

Vicky's first crime fiction series was published by HQ/Harper Collins. Her debut in this police procedural series, *Turn a Blind Eye*, was optioned for TV and was shortlisted for the CWA John Creasey Debut Dagger in 2019. She has MAs in Creative Writing and Effective Learning.

To keep up to date with Vicky's releases, special offers and promotions, please join her newsletter here.

If you like pictures of dogs, the sea, the Kent countryside and behind-the-scenes of Vicky's writing, you can follow her on Instagram at @vickynewhamwriter.

If you have enjoyed this story, Vicky would be hugely grateful if you could leave a quick review on Amazon and if you could tell your family and friends about it. Reviews and word-of-mouth recommendations are the best way to help authors.

And, please pre-order the next book in the series, *Murder in the Summer House,* here.

Printed in Dunstable, United Kingdom

76848251R00204